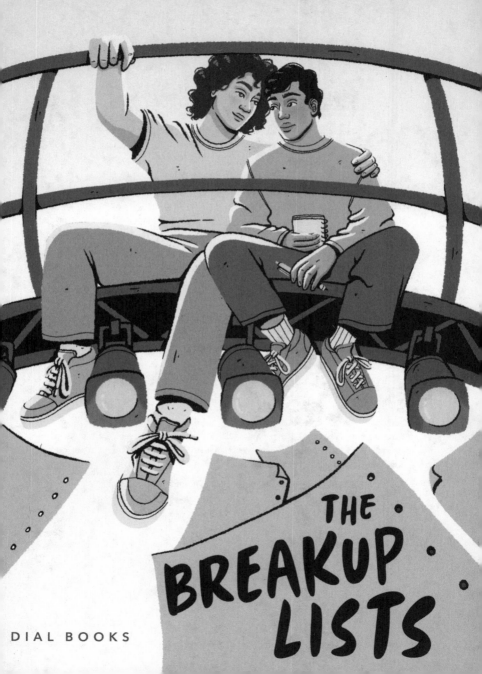

ADIB KHORRAM

THE BREAKUP LISTS

DIAL BOOKS

DIAL BOOKS

An imprint of Penguin Random House LLC, New York

First published in the United States of America by Dial Books,
an imprint of Penguin Random House LLC, 2024

Copyright © 2024 by Adib Khorram

Dial & colophon are registered trademarks of
Penguin Random House LLC.
The Penguin colophon is a registered trademark of Penguin Books Limited.

Visit us online at PenguinRandomHouse.com.

Library of Congress Cataloging-in-Publication Data is available.
Printed in the United States of America • ISBN 9780593616390
ISBN 9780593700297 (INTERNATIONAL EDITION)

1st Printing
LSCC

Design by Jason Henry • Text set in Charter

FOR ALL THE THEATRE KIDS

1

Even though I'm the Theatre Kid, my sister's the dramatic one.

"Ugh," Jasmine says as soon as she sees Nick, three lanes over in the parking lot. She rests her head against her car's steering wheel, then jolts back up when her nose sets off the horn.

"You okay?"

Jasmine mutters something into the wheel. It's got a pink fuzzy cover on it.

"I can't hear you."

She sits up, sighs, and faces me. "Sorry. It's just hard seeing him."

"It's been months."

"He broke my heart. You don't know what it's like."

I've had my heart broken before. Maybe not as often or as hard as Jasmine, but still.

"Can you do his list again?"

"Jasmine . . ."

"Please?"

Nick is Jasmine's ~~millionth~~ latest ex-boyfriend. They dated all summer before Nick broke up with her because he "didn't want

3

to be tied down senior year." But now she's stuck sitting behind him in Pre-Calculus.

I've repeated his list so many times I've basically got it memorized. Still, I reach into my backpack, pull out my black stage manager binder, and flip to the end where I keep my lists. Given how many of them there are—and how often Jasmine needs them repeated—I have to keep them close.

MAN BUN NICK'S BREAKUP LIST:
~~A CRUSTY SOCK IN HUMAN FORM~~
TOO MUCH AXE BODY SPRAY
~~NOT ENOUGH TO COVER THE WEIRD SMELL~~
SMACKS HIS LIPS AT THE BEGINNING OF EACH SENTENCE
DOESN'T LIKE PICKLES
~~ALWAYS LOOKS LIKE HE'S HOLDING IN A FART~~
BAD MAN BUN

It barely even qualifies as a bun. More like a little man garlic knot or something.

"Plus there's the whole thing where he broke up with you," I point out.

"Right. Right."

"And you said you wanted to focus on yourself senior year."

Jasmine gives me a sharp nod. She takes a deep breath, redoes her ponytail, and squares her shoulders. "Thanks, Jackson. What would I do without you?"

I slip my binder into my backpack and shrug it on, grab my shmoodies, and follow her into school.

The Riverstone High School Alumni Association ~~ruined~~

renovated the student entrance over the summer, replacing the rows of double doors set in red brick with an ugly white façade. Huge letters spell *RIVERSTONE* above the doors, but they're the same white as the wall, so you can only see them by the shadows they cast. At night, they're lit by blue LED backlight, even though Riverstone's school colors are purple and gold.

It looks more like an IKEA than a high school.

Jasmine taps my shoulder. "You staying late?"

"Auditions today and tomorrow. Callbacks on Thursday."

"All right. I'll be in the pottery studio when you're done."

Jasmine settles her backpack on her right shoulder and marches off toward the A Hall. I head up the stairs to the D Hall and my locker, where Bowie is waiting for me.

Bowie Anderson has been my best friend since we were in first grade. I don't know if it's because we were the only ~~spicy~~ non-white kids in our class (with Bowie being Black and me being half Iranian), or because even at six years old we were both already finding safety in other queer people, or because Bowie was one of the few people that never made fun of my hearing aids. But we've been more or less inseparable ever since, except that Bowie joined the Gender & Sexuality Alliance first year, while I joined Theatre.

"Hey, Jacks." Bowie stuffs their jacket into their locker.

"Hey. I got your shmoodie."

"You're a lifesaver." Bowie shakes the blender bottle vigorously, pops the lid, and takes a big swig. They've got dark brown skin, the kind that looks a little purple in a certain light, and short twists. Their lean neck bobs as they swallow, and they wipe their mouth with the back of their hand. "Mango?"

"And papaya. Dad got a huge bag at City Market." Along with two giant watermelons, a bushel of guavas, and the biggest apples I've ever seen. Dad always buys way more fruit than we can actually eat in a week, which is why I started making smoothies for me and Bowie in the first place, though I pronounced it "shmoodies" once by accident and the name kind of stuck. Normally I get ~~pissed off embarrassed~~ annoyed if people make fun of me for stuff like that, but Bowie's allowed because I know they never mean it.

"How was practice?" I shake my own bottle and take a sip.

They groan and roll out their left shoulder. "Brutal. So many sprints."

Bowie's on the swim team. I've never liked swimming, since I hate getting my head wet, but I do like watching the sport. Bowie's butterfly is a thing of beauty.

Plus, there are guys in Speedos.

I shut my locker and settle my backpack. Bowie looks behind me and cocks their chin. That usually means one thing.

Sure enough, Liam Coquyt is weaving through the hall, headed our way. He's a senior, and the swim team captain. He's tall and white and ~~annoyingly~~ classically handsome, with azure eyes and a sharp jaw and cheeks that always look a tiny bit flushed.

He smiles and runs a hand through his raven hair, which is feathery from all the chlorine.

I've heard more than one rant from Bowie about how hard it is to take care of natural hair when you spend hours a day in the pool—not to mention the racism of swim cap manufacturers and the governing bodies of the sport—but Liam looks like he doesn't even condition.

"Hey, Bowie. Hey, Jackson." He reaches behind me to tuck in the tag on my T-shirt. His smooth fingertips graze the back of my neck.

He's always doing that.

Liam nods at my shmoodie. "You got one of those for me?"

One time—one time!—Bowie was out sick, so I gave their shmoodie to Liam. And ever since, he keeps coming by my locker in the morning, hoping for another one.

It's not like he's a stranger: He and Bowie are friends, which means he's sort-of friends with me too, but not on the level of getting shmoodies. That's only for best friends.

Still, he comes by every day, smiling and tall ~~and handsome~~ and sometimes I think about making an extra.

Just to be nice.

He stands by me, radiating body heat through his T-shirt, while he talks to Bowie about practice. I tune them out and drink my shmoodie; trying to follow conversations is exhausting, and I have to save my energy for class where I can. But then Liam flaps his hand to get my attention, a gesture he must've learned from Bowie.

"Yeah?"

"See you this afternoon, right?"

"What? Why?"

"Auditions?"

"You're auditioning?"

He nods, blushing a little. "I thought it would be fun."

I glance at Bowie, whose eyebrows are arched in surprise, then back at Liam.

"Oh. Okay then."

Liam gives me another smile; his smooth arm brushes mine as he heads down the hall, so warm it makes me shiver. I stare at his back for a moment—it's wide and strong from all the swimming, straining the shoulder seams of his shirt—then turn back to Bowie and switch to sign.

"What is he doing?"

"Auditioning, I guess."

"But that's—" A terrible idea.

"What's the worst that could happen? He doesn't get a part?"

It's the fall musical—*Jesus Christ Superstar*—so everyone who auditions is pretty much guaranteed a role in the chorus if they want one. Especially if they're a senior. But Bowie's in the GSA; they don't understand the cutthroat politics of senior actors.

As a techie (and a junior) I've been ~~excluded~~ able to avoid most of it.

"Whatever," I finally mutter.

"You need a ride today?"

"Jasmine's got me. Thanks."

Bowie glances toward the ceiling. "Warning bell. See you at lunch?"

"Yeah."

After sixth hour, I power-elbow my way to Dr. Lochley's office. The door is open, but I still knock on it before I head in.

Dr. L's got her phone nestled between her shoulder and ear, and she's staring at her computer with her lips pursed. She looks up at me, smiles, then focuses back on her screen.

"Well, how am I somethingsomething done if I have to remember a million passwords?" she asks. She takes off her purple cat-eye glasses and pinches the bridge of her nose. "This isn't the Pentagon, you know."

She mutters something I don't catch, hangs up, and shakes her head, which sends the ends of her graying bob dancing around her jawline. Dr. Lochley is willowy and white, but she's got a year-round tan. She's barely lighter than me.

"Jackson. Good. Mind giving me a hand?"

Dr. Lochley nods to a cardboard box filled with random props: a small sword, a plunger, a beach ball, a picnic blanket—and that's just what I can see on the top.

"Sure."

Seventh hour, Dr. Lochley teaches Theatre IV, which is only for seniors. But because I didn't have any better classes to take, I signed up as her teacher's assistant, which means I get to sit in on Theatre IV a year early, and then take it for real next year. I grab the box as Dr. L straightens out her desk and grabs her tote bag.

"Improv today?"

"Yeah. You want to join in?"

I suppress a shudder. Improv means lots of people, all talking over each other, and maybe I can follow and get in a joke, or maybe I'll be lost and confused and people will get annoyed with me for not keeping up.

Most people seem to think that, just because I wear hearing aids, I hear ~~normally~~ 100 percent of what they say, but I don't.

"I'm good," I say. "I was thinking I could go set up for auditions?"

"All right. I still think it's somethingsomething."

"Say again?"

"It's a shame you're not auditioning. You've got the perfect look."

I'm not sure if she's saying that because I'm short, and would ~~make the leads look taller~~ create interesting mise en scène; or because I'm half Iranian, which is ~~the wrong brown~~ vaguely the right part of the world. But still: There's no way. Some people aren't meant for the stage, and I'm one of them.

"Who would stage manage, then?"

Dr. L chuckles. "Fair enough. Here, I'll write you a pass."

"Thanks."

2

I open the stage right door and poke my head out. A row of folding chairs lines the hallway, right in front of a glass case full of charcoal ~~sketches of butts~~ still lifes of peaches from one of the art classes, Jasmine's among them. Hers is clearly the best: Iranians know their fruits.

I glance around. "Liam?"

His head snaps up.

"You're next."

He gets off his chair and gives me a grin, but there's a tiny wobble in it, like he might actually be nervous, and worse, him being nervous makes me so nervous my heart does a little flutter. Which is weird, because he's basically guaranteed a role in the chorus. Everyone gets a part in the musical.

~~Well, almost everyone.~~

Still, it would be hilarious if he got a big role. The senior actors would be ~~pissed~~ surprised.

He pauses right in front of me, so close I can smell his citrusy deodorant. "Wish me luck?"

Some of the other auditioners glare at his back, and based

on facial expressions I'm pretty sure one of the sophomores just hissed like a cat.

"Never say that!"

"What?"

"You never wish someone luck in a theatre. Or even near one. That's actually super bad luck."

"Really?"

"Yeah, that's why we say 'break a leg.'"

"How am I supposed to act with a broken leg?"

I roll my eyes. I don't have time to get into the contradictory origins of the phrase.

But Liam's face lights up. "Oh. So I'll be in the cast?"

"Come on." I tug him into the theatre, my thumb sliding along the cord in his forearm, and I let go as the door swings shut behind us. He takes his mark, raising a hand to his brow to look out into the audience before dropping it back to his side.

I take Liam's audition form out to the front-of-house table where Dr. Lochley and Mr. Cartwright, the choir director, are stationed.

Liam introduces himself. He runs a hand through his dark hair as Mr. Cartwright asks, "What are you singing for us?"

Liam clears his throat. "'Gethsemane.'"

I take my seat at the end of the row in front of the table as our accompanist, Miss Dawson, starts playing.

I can't tell if his singing is very good or not; without him mic'd up, I have a hard time discriminating his voice from the piano, no matter how much he projects, and I'm pretty sure he's not even projecting.

But he looks great onstage. He's tall and ~~statuesque~~ well proportioned, and after a couple of bars he seems to relax into the song. His shoulders unclench, and his body loosens, and it's like he's leaning out into the audience, pulling us in.

And even though I can't make out the words, I can just tell. He's good. My heart beats in time with the bass notes on the piano; the hairs on my arm stand up as I notice Liam's Adam's apple jiggling from his vibrato.

Wow.

I glance back at Dr. L, who's leaning in too, lips parted slightly in surprise. The corner of her mouth has turned up a bit. She doesn't have any obvious tells, but after two years of shows, I've started to pick up on the more subtle ones.

Mr. Cartwright, on the other hand, has no poker face whatsoever. He's bobbing his head and beaming at the stage in wonder.

I can't watch them for long, though, not with Liam onstage, drawing my attention like a magnet. His eyes meet mine for a second—in the stage light, they sparkle like a summer sky—and my heart skips a beat, because there's nothing more awkward than having someone sing right at you. It's too intense.

The music finally ends. Mr. Cartwright and Dr. Lochley sit back, stunned. Onstage, Liam relaxes, breathing hard, cheeks flushed, and it's like someone turned down the dimmer on the sun. The theatre seems darker and colder, now that he's not singing. I give a little shiver.

Mr. Cartwright recovers first, pushes his glasses up his large nose. He's white, but his nose could give Dad's Iranian nose a run for its money. "Thank you, Liam."

Dr. L says, "What's your monologue?"

Liam scratches the back of his neck. "It's a poem, actually. I heard that's somethingsomething?"

Dr. L nods, her eyebrows quirking up. Poems are allowed, but not many people do them.

Liam meets my eyes again before he starts reciting, and I can't make out a single line. I pull out my phone and use the app to turn up the sensitivity on my hearing aids. When I look back up, Liam's looking right at me as he speaks, and it's still intense—his eyes really are a ~~spectacular~~ ridiculous shade of blue—but less than when he was singing, so I let myself lock eyes with him. Just so he knows I see him.

Auditioning can be really lonely. Not that I've done it since first year. Being a techie is way better.

Halfway through, the air in the theatre changes. I don't know how he does it, but we're all leaning in again, like he's cupped water in his hands and all of us are thirsty. My skin buzzes with the sensation, and suddenly I'm aware that my shirt tag is sticking up again, but I ignore it, holding my breath as Liam finishes.

"One equal temper of heroic hearts,
Made weak by time and fate, but strong in will
To somethingsomethingsomething not to yield."

My chest flutters as I finally exhale.

That was a killer audition.

I glance toward Dr. Lochley, and she's got an eyebrow raised, which is even more powerful than a lip quirk.

"Thank you, Liam."

"Thank you." Liam cracks his usual smile, and the difference is stark, like he's pulled on a coat, hiding all that talent shining within.

I sit there, staring at him, too stunned to move, until Mr. Cartwright says, "Jackson? Next?"

"Sorry."

My feet are leaden as I escort Liam out. He asks me something but I don't catch it.

"Huh?"

"Sorry." He waits until we're by the door, his face lit by the glow of the exit sign. "How'd I do?"

~~Amazing.~~ "Well, you didn't fall off the stage, so that was good."

He laughs and reaches behind me to tuck in my tag. He's got little beads of sweat along his hairline, and the scent of chlorine off him is stronger than usual. It's not bad, though. He just smells aggressively clean.

I open the door to let him out, glance at my clipboard to see who's next.

But how could I forget?

"Cameron," I say, careful to keep my voice neutral. "You're up."

Cameron studies Liam as he brushes past, then turns to me. He's got these deep brown puppy-dog eyes, the kind that make you want to automatically like someone, but I stare at my clipboard to avoid his gaze.

"Here." He lays his form on my clipboard, and I open the stage door wider to let him in. As he brushes past, bumping my shoulder, I catch Liam watching me.

"Callback list goes up Wednesday morning," I tell him.

"Got it." He gives me a thumbs-up before I shut the door and follow Cam into the theatre.

I hand over his form and take my seat, pulling out my phone

15

again to turn my hearing aids all the way down, because I do not need to hear Cameron sing. He's got a beautiful voice, and he's a phenomenal actor, but seeing him onstage is ~~the worst~~ complicated.

Cameron and I used to date, back when I was a first year and he was a sophomore. He was my first boyfriend. My first kiss too. Until he got a part in the fall musical (a gender-agnostic production of *My Fair Lady*), and I didn't. Suddenly he was too busy with the other actors and didn't have time for a boyfriend who was just on stage crew.

When Cam dumped me, I was so hurt, and angry, I threw myself into the show. Making lists of props and scene changes and costume changes and everything I could, just to distract myself, but that paid off. The stage manager for *My Fair Lady* was a senior named Caprice; she noticed all my hard work, and Dr. Lochley did too. They made me assistant stage manager—a big job for a first year—and when Caprice decided to act in the spring play, rather than stage manage, I got to take over for her.

Of course, Cam got cast in that play too, and he was even more insufferable, treating me like I was some sort of servant: walking over the stage after I swept it, ignoring me when I tried to get him to be quiet during rehearsals, leaving his props everywhere for me to chase down between acts.

He's been in every single show since, and he's only gotten worse. The problem with Cameron is, he does this thing where he'll look at you with his puppy-dog eyes and his button nose and floppy hair and you'll just want to forgive him for being awful. His was the first list I made for myself, rather than Jasmine.

I've updated it so often, the original paper's not in my binder anymore: I had to copy it over. Twice.

CAMERON'S BREAKUP LIST (V.33):
~~ARROGANT JERK~~
TOTAL PRIMA DONNA
~~FUTURE PROBLEMATIC WHITE BOY~~
TREATS TECHIES BADLY
~~GLOWED UP EVEN MORE SINCE WE DATED~~
BASIC WHITE BOY LOOKS
ALLERGIC TO ONIONS
ALWAYS MAKES THE CAST

After Cameron's monologue (Atticus Finch from *To Kill a Mockingbird,* which remains his favorite play despite all the racism and N-word and white savior-ism stuff), I show him out. His shoulders are tense. I don't know why—I already know he's going to get a part. He knows it too.

But as we reach the door, he looks back past me, toward the proscenium. He can't see Dr. Lochley or Mr. Cartwright from the door, but he bites his lip before he catches me watching him. He rolls his eyes and pushes out into the hall.

I fix my face and call in the next audition.

Once we're done, I help Dr. L close up the theatre. It's nearly five o'clock, and my stomach is growling. If this were a rehearsal, I would've ducked out for an afternoon snack, but with auditions there's no breaks. And food isn't allowed in the theatre.

Not that anyone else seems to obey the rule. Not even Mr. Cartwright, who was munching on Mike & Ikes—he calls them "the original gay candy!"—the whole afternoon. But as stage manager, I'm supposed to set a good example.

"What would I do without you?" Dr. L muses as I sweep the stage using a wide dust mop with *RHS THEATOR* (no idea) stenciled on its head.

I shrug and try not to blush. Sometimes Dr. L acts like the whole department would come crumbling down without me, but she's always careful not to say that with an actor around. Probably because she knows their ego would melt, like a halogen lamp with oily fingerprints on it, if she ever acknowledged that anyone else in the world might have talent. So she heaps praise on them and treats me like a ghost, haunting the theatre in my show blacks.

Actors get standing ovations. Techies get fiberglass splinters.

But it's fine. I like being backstage.

I rack the dust mop, grab my backpack, and head for the exit. But when I swing the door open, it stops with a soft thump.

"Sorry." I look around the door. Liam's there, rubbing his elbow and shaking his head, but he's got a tiny smile.

"My bad. I forgot they opened outward."

"Still. You need that to swim." I nod at his arm. His sleeve is riding up a bit, showing off the little vein down his bicep. Liam has really ~~nice~~ strong arms. I think I do too, but mine are just kind of big from all the work on lights and scenery. His are ~~cut~~ *defined*.

His grin widens, and I can't help mirroring it a little. He steps closer to me, and his body heat washes away the last chill of the theatre.

"Yeah. Or act, if I get a part."

I back up, but the door is right behind me. "If you're fishing for intel, it won't work. You've got to wait for the callback list like everyone else."

But I can't imagine him not getting a callback. Not after an audition like that.

I turn and head toward the Art wing, but Liam hurries ahead of me and turns to walk backward, so I can see his face as he speaks.

"Not even a hint? To make up for all the shmoodies you owe me?"

"I don't remember owing you any shmoodies. You're not on the shmoodie list."

There is no shmoodie list. I only bring one for me and one for Bowie.

"If I get a role, will you put me on it?"

"No." But he gives me the biggest, goofiest frown, and I accidentally crack a smile.

He laughs. "Just you wait. I'll make that shmoodie list someday."

And then he spins on his heel and walks next to me. His shoulder brushes against mine, and for a second I wonder if he's doing it on purpose. As far as I know, Liam's straight, and most straight guys would drop a *no homo* after brushing against another guy. Especially a gay one.

Then again, Liam's never been homophobic~~, unless you count him being nice to me: Straight guys being nice to gay guys is kind of homophobic as is~~.

Still, he makes sure to give me some space. I'm just ~~hoping~~ imagining things.

He is really beautiful; the kind of beautiful that guys shouldn't be allowed to be. The kind where I can't always tell if I'm jealous or attracted to him or both. But I shake the thought off as I stop at the door to the pottery studio; Liam keeps on going for a few steps before turning back quizzically.

"This is me. See you." I give him a wave before letting myself into the studio.

There's a weird, wet earth smell to the pottery studio, like the way the ground smells after it rains.

"I'm all done," I tell Jasmine, who's hunched over one of the tall worktables, poking a little wooden stick into the corner of a tiny box. There's a smear of brown clay on her cheek, and her hair is pulled back into a ponytail.

I don't catch her answer, but she gets up, takes her tiny box to the closet thing that stores the pottery, then grabs her tools and takes them to the sink in the back.

I hop onto one of the high stools and pull my binder out to organize my notes from today, but I pause when I feel warmth on my back, like someone's looming behind me. I jerk away.

Liam has followed me in.

"What?" I say. "Don't loom over me like that."

"Sorry." He backs away. "I was just checking this out. I never took pottery. Or any art class, really."

"Oh." I can't imagine that. I've been in one (or more) Theatre classes every year. "My sister does pottery."

I nod toward the back just as Jasmine emerges, scrubbing at her cheek with a flimsy brown paper towel.

"Ready to go?" she asks, but then she notices Liam standing over me. Her lips quirk, and her cheeks flush, and she reaches for her hair to play with it before realizing it's still in a ponytail.

Oh no. I've seen this process before.

"Hey." Suddenly her stride has a lot more hip in it.

"Hey. Jasmine, right? We had APUSH last year."

"Yeah." Her eyes slide from Liam's face to his swimmer's shoulders to his arms and then back up.

"I was just trying to convince Jackson to put me on his shmoodie list."

Jasmine laughs. "I'm his own sister and he won't put me on it. He only makes them for Bowie."

Jasmine hates shmoodies, for the same reason she hates soup: a firm conviction that food should be eaten and never drunk. But my chest tightens at her jab. Making me sound like a bad guy.

"Fine." I huff and pull my backpack on. "If you get a part, I'll add you to the list. Okay?"

Liam beams. "Really?"

I nod and move toward the door, but Jasmine doesn't follow.

She's studying Liam, bottom lip curled under the top one. "You need a ride? We've got room."

Liam chuckles and rubs the back of his head, which makes his shirt ride up, showing off the bottom of his abs. Actual abs. I've seen them at swim meets before, but never up close.

Jasmine's looking at me expectantly.

"Huh?"

"I said, let's go."

"Oh. Yeah. See you, Liam."

I push my way out the door.

3

As we walk to the car, Jasmine's got this dreamy smile, and her head's bobbing like she's listening to music only she can hear. Sure signs of a crush.

I've had crushes too, of course, though most have been straight guys. Last year, the photos for our Thespians troop were right after the photos for the wrestling team, and let's just say the parade of guys in singlets was something to behold. But that's all they are: crushes. They never went anywhere. Not since Cam.

Jasmine's crush-to-date ratio is in the ninetieth percentile. My sister is always falling in love. Or out of it. As if love is something you can toss around like handfuls of glitter. (Dr. Lochley is adamantly opposed to glitter, which, once introduced to a theatre ecosystem, can never truly be eliminated.)

And Jasmine's crush-to-love pipeline is extremely efficient. By next week, she and Liam will be holding hands. By October, they'll be making out in the little alcove by the trophy case that separates the Art wing from the Music wing, like all the other senior couples. By November, she'll be planning the wedding. It'll all be awkward and insufferable, especially since I'll have a front row seat to the whole thing.

But then by December they'll have a fight and break up. Or drift apart and break up. Slowly start annoying each other and break up. Go off to different colleges, try and fail at the long distance thing and break up. ~~Have terrible sex and break up.~~ And I'll be left making another list.

I toss my bags in the back of Jasmine's car and buckle up. She says something to me, but I don't catch it. Between classes and auditions, my brain is more or less done listening for the day.

"Say again?"

She turns to face me fully. "I said, Liam seems nice."

"I guess. He's more Bowie's friend than mine."

"Ah." That tiny smile makes another appearance as Jasmine starts the car.

My sister is a lost cause.

My predictions all come true:

Jasmine does have a crush.

Liam does make the callback list.

And the senior actors are ~~pissed~~ ~~mutinous~~ concerned.

"He's never been in a show before," Cameron tells Jenny, this sophomore who did tech for one show before falling in with the actors ~~and turning into a monster~~. "He doesn't have the chops for a lead."

I keep quiet. None of them saw Liam's audition. He does have the chops.

"You never know," Jenny says. "Sometimes Dr. Lochley does weird stuff. I mean, remember *The Bad Seed*?"

"I guess." Cam catches me watching. "What do you think, Jackson?"

"I can't talk about auditions. You know that."

"Whatever." He keeps talking to Jenny but turns away, and I lose the thread of the conversation.

I sigh and turn back to the Theatre Board, this huge corkboard to the right of Dr. Lochley's office, covered with flyers for shows in town, news about alumni, release forms, and of course, right in the middle, the callback list, with Liam's name near the top.

I pull down the old audition sign-ups and replace them with a small flyer I designed advertising tech crew: how it's fun, how it's cool, how you can earn Thespian points, how it goes toward lettering in Theatre.

Most people just want to act, though. If it weren't for Dr. Lochley's Theatre I students who have to volunteer for one show during the year to pass the class, we wouldn't have crews at all.

Last year I had to beg Bowie to run a followspot for the musical, but they drove a hard bargain: In exchange, I had to design a flyer for the GSA's annual drag show fundraiser.

It's not that I don't like drag shows—they're great—it's that Bowie knows I don't like the GSA. Ever since first year, when they did *Rocky Horror Picture Show* in the Main Theatre and managed to damage lineset 5. No one's even sure how they did it, but what used to be a straight steel pipe came out of *Rocky Horror* with a pronounced bend right in the center.

And since the GSA doesn't have any budget—all the funds they raise go to charity—the Theatre budget had to eat the costs. Granted, the GSA has been banned from using the theatre ever since, and granted, the charities are all important ones, like the Trevor Project, but still. I just don't trust them.

~~It probably doesn't help that Cam used to be in the GSA, too.~~

24

* * *

Dr. Lochley and Mr. Cartwright are huddled together at their table once more, heads bowed and muttering. I watch from my usual spot and wait for them to decide who they want to see next. Mr. Cartwright keeps shaking his head, but Dr. L does her karate-chop-for-emphasis every other sentence.

Finally they split apart. Dr. L calls out, "Jackson, could you ask Liam and Cameron to come in?"

~~Gross.~~

"Copy that."

I pop my head out the backstage doors. Liam's staying well clear this time, sitting on the floor against the opposite wall, but his head snaps up. His hair flops into his eyes for a second before he shakes it off and stares at me, his blue eyes looking guarded but hopeful.

I nod at him and clear my throat. "Liam? Cameron?"

While they settle onstage, I run out to grab their sides from Dr. L.

"For Liam." She passes me a couple pages with Jesus's part highlighted. "Cameron." Cam's sides are for Judas.

I stare at the sides. Is she really thinking of giving Liam the title role? On his first audition? Without ever being in a show before?

I knew he was good, but wow. I run the sides up and hand them over.

"Thanks." Liam looks over his script and then back at me, a ~~weirdly endearing~~ mix of panic and excitement in his eyes.

Cam takes his sides without even looking at me. He just nods,

25

like I'm a server at a restaurant refilling his water. But his brows crease before he schools his features.

I take my seat again as Dr. L gives them both a few instructions I can't hear. They're doing the scene from Act I where Judas is yelling at Jesus for hanging out with Mary Magdalene, though Dr. L has them saying their lines instead of singing. I've never actually read the Bible—Dad being a lapsed Bahá'í, Mom being a lapsed Methodist, and me being a lapsed heterosexual—so I'm not sure how much of the scene is biblically accurate.

At first, it's just Liam and Cameron reciting lines at each other. But then? I don't know how to describe it. One moment Liam is just Liam. Yeah, he looks great onstage, the lights kindling his eyes and highlighting his cheekbones, but still: just a ~~hot~~ guy talking.

Then I blink, and I'm looking at a different person entirely: His voice, his body language, everything changes. He transforms.

And Cameron responds by doing the same. He's no longer Cam, ~~ex-boyfriend~~ senior actor. No longer someone who barely knows Liam. Instead, a whole life of friendship and arguments and history blossoms between them, as if it had always existed.

The hairs on my arm stand up as Judas takes an aggressive step toward Jesus, but Jesus stands his ground. He's taller than Judas, but that's not what makes him so impressive: It's the set in his shoulders, the jut of his jaw, the blue fire in his eyes I can feel from thirty feet away. At auditions I had to lean in, but now I have to lean away or risk getting burned.

They finish their scene staring at each other, breathing hard as if they swam a race. Chests rising and falling. Cheeks flushed. They might even be sweating under the stage lights.

Then they blink. The spell bursts like a bubble. Cam looks toward Dr. L, but Liam's eyes find mine.

~~I snap my mouth shut.~~

"Thank you," Dr. L says from the table, and Liam looks to her instead. I can breathe again.

That's all: "Thank you." But I'm pretty sure, if she wasn't a professional, Dr. Lochley would be up and dancing in the aisle.

Liam clears his throat. "Um. Thank you."

He looks back down at his sides. Cam's staring at Dr. Lochley like he's not sure what just happened.

It's quiet in the theatre until Dr. L waves at me. "Jackson?"

Oh. I'm supposed to grab their sides. I run up the aisle, take the steps onto the stage two at a time. "I'll take those. Here."

I lead them both out. At the door, Liam pauses and turns to me. "Was that okay?"

"You know I can't talk about it." But then I realize maybe he doesn't actually know that. I try to soften my voice. "I'm not allowed to discuss callbacks with anyone. Sorry."

"It's okay. But don't forget your promise."

Out in the hall, Cam turns around, looking between me and Liam with a frown on his face.

"What promise?" I ask.

"If I get a part, you'll put me on the shmoodie list."

I forgot about that. But he's certainly earned it now.

"Don't worry. I'll add you. *If* you get a part."

He smiles so wide you'd think I told him he got the lead. (Which I'm pretty sure he just did.) It's alarmingly like standing in the hot spot of a Leko, warming my face while also slowly burning a hole in my retina.

Cam comes closer. "What about if I get a part? What do I get?"

He's got his puppy-dog eyes on again, dark and twinkling. Cam does that sometimes: He's attractive and charming. He knows how to turn it on. I remember how it used to be, when he'd turn his attention on me, right before we kissed. It used to take my breath away.

And he still likes to use it on me, mostly to mess with me. Remind me of how we used to be together. Of how ~~I wasn't good enough for him~~ he thinks he's better than me.

It doesn't work this time, though: Liam outshines him.

"Attention," I say. "Like usual."

For a split second his eyes widen like I've actually hurt him. Cracked him open and exposed something he doesn't want other people to see. But then his eyes narrow. "Don't you have work to do, Jackthon?"

Liam stiffens next to me. My own shoulders tense.

When I was little I had a bit of a lisp. Well. More than a bit.

And I still do, sometimes, despite the speech therapy. Especially when I'm tired, which I always am by the end of the day.

Cameron used to think it was cute. Now he's just being ~~a dick~~ cruel.

I close the door behind me and go see what Dr. L needs next.

4

Once callbacks are over, Dr. Lochley and Mr. Cartwright retreat to the Theatre Office to ~~fight about~~ discuss the cast list, leaving me to clean up the theatre: Collect all Mr. Cartwright's Mike & Ike boxes, fold up the table they were using, and put away the chairs. Gather all the discarded sides for recycling. Sweep the stage. Set out the ghost light—this big bulb attached to a tall, wheeled stand.

Dr. Lochley doesn't care either way, but Denise (Dr. L's wife, who helps out with tech) has made it clear that every theatre should always, always, always leave a ghost light for when no one's inside, especially overnight. Denise says that theatres and hotels are the two most vulnerable buildings to hauntings.

I'm pretty sure that's not true, and I'm also pretty sure I don't believe in ghosts, or curses, or anything, but Denise is very superstitious. One time she thought I'd named the Scottish Play, aka *Macbeth*, in the Little Theatre. (I said *magnets* but apparently they sound similar enough.) She didn't let me explain, just made me leave the theatre, spin around three times, spit, then knock and ask to be let back in.

I might not be superstitious, but lots of other people are, so: I leave out the ghost light.

I click it on, right as I feel something on my back.

I scream and spin around, nearly falling over, but strong hands catch me. Liam's standing there, eyes wide like *I* startled *him* and not the other way around.

"Sorry!" I think he says.

"What? Wait." I straighten out, breathing hard, take a step back because suddenly I'm warm all over. Liam radiates body heat, like, all the time. Bowie does too. Something about swimmers and thermogenesis or something.

I pull out my phone and turn my hearing aids back on.

"What?"

"Sorry." He nods at my phone. "What's that for?"

I bite my lip. Most people don't get it—sometimes even my family forgets, which really stings—but Liam's looking at me like he really wants to know. The ghost light reflects in his big blue eyes.

"I turned my hearing aids off," I say. "Listening all day is exhausting."

"Really?"

"Reading lips, concentrating, trying to infer whatever I miss . . ." I point to my hearing aids. "These don't magically make me hear like you."

"I didn't think so." He bites his lip. "I'm sorry for startling you. Your tag was sticking up."

"Oh." I reach behind me, but he managed to tuck it in before I screamed.

"Do you want some help? We don't have to talk."

"I'm done now."

30

"Oh." He scratches the back of his neck, which makes his bicep flex. I get a whiff of his deodorant too, eucalyptus and something else, something that makes my nose tingle, but in a good way. "I'm sorry. You can go ahead and . . ." He gestures at his own ears. "I don't mind."

I try not to with people around. "You sure?"

But he slides his phone out of his pocket and types for a second, then shows it to me. His Notes app is open.

> Positive.
> We can just chill.

"Thanks," I say aloud.

He nods and smiles, grabbing my backpack off the ground for me as I turn my hearing aids back off. I do one last look around, turn off the work lights, and let the theatre doors close behind us.

> You need a ride?

"Jasmine's got me. She'll be working a while yet."

> I can keep you company

"I'm just doing homework."

> I don't mind. Don't want to go home yet.

I cock my head at him, but he doesn't answer my unasked question. Finally I shrug. "Sure."

* * *

"Chicken?" Amy signs at me.

I nod, and she passes it my way. I kind of lucked out on stepmothers: Amy never tried to do any weird *I'm your mother now* stuff when she and Dad got married five years ago, like Jasmine was worried about. Instead, she said she hoped we'd be friends, and that she would grow to become someone we could trust. She's always been there for me and Jasmine.

She even learned some sign, though it's mostly food words. Still, it's more than Dad ever managed, or Mom for that matter. With them both being doctors, it was like they expected my hearing aids to solve everything, and then were personally offended when they didn't.

Truth be told, my family has been more comfortable with me being queer than they've ever been with me being disabled.

Don't get me wrong, Dad absolutely loves me and Jasmine, and makes sure we know it. He comes to all my plays, frames every single one of Jasmine's art pieces, but I don't think he gets us. It must baffle him how he, a cardiologist, and our mom, an anesthesiologist, wound up with two artsy kids.

I pass the chicken to Dad, who's looking at his phone as we eat, bushy eyebrows twitching. Even when he's not on call, he's usually glued to his phone. Dr. Iraj Ghasnavi is dark-haired, though it's thinning in the back and around his widow's peak, and brown-eyed like me and Jasmine. His skin is darker than mine, a rich sienna that never burns in the summer, just turns more golden. He's also short like me—I topped out at five-seven when I was fourteen, which doesn't bother me that much (except when people loom over me), but it does make reaching things in the theatre annoying sometimes.

Jasmine thumps the table to get my attention.

"Huh?" I wish she'd just use her Notes app like Liam did. But I stifle a sigh and turn my hearing aids back on. "Yeah?"

"What were you doing with Liam this afternoon?"

"Uh. Homework?"

"Who's Liam?" Amy asks, looking between us.

"Just a guy I know," Jasmine says, but then she looks down at her plate and lets her hair draw a curtain on her expression. No doubt hiding a rising blush.

She's definitely crushing.

Dad looks up from his phone. "Somethingsomething Liam's an Iranian name? It means 'my nation.'"

"His last name is Coquyt, though," I say.

Dad cocks his head to the side. "Probably not Iranian, then. He's your year?"

"Mine," Jasmine says. "Senior."

"What's he doing for college?"

Jasmine shrugs.

"Early decision at UT," I say. He and Bowie talk about it sometimes. "He's a swimmer."

Dad raises his eyebrows. "Good school."

It's one of the best swimming schools in the nation. Up there with Ohio, according to Bowie. They're good enough to get in, that's for sure.

I used to think me and Bowie would end up at the same school, but that's probably not going to happen: I really want to go to NYU, or maybe Northwestern in Chicago. But Ohio's not that far from either one. We'll still see each other all the time.

At least Bowie's not eyeing somewhere out in, like, California or Texas. Far, far away from me. I don't know what I'd do without them.

"Have you looked at UT?" Dad asks.

Jasmine blushes and pushes her food around her plate. Her lack of a decision on college has been a point of contention between her and Dad for pretty much the last two years. She's still not sure what she wants to do once she graduates.

Some days it's hard to wrap my head around the fact that Jasmine is graduating this year. Other times, it feels all too real, and kind of scary. It'll be weird to be at school and not be Jasmine's little brother. To just be Jackson.

Jasmine mutters something and stabs at her chicken.

"What?" I ask.

"Never mind."

I hate when people do that: Refuse to repeat something I missed. And Jasmine knows that, but she's too busy being annoyed with Dad.

The awkwardness hangs over us like an overloaded lineset. Finally I turn my hearing aids back off. Amy starts asking Dad something. Jasmine stuffs macaroni and cheese into her mouth.

"You okay?" Amy signs at me.

I smile around my salad and nod.

I'm fine.

5

*D*r. Lochley's pretty strategic with cast lists. They always go up during seventh hour, while everyone (including her!) is in class. I don't know how she does it: whether she enlists help from the front office; or gets Denise to come in and do it for her; or if she's somehow harnessed the power to be in two places at once.

If it's the last one, she's not showing any obvious signs of having superpowers. She's sitting at her desk in the Little Theatre, talking about Stanislavski and what she calls "the art of experiencing."

"Most of you spent the week in auditions, where you tried your own hand at the art of experiencing. Anyone want to share what they felt?"

Mae raises her hand. "I felt like vomiting," she says, which gets chuckles from everyone.

"Not unheard of," Dr. L says. "But not exactly what I was looking for. Cameron?"

The worst part of being the TA for Theatre IV is that Cam's in it—and Philip, his new boyfriend. Philip actually kind of looks like Cam—white, floppy brown hair, brown eyes—but he's a bit shorter, and a bit less handsome.

Not that he's not handsome: Philip's good-looking, and I had a little crush on him, up until I got to know him.

PHILIP'S BREAKUP LIST:
TRAGICALLY BORN WITHOUT A PERSONALITY
~~TALENTLESS HACK~~
MEDIOCRE ACTING AT BEST
~~SELF-OBSESSED GYM GAY?~~
TERRIBLE HAIRCUT
MOUTH BREATHER!!
~~ALWAYS TOUCHING CAMERON~~
~~ALWAYS AGREEING WITH CAMERON~~
THINKS IN CRAYON

Honestly, I'm not sure why I even made a list for him; I've barely looked at it since I tucked it into my binder, and even then only to update it when he started dating Cam.

They've been sitting next to each other on the second row bench since the year started, though lately it's devolved into Cam lying with his head on Philip's lap, Philip playing with Cam's soft hair while they listen to someone's monologue or nod along to the lecture or watch a video on the TV Dr. Lochley wheels into the theatre sometimes.

They're not sitting like that now, though: Cam is leaning in, fingers interlaced and elbows on his knees as he considers. ~~But Philip's hand still rests on the small of Cam's back.~~

"When I was auditioning, it felt like pulling on a comfy sweater. It's the kind of thing you only really get by doing the work.

Trying and failing and learning and doing better over time. Paying your dues."

I fight not to roll my eyes. Even when he's answering questions in class, Cam acts like a spotlight's on him.

But some of the others nod along. That's a big thing with the seniors: paying your dues. Doing small roles and bit parts and being in the chorus as you build up to being a lead your senior year, like a role is something that's owed to you. But somehow, paying your dues never seems to include focusing lights or painting sets or altering costumes.

Dr. Lochley taps her finger against her lips, says something to the class I can't make out. I'm still trying to parse it when she turns to me. "Jackson, what do you think?"

"Huh?" I clear my throat. "Say again?"

"Do you think there's such a thing as natural talent? A moment when lightning strikes?"

"Well." I think about Liam. How he seemed to transform himself out of nowhere. "Acting is an art, and all art is unpredictable. Sometimes you spend years on something and it never works out; sometimes you're in the right place at the right time and magic happens. I think that practice makes it easier to reach for that magic, but sometimes it's just there. Right when you need it."

"Well said. That's the ephemeral thing about it. Acting!" Dr. L karate chops as she says it, then makes a show of checking her watch. "Oh. The bell's about to ring."

It's a calculated thing; all the actors shift in their seats and stare at each other.

"Your assignment for the weekend: Find a clip of a performance you like, and be prepared to explain why you like it, and what kinds of experiences the actor might be using to inform the role. Try to—"

But I lose the rest of it as everyone starts shuffling and getting up. The bell must've rung out in the hall. The Little Theatre's got its own PA that's not connected to the bell system.

Dr. L starts stuffing her own books and binders into the giant black tote bag she carries everywhere. It's got *Act well your part* in gold letters on one side, and the comedy and tragedy masks on the other. When she stands, everyone stops to look at her. "By the way, the cast list is up if you want to take a look."

Everyone bolts from the room. Everyone except me. I take my time packing my stuff.

Dr. L taps my shoulder. "And so it begins." She's got a mischievous twinkle in her eye. "I liked your metaphor, about reaching for magic. I'm going to remember that one."

I try not to smile too big.

"Have a good weekend, Jackson."

"You too."

With a few swift strides, she's gone. Normally she hangs around after school for a little while, even on days where there's no rehearsal, to answer questions, deal with emails, do all the weird things the district makes teachers do. But on cast list days, she heads straight for the parking lot; she'll be off school property before the first buses even leave.

I'm anxious and I don't even know why. It's not like my name will be on the list.

I'm really hopeful for Liam, though. He was so good. Dr. L has to know he's the best. But sometimes there's ~~Cam's ego department politics~~ other factors to consider.

The hallway is a crush of bodies and a jumble of crackling noise so overwhelming I turn my hearing aids off. Too much cross talk, too many shrieks of joy or cries of disappointment.

And holy shit, the cast list is huge. Not huge as in the number of people in the show, but huge as in Dr. Lochley must've used the plotter printer, because the cast list is like twelve feet wide and three feet high, draped across the Theatre Board and onto the brick wall beyond.

This is the most extra Dr. L's ever gone for a cast list.

Tension ripples through the crowd as some people have their year made and others have their dreams crushed. Tori, a Black girl and one of the few senior actors who's genuinely nice to me, raises her hands to the sky and cries out so loud I feel it in my chest.

I figured she was a shoo-in for Mary Magdalene.

A few feet away, Cameron stands rigid, staring at the list, Philip's arm around his waist. Then he turns, and for a second his eyes meet mine, big and shiny like he wants to cry. His lip even quivers.

And for the briefest of moments, I remember what it was like when we were together, and he got into a nasty fight with his brother and cried on my shoulder. Or his mom threatened to ground him for getting a C on an Algebra II test.

But then his expression hardens. He keeps his eyes fixed on me while he whispers something that makes Philip chuckle. And then they both skulk off toward the stairs.

Whatever. I'm used to it. I ignore them and push my way toward the board.

Sure enough: *Mary Magdalene–Tori Tanner.*

And just above that: *Judas Iscariot–Cameron Haller.*

And at the very top: *Jesus Christ–Liam Coquyt.*

A shoulder brushes against mine. Liam. He's looking pale, eyes wide with panic, mouth hanging open.

"Hey. The list is up," I tell him, as if he wasn't staring at it unblinking.

He nods, silently mouths *Jesus Christ.* Slowly the shock melts into a smile like the sunrise, and I find myself smiling in sympathy. He deserves this. As he turns to face me, smile even broader somehow, I laugh and say, "I guess I owe you some shmoodies."

6

Jasmine drops me off at Bowie's Saturday afternoon, but before I can get out she taps my shoulder.

"Huh?"

"What happened with the play? Did Liam get a part?"

"Musical. And yeah."

"Why didn't you tell me?"

"You didn't ask?"

She's never cared about Theatre before. This crush must be serious.

"You like him."

"What? No. I just . . ." She sighs, and it turns into this sweet smile. "He's really cute."

"I thought you were focusing on yourself this year."

She straightens in her seat. "I am. Forget I asked."

I wave as she drives off. But she definitely doth protest too much.

Jasmine's never had a crush on one of my friends before. I'm not sure how I feel about it. Still, he'd be a big improvement over her past boyfriends: in personality, and in hygiene, and yeah, in looks too.

Bowie answers the door, dressed in a black crop-top sweater

and black shorts that are almost capris, showing off the rich, dark brown of their legs and stomach. They've always been in good shape from swimming, lithe and long, but this last year they've actually started to get some abs showing. I try not to be jealous.

They've also done their makeup, metallic purple eye shadow and equally vibrant aquamarine lipstick. A plain black headband holds back their twists.

Bowie's really good-looking, which is maybe why people always think we're dating. Like, because they're good-looking, they should want to date people. And like, because Bowie is beautiful, I can't be just friends with them. According to Bowie, last year, one of the other GSA kids actually told them, to their face, that they "couldn't wait for you and Jackson to finally hook up."

I sign hello to Bowie's mom as we pass the kitchen. Both of their parents are deaf, and I learned ASL from all the afternoons and weekends spent at their house. Well, technically it's a mix of ASL and BASL, Black American Sign Language, which I didn't realize until I started talking to white signers, and people said I had an accent. Bowie's mom had to explain it to me.

She greets me back, asks about school and how Dad and Amy are doing. Her skin is the same rich brown as Bowie's, and her head is shaved. She has the perfectly shaped head for it. Her hands are small and deft as we talk.

"Mail came," she tells Bowie as I grab a bag of snack-size Twizzlers from the pantry. The Andersons have started stocking up on Halloween candy early.

Mrs. Anderson hands Bowie a white envelope, one of the big nine-by-twelve ones, stuffed with papers. It's got the UT logo stamped across one side.

"Thanks." Bowie tucks it under their arm and turns to lead me upstairs, where I sprawl on the floor and they flop onto their bed and we fight through our AP Chem homework.

As I rip into another Twizzler, my phone buzzes with a text from a strange number.

Is there anything I should know before Monday?

Who is this?

Oh sorry.

It's Liam.

I got your number off the board?

I always put my number on the crew signups in case anyone has questions, but I can't believe someone actually looked at them. I can't believe Liam actually bothered.

We've been friends for a while, but not *texting* friends. I add him to my contacts.

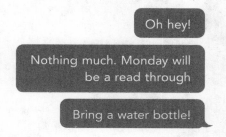

Oh hey!

Nothing much. Monday will be a read through

Bring a water bottle!

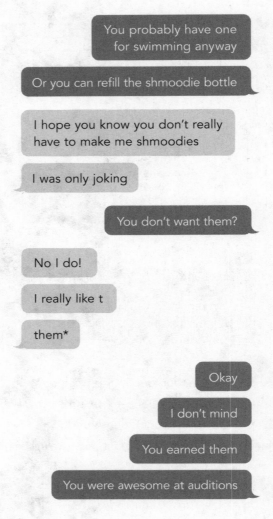

You probably have one for swimming anyway

Or you can refill the shmoodie bottle

I hope you know you don't really have to make me shmoodies

I was only joking

You don't want them?

No I do!

I really like t

them*

Okay

I don't mind

You earned them

You were awesome at auditions

It's safe for me to tell him that now.

Bowie scoots toward the end of their bed. "What are you doing?"

"Nothing. Liam had some questions about the show."

"Tell him hi."

Bowie says hi

Oh

You're with them now?

Yeah

Sorry for interrupting

See you Monday!

I shrug. He wasn't interrupting much. AP Chem kind of sucks. I turn back to my work, but Bowie flaps their hand.

"I didn't know you texted Liam," they sign.

"I guess he got my number off the Theatre Board."

Bowie studies me for a long moment.

"What?"

"Nothing." They press their lips together—the aquamarine really does look good on them—and blow out a long breath. "He's been talking about trying out for a while. Didn't think he'd get a lead on his first try."

"He was amazing. You should've seen him."

"Yeah?"

I nod, but Bowie's got a weird smile.

"What?"

"Do you like him?"

"Yeah, he's fine."

"Jacks."

"Just as a friend."

No way am I crushing on another boy that won't like me back. All signs indicate he's straight, anyway. And if Jasmine likes him? No way.

Bowie's face scrunches up. "Well, look out for him, okay? He's not used to Theatre Kids."

"Hey! I'm a Theatre Kid!"

"You know what I mean. Now come on." They throw a Twizzler at my nose. "Finish up so we can play *Smash*."

"You're going down."

7

When we pull into our spot Monday morning, Jasmine flips down her sun visor and examines her face in the mirror, licking her finger and smoothing down her eyebrows. We both got Dad's thick, dark eyebrows, and Jasmine inherited a teeny bit of Dad's unibrow too. She's super self-conscious about it, and gets it threaded once a month.

My sister's beautiful, though, unibrow or not. She's got more makeup on than usual for a Monday, foundation and lipstick and some concealer on the pimple in the fold of her nose. I hate when I get one there.

She's dressed up too, in a pink blouse and jeans, with her hair down in loose waves, like she's trying to impress ~~Liam~~ someone.

I grab my backpack and the shmoodies, hooking my fingers through the plastic loops on the lids. The cold bottles smack against each other as I shut the door.

Jasmine jogs to get in front of me. "Who's the extra for?"

"Liam. I told him I'd make him some if he got a role."

"Aw, that's sweet. Need help carrying them?"

"I'm good." It's a shmoodie, not a set piece.

Jasmine shrugs and waves at her best friend Ellie. I head for the stairs, taking them two at a time, round the corner for the Theatre Hall—

And stop dead when my eyes land on the disaster that is the Theatre Board.

I don't mean the giant cast list Dr. Lochley made, though that is a bit of a disaster. No. I mean the duct tape letters stretched across it.

LIAM COQUYT SHOULD CO-QUIT.

An angry fire burns behind my sternum.

First, duct tape? Really? It leaves a disgusting residue everywhere you stick it. Denise doesn't allow it anywhere near the theatre; we only use gaff tape.

And second, it's not even clever. Coquyt, co-quit. Not exactly Shakespearean wordplay.

Third: Liam absolutely does not deserve it. Theatre is supposed to be welcoming to everyone.

This has Cam written all over it. I knew he was upset on Friday, the way he was muttering to Philip, the look he gave me. Cam's always been a jerk, but I didn't think he'd do something like this.

Not that I could ever prove it.

I knock on Dr. Lochley's office, but no one answers. Must be in a staff meeting or something, since she's usually here long before first bell. But I can't let anyone see this, least of all Liam. I told Bowie I'd look out for him, and I meant it.

I set the shmoodies on the floor with my backpack, snap some photos for evidence, then get to work.

I pull down the destroyed cast list, along with half the flyers beneath where the duct tape stuck; thankfully the corkboard itself seems fine. When it's down and wadded up, I've got a decent-sized paper-and-tape wad, about the size of a misshapen volleyball. I tuck it under my arm—I've got to find a big enough trash can to dispose of it—and head to the computer lab.

By the time I return, Dr. L is back, facing the empty board with her fists on her hips and her legs akimbo, like she's ready to remake the world. She wears her scarf like armor.

"Jackson! Did you clean the board off?"

"Yeah. Here."

I hand her one end of the fresh cast list, and she helps me pin it up.

"What brought this on?"

I show her the pictures.

"Who would do something like this?" She pulls her glasses off and zooms in the photo.

"Someone who wanted Liam's part, probably." Like Cameron. "Or who was mad at him for not paying his dues." Again: Cameron.

"Emotions always run high around casting," Dr. Lochley says sagely. "You know, when I was in college we did Eve Ensler's *The Vagina Monologues*, and the first day of rehearsals, someone left a bunch of tampons in the studio."

I blink and fight the urge to check my hearing aids.

"They were used too. It was a whole mess. We had to shut down rehearsals so a cleaning company could come in. Blood's a biohazard."

Dr. Lochley's college days were super weird.

"Anyway. Maybe you should talk to the actors? About

49

welcoming in new . . ." I was going to say *blood,* but not now. "New talent to the department?"

"Oh, everyone knows that. Don't worry about it."

Dr. L has a much higher opinion of the senior actors than I do.

"But Liam's not used to this, and if people are going to be terrible to him—"

"Jesus was misunderstood and persecuted in his time too." She hands back my phone. "I think you underestimate the actors. I'm sure they're going to welcome Liam with open arms. But even if they don't, he can always use it for the role."

Liam doesn't deserve that.

No one deserves that.

Dr. L looks up toward the ceiling. "Oh. Warning bell. You'd better get to class."

8

After last bell, I fight the tide down to the Main Theatre. There's always lots to do on the first day of rehearsals. I clear off the stage, then start pulling folding chairs off the rack. Dr. L always starts with a full read-through, and she likes for everyone—from leads down to chorus—to sit in a big circle onstage, to *take in the performance space.*

I count out the chairs, adjust the spacing (it ends up being more of an oval than a circle), then head to the stage manager station to bring up a stage wash. The backstage doors open and Liam comes in, arms full of scripts.

"Oh. Hey." I rush over to take them from him. "Thanks."

"Sure. Did I make it in time to actually help?"

I shrug and try not to smile. None of the actors have ever actually offered to help me before. I'm not sure what to make of it.

"Thanks again for the shmoodie. I love pineapple."

"Good." Today's were pineapple and vanilla Greek yogurt. After fixing the cast list, I barely had time to throw the shmoodies at Liam and Bowie on my way to first period.

I look over the pile of librettos; they're rented from the rights company, and we have to return them at the end of the production.

Each has a character name stamped on it. I go around the circle, starting with the leads together at upstage center, leaving two seats empty for me and Dr. Lochley.

"Is there a somethingsomething?" Liam asks.

I look up and shake my head. "Say again?"

"Is there a method to the madness?"

"Not really, just try to keep groups together, like Apostles and stuff."

Liam nods and holds out his hand; I give him a stack of various Romans to lay out. But he doesn't move.

"Everything okay?"

His Adam's apple bobs up and down; his eyes flit to mine and then away.

"Thank you for what you did this morning. With the cast list." He blushes, pink cutting a sharp line along his cheekbones.

"Oh." My own cheeks start heating. I scratch my nose. "It's nothing."

"It wasn't nothing to me."

"How'd you find out about that anyway?"

"Dr. L told me." He grips the scripts tighter, the little tendons on his hands flexing. "She said she wanted to make sure I knew I was welcomed in the department."

I try not to frown, but I can feel my nostrils flaring. The whole point of me taking it down early was so Liam wouldn't know. All I can think to say is "Sorry."

Liam looks right at me, his blue eyes wide and open, and even though there's only a general wash on the stage, I feel like I'm stuck in a spotlight. His gaze is way too intense. It's like Cam's puppy-dog eyes but ten times worse, because behind Cam's look there's always the sense that he wants something. But Liam's sharing something instead. Something small and vulnerable.

"I didn't want you to find out," I tell him. "You don't deserve that."

He just keeps looking at me, and I think my face might be melting off, it's so warm. "Thanks."

"You're welcome."

Liam finally blinks, and I can breathe again.

"Come on. The rest of the cast will be here soon."

I get everyone settled for read-through, handing out fresh pencils for people to use. "Don't use ink. Pencil only."

I've got to go through and erase everyone's notes at the end of the show, which is tedious enough, but if people use pen we get charged for the damage.

Liam's already seated, libretto in his lap, bouncing his knees. Dr. Lochley is talking to Cameron over by the stage door. He's got his arms crossed and a frown on his face. Maybe she realized he was the one who vandalized the cast list after all.

He spares a look in Liam's direction, and I can't tell if he's mad or sad, but then he sees me looking and gives me a definite glare.

Dr. Lochley doesn't notice, though; she nods firmly, pats him on the shoulder, and turns so fast her scarf nearly smacks his face.

She makes her way center stage and claps her hands once to get everyone quieted down. "Welcome, everyone, to the read-through for *Jesus Christ Superstar!*" She pauses while the cast applauds. "For today, just speak your lines, don't worry about singing. I want everyone to get a feel for the somethingsomething."

Everyone nods and mutters as she takes her seat. "I'm Dr. Lochley, I use she/her pronouns, and I'm the director. Let's all introduce ourselves and our roles before we get started. Jackson?"

"Jackson. He/him. I'm the stage manager." I open my binder, check the lead on my mechanical pencil, and keep my head down as Liam introduces himself. Everyone goes around the circle, but I don't pay attention: I already know everyone's names and pronouns, and besides, tracking people talking in a big circle?

I'm already exhausted and we haven't even begun.

Instead, I open my binder. My libretto is actually a photocopy, even though that's technically illegal. But with the amount of notes I make, I would destroy the paper trying to erase everything.

I cross my left leg over my right to make a better platform for my binder, and my knee accidentally bumps into Liam's. He's still jiggling nervously, but he stops as soon as we touch.

I glance his way, and he smiles back at me, small and nervous, pressing his knee against mine.

I try not to hold my breath, but he pressed back against me. He definitely did that. Why would he do something like that?

I'm in black jeans, and he's in shorts, showing off his long legs. There's a little hair along his calves. I guess he hasn't shaved for a meet yet. And even through the denim I feel his warmth.

I swallow and shift my binder a bit to cover the sudden tightness in my jeans, which is definitely a reaction to my nervousness about the read-through and not to Liam's knee. But suddenly I can smell his deodorant a lot more too, and that subtly sweet chlorine scent that's all him, and I wish my tag would stick up so he could fix it for me.

I shake my head. My imagination is out of control. There are plenty of straight guys that don't mind bumping knees with a gay guy. It's not a big deal. And besides, Jasmine likes him.

Dr. L taps her pencil against my binder, and I realize intros are over. I'm supposed to read the stage directions.

I clear my throat and ignore Liam, and my pants, and the scenarios my brain is trying to spin out of the fleeting contact.

"Act one. Scene one . . ."

9

*B*owie and Liam have their first swim meet of the season at the end of September.

Rather than drop me off at the doors to the Community Center, Jasmine pulls into the parking lot.

"What are you doing?"

"I thought I'd watch too. Is that a problem?"

No, except Jasmine spent an hour "getting ready" this afternoon, and I figured she was going to hang out with Ellie. Not come to a swim meet with me.

I suppose it was inevitable, though. All week long, she was waiting outside the theatre after rehearsals, instead of making me find her in the pottery studio. All so she can say hi to Liam.

Last time she even "accidentally" brushed against his shoulder, so she could comment on how swimming must keep him in good shape. Which led to him mentioning the meet.

So maybe that counted as him inviting her? Maybe he wants her here. Maybe he likes her too.

~~Maybe that whole touching knees thing was a fluke. It's not like it happened again.~~

He still tucks in my tags, though.

Jasmine waves her hand in front of my face; I hate when she does that.

"What?"

"Are we going in?"

"Yeah." I grab the two shmoodie bottles—they've got extra banana for more potassium—and lead the way.

The Natatorium is attached to the Community Center: I suppose the city must split costs with the district or something. It's a huge, cavernous thing, with a short-course pool, diving well, and bleachers on both sides.

I turn my hearing aids off before we even step inside: With concrete floors, high metal ceilings, lots of water, and huge crowds, there's no way I'll catch anything except a headache. With them off, everything sounds far away, soft and squishy, but way easier to manage.

Jasmine says something as I lead her toward the spectators' bleachers, which are opposite the team bleachers. I spot Bowie and Liam and the rest of the team in their purple warm-ups, sitting beneath the purple-and-gold Riverstone Raptors banner.

Jasmine tries talking to me again, but I shake my head. "I turned my hearing aids off. Too much noise."

She nods and pulls out her phone to type notes.

When do they go on?

"They're both in the medley relay." Bowie for butterfly, Liam for freestyle.

But Jasmine raises her eyebrows at me.

"First event."

More spectators trickle in, but it's a swim meet, not a football game, so the crowd is ~~sparse~~ small but dedicated. Eventually, people settle. The teams stand. Someone plays what I assume must be the national anthem on a harmonica.

Bowie and Liam and the rest of the team take off their warm-ups, heading toward the blocks. Jasmine stiffens next to me. I get it: Liam ~~in a Speedo~~ shirtless is a sight to behold, even from a distance. Bowie's looking good too: Their back has grown broader since last season. They fight with their cap—most swim caps are made for white people hair—and adjust their goggles as Trevor, a senior who swims backstroke, gets into the pool and grabs the handles for his start. While Bowie bounces on their toes to keep warm, Liam looks our way and gives a wave. Even from across the Natatorium, I can see the way his muscles move. ~~I almost forget to breathe.~~

Jasmine nearly knocks me over as she leaps to her feet to wave back. Liam laughs and faces the blocks, flapping his long arms back and forth to ~~lubricate~~ loosen up his shoulders.

When Jasmine sits again, her cheeks are flushed. She shows me her phone.

He waved at me!

I want to tell her he waved at *me,* but I can't be sure. And there it is again: Is he being nice? Or does he like her?

The uncertainty is killing me.

As the crowd streams out, I grab for the shmoodies, but only one of them is there. I look beneath our bench, and the one behind us, to see if it fell over, but it's just gone. Then I catch Jasmine already moving down the stairs, with one of the bottles—the one with a blue cap, which I use for Liam—in her hand.

I grab Bowie's and join the queue.

The lobby is packed, but I head for the doors; Bowie knows to meet me outside. I gesture for Jasmine to follow, and we escape out the double doors onto the lawn. The afternoon sun is shining, and it's warm with summer's last gasp. (I assume. You never know with Missouri weather. Or climate change.)

Jasmine's already trying to talk to me while I'm still adjusting my hearing aids.

"—awesome. Right?"

It was awesome: Bowie had a terrific meet, placing first in three events and even setting a new personal record. And Liam? He took first in five. That's not even counting the relays.

"Yeah." I nod at the shmoodie she ~~usurped~~ grabbed. "I can take that."

"Oh, I don't mind." She shakes her hair off her face and watches the doors, bouncing on her toes.

Finally Bowie emerges, flanked by their parents; Liam's not far behind, his swim bag slung over his shoulders. He jogs over while Bowie is stuck saying bye to their parents.

"Hey. You came."

He's looking at me, but Jasmine says, "Of course I did!" and shoves his shmoodie at him.

"Oh. Uh. Thanks." He looks from her back to me; I give him a little shrug.

"It's—"

"Peanut butter and banana," Jasmine answers.

"And spinach."

"Mmm." Liam shakes it and pops the top to taste it while Bowie finally joins us. I high-five them, pull them into a hug, and hand over their shmoodie.

"You did great," I sign. "Proud of you."

"Thanks. If I can shave another second off my fly, I can set a new pool record."

"You can do it."

Bowie turns back to Liam. "You ready to go?" they ask aloud. Liam ~~licks the shmoodie off his lips and~~ nods.

"Oh. You three going somewhere?" Jasmine asks.

"Perkins. Don't worry, I can get a ride home from Bowie."

She plays with her hair. "What, is this an exclusive thing?"

I blink at her. It's not exclusive so much as it's a thing me and Bowie always do, and I invited Liam this time since we're friends now.

"You don't want to be those two's third wheel, do you?" she asks Liam, gesturing between me and Bowie. "I can something-something."

Liam purses his lips and glances toward me, but Jasmine says something else and he follows her toward the parking lot.

"What just happened?" I ask Bowie.

Their eyebrows raise. "She said she'd drive us."

"Great."

We pack into Jasmine's car: Liam in shotgun, since he's got the longest legs, and me right behind him since I'm the shortest (not counting Jasmine). Jasmine immediately engages him in conversation I can't make out.

Bowie turns to me. "What is she doing?"

I sigh. "She has a crush."

"On Liam?" Bowie's eyes go wide, but then they cock their head to the side. "Actually, that tracks."

"It's a nightmare. She's never crushed on one of my friends before."

Bowie frowns.

"What?"

"Is that all it is?"

"All what is?"

But Bowie glances toward the front of the car. They turn back to me and roll their eyes.

"Jasmine wants to know what we're talking about."

"Don't tell her!"

"I told her if she learned sign, she could follow along."

I snort. But Liam twists around in his seat so we can see him. And then he fingerspells, very slowly, "I'm trying."

"Really?" I ask aloud.

He nods. "Bowie's been teaching me."

"Bowie's a good teacher."

"Yeah." Suddenly the car is too hot, even though Jasmine's got the air conditioner going. She says something again, and Liam turns back around as we pull into the Perkins parking lot.

10

I don't know how exactly Perkins became me and Bowie's designated hangout spot, but there's not many places where you can get huge amounts of carbs for cheap, and that are open twenty-four hours a day—my shows get out late. Plus it's usually full of older folks having quiet conversations, and there's no loud music playing. So it's all around kind of perfect.

Our host, Janice—she's taken care of me and Bowie loads of times—leads us to a booth toward the back. When Liam sits, Jasmine slides in next to him without a word. Bowie likes to be on the outside of the booth, so I take the inside, right across from Liam. My knees bump up against him, but he straightens out and we don't touch again.

Janice comes by to take our orders: an omelette and hash browns for me, like usual; a huge stack of pancakes for Bowie, of course; but then Jasmine takes forever before ordering a salad.

Jasmine never used to order salads at restaurants, until she dated Tristan last year.

STANKY TRISTAN'S BREAKUP LIST:
~~ENCOURAGED JASMINE TO ORDER SALADS~~
TOLD JASMINE TO WATCH HER WEIGHT
~~FUTURE INCEL~~
NEVER EATS GREEN FOODS
FATPHOBIC
~~PROBABLY DOESN'T WASH HIS ASS~~
FUNKY BODY ODOR
~~LIKE SERIOUSLY, DOES HE USE SOAP WHEN HE SHOWERS??~~
POOR HYGIENE

I can still kind of smell him every time I see his list in the back of my binder.

Jasmine got out of the salad habit after they broke up. Mostly. Sometimes, when she's around a crush, she falls back into it.

I order some mozzarella sticks for the table, so maybe she'll feel okay having some if she wants, and then Liam orders an omelet too.

"Twins," he fingerspells at me, and I laugh.

"What was that?" Jasmine asks.

"We're order twins," Liam explains.

"So how long somethingsomething?" Jasmine asks, and pulls Liam into conversation. I sigh and turn to Bowie.

"So you're teaching Liam sign?"

"Yeah. After practice, or at school. Whenever we have time."

"When did he start?"

"Right after he got cast."

My chest feels warm again. Did he start learning because of me? That's not a leap, is it? Maybe it is. Maybe he always wanted to learn. Maybe he knows other deaf folks. Maybe he's tired of taking AP Spanish and wants to know a different language.

"What am I missing?" Liam asks aloud.

"Nothing." Bowie elbows me in the side, but I ignore them.

"You know how those two are. Always off in their own little world." Jasmine rests a hand on Liam's arm. "Oh wow, you're really warm."

Liam's cheeks color. "Most swimmers are."

Bowie swivels my way again. Their eyebrows are nearly through the roof.

"Oh my god!"

"I know. She's got it bad."

Bowie purses their lips. "What are you going to do about it?"

"Me? Nothing. If she likes him . . ."

"You're really fine with . . . that?" They gesture across the table, where Jasmine is comparing her hand size to Liam's.

"I mean . . ."

It might be awkward, being friends with Jasmine's boyfriend. My heart hammers just imagining it. Then again, after the string of ~~deplorable~~ incompatible people she's dated, maybe Jasmine deserves someone nice like Liam.

"If they like each other, sure. Liam's a really good guy."

I glance across the table. Jasmine's moved on to playing with Liam's hair. It's still shiny and damp from the pool, ~~an adorable~~ a wispy black mess.

"Your hair is really soft."

"Thanks?"

Liam blushes again, his lips curved into a shy smile, and yeah, he might actually like her too.

We're saved from any more awkward flirting by Janice, hoisting a huge oval tray of laden plates.

"All right, loves," she says. "Who's hungry?"

Jasmine has to use the bathroom before we go, but it's so nice outside—the sun setting, a pleasant breeze rising—we wait by the car. Liam leans against the trunk, all long legs, arms crossed, while Bowie checks their phone.

"My parents want me to grab a pie. Be right back."

And then it's just me and Liam, waiting. I lean against the car next to him; his fingers brush my neck as he tucks in my tag.

"Thanks," I say. "Sorry for . . . you know." I gesture toward the restaurant.

"What? No. It was fine. Your sister is cool."

"Yeah?"

He chews on his lip for a moment, staring past me at the doors. His fingers drum against the trunk.

And I know what he's going to ask. I can see it in his eyes. In the way his cheeks are colored by more than just the sunset. In the way Jasmine was all over him tonight.

"I actually wanted to ask you something," he says.

My throat closes off. But it's not like I didn't know this was coming.

"Yes," I tell him. "You can."

"Huh?"

"You can ask her out. It's okay with me."

"Oh . . ." He blinks down at me. "Uh. Really?"

"Really." My throat feels sandy—a little hash brown stuck in it, probably—but I swallow hard. "I think you'd be really good together."

"Oh." He scratches the back of his head. "I haven't dated any-one in a while."

"Really? Why?"

He looks at me, then down at his feet and says something I don't catch.

"What?"

"Sorry. It feels weird to say."

"You can sign it."

A smile crests his lips. "I'm not that good yet." But then it fades, and he runs a hand through his hair. "Sometimes I feel like people only want to go out with me because of how I look. Like my outside is all that matters."

"Well, have you seen yourself in a mirror?" I blurt out. And immediately wish I could take it back. My cheeks are burning, and Liam's look ready to go supernova. I have to salvage this.

"It's a miracle you can swim without getting distracted by your reflection in the pool."

The tension snaps, and Liam cracks up, squinting and showing his canines. "Oh, god, that makes me sound so conceited."

"That's what I always tell people. Only someone as conceited as you would bother hanging around to help me clean up after rehearsals."

"I like doing it."

"I really appreciate it." I swallow. "I get it, though. For real. You feel like people don't really see you."

I know what that's like. Stage managers are supposed to be invisible.

"Yeah. Exactly."

"Well, for what it's worth, Jasmine isn't that shallow."

Historically, her boyfriends have been the shallow ones. ~~I guess that's what happens when you date from the inflatable backyard dating pool.~~

Liam bites his lip, like he's about to say more, but then he straightens and looks past me. Jasmine and Bowie are headed our way, Bowie with a pie.

"What are you two talking about?" Jasmine asks. "Nothing bad, I hope."

I shake my head. Liam scratches the back of his neck, giving me a huge whiff of his chlorine scent and deodorant. Jasmine probably smelled it through the whole meal.

She gives Liam a sweet smile. "We'd better get going."

That night, I sit up in bed, going over my trig homework. I'm not part of the Toxic Math Fandom, but I try to do well, because you need math a lot in Theatre.

As I'm calculating another tangent, my phone buzzes. Liam.

Thanks for dinner tonight!

Sure!

Thanks for coming.

Thanks for inviting me.

And congrats again!

Thanks

And then there's three dots. They appear and disappear and reappear so many times my phone locks itself. I turn back to my homework.

But then it buzzes again.

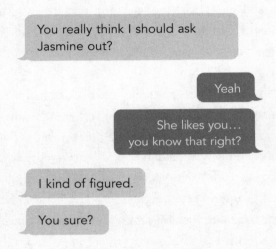

You really think I should ask Jasmine out?

Yeah

She likes you... you know that right?

I kind of figured.

You sure?

I can't believe I've turned into Jasmine's wingman. But she's my sister. I want her to be happy.

Positive

11

"**H**ow's the fit?" Denise asks the door.

I really like Denise~~, maybe even more than I like Dr. L~~. She's super smart, but not the kind of smart that demands to be acknowledged: more the kind of smart that makes you want to bask in her knowledge in the hopes of absorbing it via photosynthesis. She's got porcelain skin, hazel eyes, deep dimples, and hair that would probably be curly if it wasn't buzzed short. She's in a black Foo Fighters T-shirt that stretches across her big boobs and bigger belly.

Behind the door, Liam says something I can't make out. We're in the dressing room, backstage left. Racks and racks of costumes line one wall; a row of mirrors and lights line the other. Two doors lead to the actual changing rooms.

Denise bites her lip. "Well, come on out and we'll take a look. It's just me and Jackson here. If you're comfortable with that."

The door swings open. Liam steps out, and I have to try really hard to not let my jaw drop.

Dr. Lochley's going for a sort of ~~vaguely-apocalyptic~~ post-modern vibe for the show, so people are in distressed jeans and

69

tank tops and T-shirts. Liam's in a pair of low-slung black jeans with the right knee ripped. And that's it.

My mouth goes dry.

I've seen him shirtless before, in a Speedo no less, but that was with the whole Natatorium between us. Not close enough to touch.

He's too tall, taking up all the space and all the air in the dressing room. His chest is the same alabaster as his face, though it looks carved, his pecs firm and strong, rising and falling with his breath. The cords of his neck slope gently into strong shoulders. The warm overhead lights turn his abs into a valley of shadows. The jeans are low enough to show the V leading from his hips to his ~~crotch~~ lower waist.

"Are these okay?" He tries to catch my eye, but I look at his knees instead.

I've lost all power of speech, but thankfully Denise speaks up.

"Turn around. Let's see the fit."

Liam does so, and I can see exactly what years of swimming have done to his back, because it's Dorito-shaped, with little dimples at the bottom of his spine.

Right above the flattest ass I have ever seen in my life. I've never had a close-up look before. Despite what swimming has done for his back, it hasn't done anything for his ass.

Denise steps closer to him, which is a relief, because then she can't see me ~~readjust my pants~~ blushing.

"Are you okay if I touch your waistband?" Denise asks.

Liam looks over his shoulder, and this time he catches me studying him. My face burns hotter.

"Sure."

Denise grabs the belt loops and tugs them up. The jeans rise three inches, exposing his ankles and probably giving him a wedgie from the way he flinches. She turns, pulls down another pair off the rack. "Try these instead?"

Liam nods and heads back into the changing room. I remember that I have lungs and start breathing again, willing my heart to beat normally and keep blood flowing to my brain and nowhere else.

Because he's absolutely, 100 percent off-limits. He and Jasmine like each other, even if they're still doing this weird dance around the issue. But *damn*.

"Jackson?"

"Huh?"

"Can you stay here in case Liam needs anything? I've got to check on the scene shop."

"I can check—"

But she's already on her way out. There's a bunch of Theatre I students getting their volunteer hours by helping clean out the scene shop.

I cross my arms and pace, until the door cracks. Liam pokes his head out.

"Where'd Denise go?"

"Scene shop."

"Oh." Liam's face turns a bit red. "These don't work."

"What's wrong with them?"

Liam opens the door a bit wider to show me. Despite him having an ass flat as the Kansas prairie, the jeans won't go up past his thighs. He's in a pair of black boxer-briefs, and though the ass is flat, the front is definitely not. ~~The image is seared into my~~

71

brain; even when I blink I see it. I keep my eyes fixed on his face.

"Oh. Yeah. Let me look through and see. It's funny, you know, sometimes the costumes get mislabeled or just organized wrong. I guess I need to do a proper sorting, but that'll have to wait until we're through with the show. Maybe that'll be my winter project, especially going into the spring play, you know, just to make sure everything's in good shape." I realize I'm rambling and clamp my mouth shut, digging until I find a better pair of jeans.

"Try these." My mouth tastes like I've licked a fire curtain.

"Thanks."

He takes them with one hand, and reaches behind me to tuck in my tag with the other, and I stifle a squeak, because I hate it when he does that.

Except I don't hate it. No matter how much I lie to myself, the truth is, I like it. I like him.

I like Liam.

"You okay?" he fingerspells. It's still weird, seeing him do it. I guess he and Bowie had a few more lessons this past week, though, because he's a little more fluid and confident with it.

But it snaps me out of my panic.

"I'm fine." Even I can tell my voice sounds weird. "I'm thirsty. You need any water?"

He already drank the shmoodie I brought him. Frozen blueberries and vanilla Greek yogurt. There was no more fresh fruit: Dad wasn't back from City Market by the time Amy had to drop me off for our Saturday work day.

"I'm good," he says. Then he signs, "Thanks," and disappears behind the door.

Once we finally find the right jeans for Liam, I label them. He's the last fitting for today, so I go find Denise, who's closing up the scene shop.

"Good work today," she tells me. "You get Liam squared away?"

"Yup. Labeled and everything."

"Great. Hey, do you know Paige?" She gestures, and a girl comes over, white with brown hair and striking green eyes that are only enhanced by an epic application of eyeliner.

"Hey," she says.

"Hey. I'm Jackson." I shake her hand; it's got a few calluses on it, like mine. "Thanks for all your hard work today."

"Sure."

Denise says something to her; she nods and goes to collect her backpack, while Denise turns back to me.

"I was thinking somethingsomething."

"Say again?"

"Sorry. What do you think of her being your assistant stage manager?"

"Really?"

"Yeah. She's interested. Hard worker. I think she'd be good at it."

I've never had an ASM before. But maybe I could mentor her, like Caprice mentored me.

"Yeah. That'd be great."

Denise grins. "Good."

Me. With an assistant. I'm still kind of floating as I head back to the dressing room to grab my backpack, but Liam opens the door before I can. He's dressed again, in a worn RHS Swim & Dive T-shirt and black sweats. I back up before I bump into him.

"Oh. Sorry."

"It's fine. Just . . ." I point inside, and he opens the door a little wider. I still have to squeeze by him, though; he smells like the pool, and soap, and blueberries.

I shake myself off and grab my backpack.

"You good?" he asks. "Need a ride?"

"Bowie's got me."

His brow furrows. "They're here?"

I nod; wave at Denise, who's wheeling out the ghost light; and head down the hall toward the choir room.

"GSA thing."

Mr. Cartwright is the GSA Sponsor, so they use the choir room for planning.

Sure enough, Bowie's in there, along with a couple other GSA members—including Braden Campos, who's kneeling over one of the risers, working on a poster board.

"Jackson!" He smiles at me as I come in. He's got inky black hair that does the sort of effortless swoopy thing mine will never do, and a tooth gap that ~~is kind of adorable~~ gives him character. "How's it going, bro?"

Braden joined the GSA last year, after coming out as bi. I actually used to have a little bit of a crush on him. We had PE together first year, and he was always really nice to me, which felt homophobic at the time, but then I realized he was just . . . genuinely nice. And I guess the crush resurfaced, once he came out, but then he went and joined the GSA.

BRADEN CAMPOS'S BREAKUP LIST:
PLAYS FOOTBALL
WHAT IS A LINEBACKER ANYWAY?
WHAT LINES ARE BEING BACKED?
~~CUTE TOOTH GAP~~
~~GOOD HAIR~~
CALLS ME "BRO"
~~TRIED TO USURP BOWIE~~
RAN AGAINST BOWIE FOR VICE PRESIDENT
GSA MEMBER!!!

Actually, aside from the GSA stuff, it was hard to come up with items for Braden's list. It would be like making a list for a golden retriever.

"You've got some . . ." I gesture to my own cheek; Braden's got glitter across his. I stay well back to avoid contamination.

Braden scrubs his cheek with the back of his hand. "Thanks. Hey, bro."

He cocks his chin in Liam's direction.

"You guys here to help?"

The whole crew is spread across the choir room, making posters for National Coming Out Day. Some are already finished, with slogans like *Take pride in who you are* and *Welcome to the family* and *Come out at your own pace* and *Out or not, you are valid.*

I wish someone had told me that when I was younger. But in seventh grade, when everyone was talking about crushes and dating and first kisses, it felt like I had to come out. Like if I didn't I'd just . . . disappear.

I kind of wish I could've taken my time with it.

Braden waves his hand. And not in the *politely trying to draw your attention* kind of way but in the *is there anyone in there?* kind of way.

"What?" I say, harsher than I mean, but I hate when people wave at me like that. And I hate that I snap at Braden ~~in front of Liam~~ because he probably didn't know any better and is mostly cool to me. Even if he does *bro* me.

"I said, Bowie's in the office."

"Thanks."

I weave my way toward the back, careful to avoid anything that looks even slightly sparkly; Liam follows close behind.

"Uh," I say. "Did you . . . did you need Bowie for something? Another sign lesson?"

"No. Just . . . didn't feel like going home yet."

"Oh."

The office door is open, so I poke my head in. It's a small, cramped space: a desk, a laptop, way too many coffee mugs, and shelf upon shelf of music. The soft scent of paper and toner fills the air.

"Hey, Jacks. Hey, Liam. You all done?"

"Yeah."

"Sorry. I need another hour."

"I can give Jackson a ride," Liam says. "If you need to stay."

If I have to ride in a car with Liam, alone, I think I might explode.

"It's all good, me and Bowie are hanging out after anyway." I turn to Liam. "You don't have to hang around. Hey, did Jasmine text you?"

Deflecting seems the only safe choice. Jasmine likes Liam. Liam likes her.

I'm not crushing, I'm not anything. I'm just a gay boy that saw Liam's abs up close and needs some time to decompress. That's totally normal.

Liam's cheeks color. He looks at me for a long moment, and then past me at Bowie, and then back.

"Uh. Okay. See you, I guess."

"Yeah. See you."

Once Liam's gone, Bowie switches to sign.

"What was that?"

"What was what?"

Bowie's nostrils flare. "Why are you trying to foist him on Jasmine?"

"She likes him. He likes her. They're just being weird."

"You sure about that?"

"You didn't see him after Perkins. He was all . . ."

"All what?"

But I don't want to tell Bowie what Liam told me. That felt like the kind of thing told in confidence.

"Trust me. He definitely does."

Braden appears in the doorway.

"Hey, bros." To him, everyone's a bro, regardless of gender. "You two done fighting?"

"We're not fighting."

He just laughs, showing off his tooth gap. "Okay. You two somethingsomething."

"Huh?" I glance at Bowie.

"Fight like a married couple," they sign to me.

"We do not!" I say aloud. Too loud. Liam's still watching from the doorway.

"If you say so." Braden runs a hand through his hair. "You got any more glue sticks?"

Bowie stands to help. I give Liam a last wave goodbye and watch as he finally leaves.

12

Friday morning, Jasmine's still looking for a parking spot when my phone lights up with a text from Dr. Lochley.

Dr. L almost never texts. She thinks it's an inappropriate blurring of teacher-student boundaries.

But this text says:

> CODE RED

"Stop!" The car lurches to a stop halfway up one aisle. "I've gotta go!"

I grab my stuff, leap out of the car and run for the entrance, ignoring Jasmine's confused shouting.

There are three common Theatre Emergencies that I have to deal with:

* TEACHER CAN'T FIGURE OUT HOW TO TURN ON LIGHTS/MICROPHONES
* WARDROBE MALFUNCTION (COSTUME OR NORMAL CLOTHES)
* ~~FIRE MARSHAL INSPECTION~~ CODE RED

Since Denise plays in a softball league for queer femmes with an administrative assistant for the fire department, she usually gets a heads-up when Riverstone's about to be inspected. And Riverstone's theatres are not ~~anywhere near~~ technically up to code.

It's not for lack of trying: It's just impossible to comply with the fire code when the prop closet has to double as textbook storage for Language Arts, the spot booth also hosts in-school suspension, and the Little Theatre's lighting system hasn't been updated since the late 1900s.

I sprint up to the Theatre Office, taking the stairs two at a time. I dimly register Liam, sitting beneath the Theatre Board, playing on his phone.

Dr. L is furiously stuffing loose papers and old script books onto the shelves in the corner of her office, but her shoulders relax as soon as she sees me. "Jackson. Good."

"I got your message. Code red?"

"Can you take the catwalk? I'll get the prop room, and Mr. Giacomo is taking care of the spot booth." Mr. Giacomo is the assistant principal who runs in-school suspension.

"Got it."

I tie my crescent wrench to my belt loop, stick my hand through a roll of gaff tape like it's a chunky bracelet, and follow Dr. L to the catwalk door. It's technically always locked, but before she graduated, Caprice showed me how to open it with a student ID in case of emergencies. I don't know if Dr. Lochley knows you can do that or not. So she leans in, using the key on her lanyard to open the door.

The air gets hotter as I climb the red metal ladder. Scents of mothballs and plywood and burnt dust and decades-old cigarette butts assail me.

At the top of the ladder is our old dimmer rack, a twenty-four channel one with red side panels, still emblazoned with the faded logo of an old production company that went bankrupt after its owner was convicted of embezzling equipment from a local news station.

Half the channels have stopped working, the broken modules labeled with pink gaff tape over the breakers. I double-check the working modules are breaker'd off, then duck under a dusty beam onto the catwalk proper: a set of wooden planks that have been nailed down to make a walkway all around the theatre.

The lighting rail runs at chest height, lights clamped every six feet or so, mostly old incandescent PARs and Lekos that got sent up here after the Main Theatre's rig got upgraded to LEDs. A tangle of orange extension cords runs all around, connecting lights to whatever working circuit we could find.

Orange extension cords (especially ones that have had their ends hacked off and replaced with stage pin connectors by Denise) are very much not up to code.

Neither are the plastic tubs stacked haphazardly on the wooden walkways, shoved halfway into the dusty recesses of drywall that make up the theatre ceiling and cloud.

Something touches my back. I jump, banging my elbow against a Source Four on the rail, and let out ~~an embarrassing~~ a totally justified scream.

"Sorry!" Liam looks sheepish, his hand still raised.

"What are you doing up here?" I rub my elbow; it's going to bruise. "Your shmoodie is downstairs."

"I came to help you. And your tag was out."

"I can handle it." I tuck in my tag.

Liam doesn't even know how to do lights, much less how to speed-strike a rig before the fire marshal shows up.

"But I want to help. Dr. L said it was an emergency."

No one's ever offered to help me with a code red before. But here Liam is, being all tall, smelling like the pool and clean laundry and lemon candy. He does have long arms, which might be useful. ~~As long as he stays on the other end of the catwalk, I'll be fine.~~

"Okay. But watch your step."

I lead Liam to the corner opposite the dimmer rack, where the longest cables are run. "We've got to unplug all the orange cables, wrap them, and store them above the cloud."

He starts to unplug a light, but can't get the stage pin connector apart.

"It's stuck."

I fight a grin. "You've got to wiggle it." I show him, wiggling the connector until a gap widens and it's easier to pull apart. In the warmth of the catwalk, his skin smells especially chlorinated. "It's for safety."

Safety third, Denise likes to joke. Speaking of which, I should double-check that all the fixtures have their safety cables.

Liam grips the end in his hand and starts coiling the cord around his elbow.

"Stop!" I take the cable from him. "Don't coil it, it'll get tangled. Wrap it instead." I show him, doing a loop, then a counter-loop, over and over as I follow the cable to the end of the row, where I unplug it from the circuit. The cable is missing its tieline, so I pull off a strip of gaff tape and use it to tie the cable.

I stand on my tiptoes and drop it over the edge of the canopy, where no one will look.

"Like that."

Liam's got a smile in his eyes. I don't know why.

"Don't make fun of me. Doing it this way means the cable will unwrap smoothly when you need it."

"I wasn't. I'm impressed."

"Oh." I'm starting to sweat; my lip tastes salty as I chew it. "Okay. Well. Like that."

I leave him to cabling while I start clearing the walkway of plastic tubs and broken lights and whatever detritus is in the way. The fire code says there has to be a clear path to the ladder in case of a fire, not that anyone is ever up here except during shows.

The work goes quicker with two. Liam gets the hang of wrapping cables, while I do all the little things it takes to make the catwalk ~~safe~~ fire code compliant. I keep my space, because the catwalk wasn't built for tall swimmers with broad shoulders who are too nice for their own good. Who help when they don't have to, just because.

Who like my sister.

I'm tightening the last Leko down on the rail, just to get it out of the way—it's got a broken reflector, but for some reason we're not allowed to throw it away, the district has to "remove it from inventory"—when Liam comes up to me. He's got a smear of black dirt under his left eye, so it looks like someone punched him.

"One of the lights get you?"

He cocks his head to the side. I point at his eye.

"What?" He pulls out his phone to study it in the front-facing camera. "Oh. Oops."

He pulls up the hem of his shirt to wipe at his face, ~~giving me another front-row seat to his abs and left nipple~~.

I realize he said something.

"Huh?"

He drops the shirt and scratches at his arm. "Sorry. Are there ~~something~~something? My arms keep itching."

"It's the lights." I pinch the Leko's power cord. "Fiberglass insulation. We've got scrubby soap downstairs."

"Thank god." He fingers the long sleeve of my black shirt. "I guess this makes sense."

I nod. He's hunched over me to avoid hitting his head on an air duct. Looming again.

I clear my throat. "You get all the cables?"

"Yeah."

"Good. Let's go before—"

The house lights in the theatre snap on. I lean over the rail to see. The principal, Mrs. Bashir, is crossing the stage, leading a man in black pants and a white polo shirt with a red-and-white patch on his chest. The fire marshal.

We're trapped.

"We need to hide," I say as quietly as I can. At least I hope it's quiet.

Students aren't allowed in the catwalk without teacher supervision.

Liam glances back toward the ladder, but I grab his hand. "No time."

I lead him around the catwalk, trying to balance speed with stealth, until I come to one of the panels on the south side of the theatre.

When Riverstone High School was originally built, it didn't include the second level with the Little Theatre; that got added on as an expansion in the 1970s. There are still weird hidey-holes in the catwalk, from where they connected the new part of the building to the old; most were drywalled up, but some were left with covers instead. I open the panel—a thin sheet of aluminum or something—and gesture Liam inside.

It's dusty and small, just enough room for the two of us to sit inside, shoulders pressed together. I pull the panel closed, shutting us in darkness.

My whole side is pressed up against Liam, and I try to lean away so we're not touching so much, because otherwise I will hyperventilate and die and that will definitely not be up to code.

But the sharp points of nails that weren't completely filed off keep poking me, so I'm trapped against Liam's firm side.

The air is getting hotter, Liam's body heat turning the tiny space into an oven. He shifts against me and whispers something in my ear. I jerk away before he can cause any feedback in my hearing aid; not only is it painful, but it might give us away.

I pull my phone out and open the Notes app.

Don't do that!!!!

He takes my phone and types:

Sorry. Are you ok?

How long do we stay here

I answer:

Until Dr L gives the all clear
It can cause feedback

I text Dr. L to let her know we're trapped. In the dim blue glow of my phone, I can make out Liam's face a little. His mouth is pinched, and his blue eyes are wide. He looks . . . frazzled.

You okay?

I hand him back the phone. His hand shakes slightly.

I'm a little bit claustrophobic
Sorry

He's shaking next to me. If he doesn't stop, he'll give us away, and that would be terrible.

Not only for the trouble we'd get in with Mrs. Bashir, and possibly messing up the fire marshal inspection, but because of the rumors. Two guys caught hiding in the catwalk? No one ever comes up here except for shows or—legend has it—to hook up.

Would people think *we* hooked up? My armpits sweat. Jasmine would kill me if people thought that.

Liam drums his fingers against his knees. I put my hand over his, give it a squeeze, and he lets me take his hand to calm him.

~~Holding Liam's hand is a mistake.~~

His hands are big. The one I'm holding is clammy, but smooth, soft enough to make me self-conscious of my own calloused palms and fingers. I wonder if swimming did it for him or if his hands are just naturally perfect ~~like the rest of him~~.

As I squeeze his hand, he relaxes, his whole body softening against my side, and I can't breathe.

The floor shifts beneath us slightly. The heavy stomp of boots reverberates in my butt. I lock my phone to make sure no light spills out from the hidey-hole. But now I'm alone in the dark. With Liam.

Last year I was plugging in an old PAR and got electrocuted. That might be too strong a word: It was a tiny zap, and it didn't hurt me, but it made my skin buzz and my tongue feel fuzzy.

I've got that buzzing again, but it's not electricity.

It's Liam. Liam's hand in mine. Liam's shoulders pressed up against me. Liam, who likes to tuck in my tags, and beg for shmoodies, who offered to help just because I looked like I needed it.

Liam, who worries no one sees him, but who sees me just fine.

And I wonder if I've been wrong this whole time, and maybe he's not so straight, and maybe he could like someone like me. Even though he's him and I'm basically a background character.

What if every time he touches me, every time he waits around after rehearsal, every time he haltingly fingerspells a word because he knows how tired I get listening and guessing and reading lips all day, he's trying to tell me something? Something more than just "we're friends."

My armpits are sweating so hard I worry the fire marshal will notice a puddle. Should I say something?

What if I've read him all wrong?

What if he does like me, and it goes bad anyway? What if I'm just like Jasmine and we break up because I'm too much? What if we're just like Mom and Dad and we break up because we can't stop fighting ~~and making our kids miserable~~?

Worse, what if it's good, but then he goes off to college and leaves me anyway?

I don't know what to do. But all of a sudden, I've got a lump in my throat that has nothing to do with the fear of discovery, and everything to do with the possibility that maybe, just maybe, he feels something for me.

I should ask him. I have to. Just as soon as we escape this mess.

Outside our hidey-hole, the footsteps tromp off, the reverberations in my butt gradually receding. And then all I can feel is Liam's hand in mine. He's still quivering a bit.

I squeeze his hand to let him know it's going to be okay. That I'm here for him. And he squeezes back.

We sit in the dark and wait for the all clear.

~~All too soon~~ Finally the fire marshal finishes, and Dr. L texts that we can come back down. I'm almost sad at how fast Liam scrambles out of our hidey-hole, but I don't blame him.

"All good?" I ask when we get back down.

Dr. L tosses her scarf over her shoulder. "Passed with flying colors. Thanks for helping, Liam."

"Sure." He scratches the back of his neck. "It was really something-something."

Really what?

Really nice, pressed up against me? My heart hasn't quit hammering this whole time.

Dr. L smiles and nods. "I'll go write you passes."

She heads into the Theatre Office, and I look anywhere but Liam's face. My backpack is still lying against the wall, next to Liam's shmoodie. I grab it for him.

"Thanks." He gives it a shake and uncaps it, while I take a few deep breaths and try to summon my courage.

But we were just crammed into a tiny box together, holding hands, and he didn't mind. He even squeezed me back a few times. So maybe I'm not imagining things. Maybe I've been reading him wrong this whole time. Maybe he's not so straight.

So maybe . . . just maybe . . .

"I was wondering," I say, but I've got a frog in my throat. I clear it. "Um. I mean . . ."

His eyebrows raise, looking at me patiently.

"I was thinking . . ."

"Oh, sorry." He pulls his phone out of his pocket. "Thought it was on vibrate. Thank god it didn't go off when we were up there, huh?"

"Yeah." The consequences are too dire to imagine.

"Sorry, lemme just . . ." He taps away, lips twitching into a shy smile. "Okay. Sorry."

"It's fine." I take a deep breath.

I can do this.

"You doing anything this weekend?"

"Yeah. Actually, that was Jasmine."

"Oh?"

"Yeah." He bites his lip for a second. "We're . . . going on a date tomorrow."

"Oh."

I can't breathe.

I wish I'd said something sooner. I wish I'd never let him and Jasmine get to know each other.

But that wouldn't have made any difference. I was just imagining things. Imagining that he wanted anything other than friendship from me. And friendship is fine. It's fine.

I'm fine.

ACT II

13

'm not fine.

As soon as Dr. L gives us our passes, Liam heads back downstairs, while I head toward the A Hall. I take my seat in American Literature and pretend I'm taking notes. But I'm not.

LIAM'S BREAKUP LIST:
HE DOESN'T EVEN LIKE ME LIKE THAT
HE NEVER LIKED ME LIKE THAT
MIXED SIGNALS
DATING MY SISTER

It's not helping, though. Because even if he doesn't like me like that, he does like me. He's my friend. He helped me with the code red. He tucks in my tags. He's even learning ASL, something my own family will barely do.

Making a list about him feels weird and wrong. I rip the page out of my binder, crumple it up, and throw it in the first recycle bin I can find.

Liam is my friend. I was only dreaming of more.

I need to wake up.

* * *

"All right. Let's try something," Dr. Lochley says.

Onstage, Liam and Cameron nod. We're in the Little Theatre, since the Main Theatre is all set for a band concert tonight. It's just Liam and Cam today: Dr. L wants to work on the scene where Judas betrays Jesus, and decided it would be easier to work with the two of them alone first and add the soldiers later.

"I want you both to center yourselves."

"Center . . . myself?" Liam asks. His eyes spike mine, but I pretend not to notice him as I help Paige put together her ASM binder. She's officially come on board as my assistant, which is great, because she's a hard worker and a quick learner.

"Internally," Dr. L says. "Cam, what do you do?"

"I like to count backward from ten, somethingsomething into the role."

"Very good." Dr. Lochley taps her lips. "I had a classmate in college who once stripped naked and climbed atop one of the giant shuttlecocks at the Nelson-Atkins on the night of the full moon, but that's still a week away. And she only used that method in extreme cases." She tilts her head. "Actually, now that I think about it, I'm not sure if it was the naked climbing or the getting arrested that she found centering."

Paige's mouth drops open. I just shrug.

"So. What do you do?" Dr. L asks Liam.

"I'm not sure." He looks my way again, and this time I don't look away fast enough.

I can't just leave him high and dry.

"What about that thing you do before a race?" I demonstrate, stretching my arms wide, then hugging myself, careful not to elbow Paige in the face.

Dr. Lochley nods. "Perfect! Why not try that?"

Liam bites his lip, then starts flapping his arms like he does on the starting blocks. His shirt rides up his abdomen as he moves, and I look down at my blocking diagrams to distract myself. It doesn't work, though. The briefest flash of skin and it reminds me of all the ~~sticky~~ embarrassing dreams he's featured in recently.

He's going on a date with Jasmine. I'm a horrible brother.

"Good," Dr. Lochley says. "Embrace physicality. Take a few deep breaths. Now, let's get to work on this kiss."

Liam studies Cam warily.

"I want you to forget about the blocking for now. Just do what feels authentic."

Liam and Cameron run through the scene, glancing down at their scripts occasionally. When they get to the kiss, Cameron leans in and kisses Liam on his upstage cheek.

"Stop," Dr. Lochley says. She mutters a long string of direction I can't catch. "And then, I want you to pause and kiss him again on the lips. Are you both comfortable with that?"

I grip my pencil so tight I'm surprised it doesn't snap. I don't want to see Liam and Cam kiss. I don't want to see Liam kiss anyone. Even if it's just for the show.

I want him to say *No, I'm not comfortable.* ~~I want him to say, What if I rehearse with Jackson instead.~~

I want to go hide in the theatre office and let Paige take over this rehearsal. But she's not ready yet.

Liam and Cam run the scene again. This time, after Judas

kisses Jesus on the cheek, he adds a closed-mouth peck on the lips.

"No," Dr. Lochley says as they pull apart. "Something is still missing."

She gets up onstage, takes Liam by the shoulders to bring him closer to Cameron, then adjusts Cameron's stance, steps back to look at the picture they make.

I can't quite tell what she's saying, so I get out of my seat and get up onstage, standing a few paces to Liam's right. Paige stands next to me, notebook in hand, even though she can probably hear just fine from her seat.

"Remember," Dr. L says to Cam. "This is the most intense relationship you've ever had. You think you're protecting him. You've seen what people want from Jesus. This is the only way to save him from something worse."

She turns to Liam.

"And you know exactly what's happening. You know what comes next. But you love Judas, flaws and all. This isn't just goodbye. This is 'I love you.' This is 'I forgive you.'"

I'm pretty sure we've veered even more outside the Bible than the musical already is. It's definitely not in the script. I doubt the ~~Toxic Jesus Fandom~~ Toxic Andrew Lloyd Weber Fandom will appreciate all the homoerotic liberties Dr. Lochley is taking with the show.

Then again, being gay and doing crime is sort of Dr. Lochley's thing.

"All right, let's go again, from 'Judas, must you betray me with a kiss?'"

I'm still onstage, next to Dr. Lochley, which means I'm close

95

enough to see it when Cam turns on his puppy-dog eyes, the way he used to do before he kissed me.

It also means I'm close enough to see the way Liam's eyes dart between Cam's eyes and lips and back to his eyes.

And when their lips meet, it's different. It's . . . intense.

It feels so intimate, I want to look away. I can't, though. I can't even breathe.

Liam's lips are thin, much thinner than Cameron's, and he's got one of those mouths that look like it's always holding a frog in it. But there's a tenderness to the way he and Cam touch their lips together, how their bodies lean in. It's sad and beautiful and ~~I hate it~~ perfect.

The air in the Little Theatre feels too close, like the air conditioner has shut off again, which it does sometimes in early fall, when parts of the building are too hot and parts are too cold. The back of my neck burns.

When Liam and Cameron finally pull apart, they hold each other's eyes for a beat.

Finally, Dr. Lochley claps her hands, and the spell is broken. "Excellent! That's the energy I need. Now let's tweak the blocking."

"Hey, can you take over for a second?" I ask Paige as we back off the stage. "I need some water."

I let the theatre door slam shut behind me, run for the bathroom, and hide in the first open stall. The bathroom is on the west side of the building, and the afternoon sun streams in through the high blocky windows, turning the ~~toilet paper particles~~ dust motes in the air into golden glitter.

I need to get it together.

I've done how many shows with my ex now? This will be number four. I'm fine. Liam's not even an ex. He's just a friend. A very kind, ~~very hot,~~ very talented friend. Who is taking Jasmine out tomorrow.

And I'm a professional. I'm a stage manager. It's my job to make the show go well. Not to go around crushing on the actors. Dr. L would be so disappointed in me.

I shake myself off. I can do this.

I wash my hands, grab some water from the drinking fountain, and head back into the theatre. Cam and Liam kiss over and over and over; eventually Dr. L has Liam bring his hand up to cup Cam's cheek as they're doing it, and I don't want to set myself on fire because it looks so real, and I don't let myself remember how Liam's hands feel. ~~I don't even think about how I hate my sister a tiny bit.~~

I've got a show to do. That's what I've got to focus on.

Except then, between kisses, Liam catches my eye again. And I'm like a notice pinned to the Theatre Board, stabbed right through the heart, because for a split second it's like he knows what I'm thinking. But he doesn't.

He can't.

No one can.

"Right, so we'll work the trial on Wednesday instead," Dr. L says as I make the changes to our schedule. "And that way Mr. Cartwright can have time to work on 'Superstar' with Judas."

I nod. "Great. And then, next week, we've got Tori double-booked—"

"Dr. L?" Cam's come up on her other side.

"Hm?"

"I've got a couple questions about the scene, if you've got a moment."

"Sure. Just a sec, Jackson."

Cam shoots me a smirk as Dr. L abandons our planning to go massage his ego. I sigh and turn to grab the dust mop, but Paige is already sweeping the stage.

"You okay?" Liam asks. He's already got his backpack on.

"Huh?"

"Is it just me or somethingsomething?"

I shake my head. "Sorry. I'm really tired."

He nods, pulls his phone out.

> Is it just me, or does Cam do that on purpose?
> Like he always needs Dr. L whenever you're
> talking to her

I shrug. "It's whatever." It does happen more than I'd like. But Cam is kind of ~~an attention hog~~ needy. I glance back; he and Dr. L have stepped out of the theatre entirely.

> It's not whatever
> He's being a jerk
> And Dr. L shouldn't let him get away with it

Part of me wants to bask in the fact he's trying to defend me. But the other part of me is mad. Because this is my job. I've been doing this for two years now. I know how to handle Cam.

He's brand-new and he doesn't know how things work

and he's got a date with Jasmine anyway.

"It's fine. Dr. L knows I can handle it," I snap.

But he just stands there, being all tall, and now he looks hurt.

"Sorry. Like I said. I'm tired. I didn't mean to snap at you."

"I understand," he signs.

He's doing little words now. I can't help smiling, no matter how hard I try to stop it.

"You're improving."

He beams at me. "Thanks, Jacks."

I snort.

"What?" I make out on his lips. He goes for his phone again.

Isn't that your name sign?

"That's what Bowie calls me. Like . . . calling me Jacks instead of Jackson." I make my regular name sign, a variation of the letter J. "That's Jackson."

Oh. Sorry.
Should I not call you that?

I want to tell him no. That it's too intimate.

That it's something special between me and Bowie.

But his smile starts to fade, and I never want him to stop smiling.

"You can call me that too."

Liam's smile makes a comeback. Despite his thin lips, it lights up the stage.

"Okay."

14

When I come downstairs Monday morning, Jasmine's at the blender. The pitcher is filled with a bunch of ice cubes and topped with blackberries, and she's spooning strawberry yogurt on top.

"Jasmine?"

"Oh, hey. I'll be quick."

"What are you doing? You hate smoothies."

"It's for Liam."

"But . . ."

I'm in charge of shmoodies.

That was the deal: Liam gets a part, I make him shmoodies.

Totally platonic shmoodies.

She can't take it over just because they went on one date. A date that went really well, according to Jasmine. She spent all weekend smiling.

"I was going to make it when I make mine and Bowie's." Like always.

Jasmine shrugs. "I figured making his smoothie is the sort of thing a girlfriend should do."

"You're his girlfriend? After one date?" I get a wave of cold in my chest, like she's dropped an ice cube down the front of my shirt, but they're all buried at the bottom of the blender. Way too much ice for one shmoodie. It'll be watered down and gross.

"Well, obviously not." She turns back to the blender and keeps talking, but I lose it.

"What?"

"Never mind."

That ice cube in me turns to steam. "Don't *never mind* me."

She looks back, at least a little chagrined. "Sorry. Just, I really like him."

"That doesn't make him your boyfriend."

"No, I know, but . . . well, if things keep up, then maybe."

One date and she's already planning their future. But that's how Jasmine is.

At least they've actually had a date. Last year she managed to go all-in on a zero-date scenario, when she'd convinced herself this guy in her French class liked her, but later found out he didn't actually know who she was.

That one had been tough. I didn't really get why Jasmine was upset in the first place, but she'd been inconsolable, and the only thing that had gotten her smiling again was the breakup list I'd had to improvise despite never having met the guy. I still had it tucked in the back of my binder. It actually was kind of funny.

MONSIEUR BAGUETTE'S BREAKUP LIST:
TERRIBLE AT CONJUGATING VERBS
POOR ~~POSTURE~~ *POSTEUR*
CROOKED BERET
DOESN'T WASH HIS LEGS

FAMILY SHELTERED KHOMEINI DURING EXILE
ONLY WEARS STRIPED SHIRTS
EATS MOLDY CHEESE

For some reason that last item had gotten Jasmine laughing so hard she nearly peed herself, but she'd felt better after.

And now here she was, throwing herself head-first into this thing with Liam. Usurping his shmoodies.

"I liked making him shmoodies," I say. "I mean, he's my friend."

Jasmine flutters her lashes. "Aw, are you jealous I'm stealing him?"

~~Yes.~~

"That's not . . . you're not even making them right."

"Can't you just be happy for me? He's really nice." She bites her lip. "And really hot."

He's more than just a body.

"I know he's your friend. But you're my brother. I need you."

I sigh.

"You know I'm happy for you."

"I know." She eyes the blender. "What am I doing wrong?"

"Huh?"

"With the smoothie."

"Oh." ~~Part of me wants to not tell her.~~ "You should put the yogurt in the bottom to help the blades spin. Then fruit. Ice on top. Otherwise it'll get all chunky."

It's better if you do the blackberries separately too, so you can strain out the seeds, but it's far too late for that.

"Thanks."

She turns the blender back on, ignoring the high-speed setting that, to be fair, she might not realize exists.

The ~~shmoodie~~ smoothie is a bit gloopy as she pours it into a bottle. She takes the pitcher to the sink, like she's about to wash it, but I stop her. "I'll take care of it."

"Okay. I'm going to get dressed." She sets the smoothie on the counter, not even bothering with the fridge. "What would I do without you, Jackson?"

I shrug, and she floats back up the stairs.

I put Liam's smoothie in the fridge before making mine and Bowie's. And I don't let myself wonder just how well their date went. If she held his ~~perfect~~ smooth hands. Or kissed his ~~beautiful~~ frog-holding lips. Or played with his ~~silky~~ chlorinated hair.

If he reached back and tucked in her tags. Or laughed at her jokes. Or leaned in and whispered secrets to her without risking feedback.

I don't wonder about any of that.

"Let's try it again from the top of the scene." Dr. L adjusts her scarf as Liam retreats stage right and Cam prepares to enter from stage left.

"Superstar" is the last number that needs to be worked on— Dr. L likes to save the big showstoppers for the end, so that the actors have as much time as possible to inhabit their roles before they get overwhelmed with choreo and music.

And of course, it's Cam's big moment: a real showcase of his talents as an actor and a singer and a dancer. He's about as much of a triple threat as someone can be.

I stand next to Dr. L in the pit as Cam goes through the number, half speaking, half singing the lyrics.

"And Jesus, go!" Dr. L calls, halfway through, and Liam emerges from backstage right once more, bowed under the weight of an imaginary cross. (We've got another workday the Saturday after Halloween to get more of the set done; Denise has been swamped lately.)

"Judas, keep going."

So Cam does, but he only gets a few more bars before Dr. L stops him again.

She shakes her head, taps her lips with her forefinger, then stomps up the steps from the pit to the stage. Paige and I follow.

Dr. L goes up to Cam and says something I don't catch, but Paige does, scribbling in her notebook. It's much slimmer than mine, ~~probably due to a lack of breakup lists,~~ but she's got her script arranged the way I taught her, with the pages hole-punched on the wrong side so they lay on the left, with a blank reverse on the right for notes.

While Dr. L ~~stokes Cam's ego~~ discusses his motivation, Liam catches my eye and gives a little smile. He didn't mention the change in smoothies, and he doesn't have blackberry seeds in his teeth, so maybe he didn't mind. Maybe he liked Jasmine's better after all.

"Okay?" he signs to me.

"Okay."

When I look back at Dr. L and Cam, they're both staring at me.

"Huh?"

"I said, do you have the diagrams from the 'The Arrest?'" Dr. L asks.

"Oh." I shake myself off and thumb through, but Paige finds the chart in her own binder faster.

"Great. Thanks," Dr. L says. "Jesus?"

I retreat while she works with Cam and Liam to try and mirror their kiss in this bit, where Judas is supposed to watch Jesus trudging across the stage with his cross, and they share one last look. Paige stays close to make more notes.

And then they run the scene again, and again, and it's ~~a little tedious~~ way better than having to watch Liam and Cam kiss over and over.

"All right," Dr. L says after their third time through. "Good. Tomorrow we'll do it with the whole chorus."

She starts packing up, while Paige and I hop back onto the stage to close up for the night. While Paige grabs the dust mop to sweep the stage, I run to the scene shop to grab the ghost light, but Cam and Liam are blocking the door. Cam's gesturing emphatically with his hands, and Liam looks like he wants to escape.

Liam spots me first; when he realizes he's lost Liam's attention, Cam turns around too.

"What do you want, Jackthon?"

Liam's eyes flash. "What did you just say?"

"I need in. Can you take it offstage?"

Cam rolls his eyes but steps around me, knocking my binder out from where I've got it tucked beneath my armpit.

It smacks the stage floor hard; papers rip and spill out between the scene shop and the dimmer rack. Cam keeps going as I drop to start picking everything up. Thankfully I have those little hole-reinforcing stickers.

Liam kneels to help me. After a moment, he flaps a hand for my attention.

"Yeah?"

"Why do you let him call you that?"

"What?"

He presses his lips together.

"It's fine. It doesn't bother me."

Liam doesn't seem convinced.

"I used to have a lisp. It's whatever."

"He's being a dick. I should . . ."

But Liam pauses as he holds out a paper to me. At the top is written, in bold Sharpie, *Dominic's Breakup List*.

"What's this?"

Heat races along my skin.

"Nothing."

"Who's Dominic?" He scans the list; his eyebrows shoot up. "Dominic Ryan? Graduated last year?"

I nod. "Jasmine's ex."

Her first ex. In high school, at least. The first list I made for her.

"What . . ."

"Don't tell her I told you. But Jasmine took their breakup really bad. I had to keep reminding her of his flaws to help her get over him."

Liam laughs. "Do you somethingsomething for all her exes?"

I shrug, because yeah, but I've never talked about them before.

"You gonna do one of these for me?"

"Why? Are you going to break up with my sister?"

Liam presses his lips together. The harshness of the work

lights turns the blue of his eyes the gray of a winter sky. "I wasn't planning on it, no."

~~I kind of wish he'd said yes.~~

"Well, you were my friend first. So no, I won't make one, even if you do. Besides, what would it say? 'He's too good at swimming'?"

Liam laughs. "I don't know. 'People pleaser.' Or how about 'too handsy.'"

"'Cause of the tag thing? I don't mind that." I look down to scoop up the rest of my papers so he doesn't see me blush.

"Okay, how about 'razor bumps in weird places.'"

I snort. "I do not need to know that."

Liam laughs too, and when I look up at him he's smiling like I've given him some precious gift.

He signs and says, "I'm glad you're my friend."

"Me too."

Even when it aches.

15

Amy drops me off at Bowie's Saturday night.

"Have fun! Don't eat too much candy!"

"Love you."

Bowie's parents have already gone to a costume party, but they left us a credit card to order pizza. Unlike Dad, who won't let me have Bowie over if we're alone, Mr. and Mrs. Anderson are cool with it. Granted, Dad doesn't know: He's with Jasmine in St. Louis for the weekend, ostensibly to visit our grandparents, but he's no doubt going to drag her on a tour of Wash U or SLU while they're out there.

I feel sorry for Jasmine, but only a little sorry, because her being gone means Liam is free to hang out with us.

Liam beams as he opens the door. He's in a worn blue T-shirt that matches his eyes, and another pair of those soft black sweatpants he seems to own dozens of. "Hey! You finally made it."

"Hey."

Bowie orders our usual: thin crust, with pineapple and bell peppers and pepperoni. It's a top-tier combination, if a little unorthodox.

I know there are members of the Toxic Pizza Fandom who

reject adding pineapple to pizza, but thankfully Liam isn't one of them. Besides, it's delicious: sweet and sour and salty. Maybe I like it so much because that balance is at the heart of so much Iranian cooking.

Pineapple used to be Mom's favorite too, before she moved out to Colorado to ~~get away from us~~ ~~make a fresh start~~ be closer to her parents, and started getting pan pizza with honey (honey!) drizzled over it. We still see her a few times a year, for holidays or summers, and despite her now-warped taste in pizza, I do miss her ~~sometimes~~.

Not as much as Jasmine does. She was always closer to Mom. She took the divorce a lot harder than I did. I think in her mind, love was supposed to be forever. Indestructible. Magical.

Maybe that's why, despite all the evidence that love is none of those things, Jasmine keeps chasing it with a never-ending list of boys at school. Like she's trying to capture something that's long gone.

Granted, I got sent to therapy after the divorce, so it's not like I was entirely unscathed myself. But at least I don't cling to the past the way Jasmine does.

We set up in the living room, using the big TV to play some *Smash Bros* since we have the house to ourselves. Somehow I end up sandwiched between Liam and Bowie, both their shoulders pressing against me, the smell of chlorine hitting me from both sides. They trash-talk each other as we play: Bowie's legitimately terrible, and Liam's pretty good. I don't catch much of what's said, but I'm not too bothered. Bowie will pause and tell me if it's something important.

Sometimes it's nice to turn my brain off and just be with people without constantly worrying if I'm understanding them right, or wondering if I'm missing things. So I relax and enjoy the ~~body contact with Liam~~ game, the feel of my friends laughing at my sides, the rumble of my controller as I use Ness's baseball bat to send poor Pichu (Bowie) flying off the stage again.

I'm just about to get Liam's last life—he's played a passable game as Cloud, but he's no match for me—when a phone buzzes against my hip. It's not mine, though.

Liam pauses right before my PK Thunder hits him.

"Sorry," he says, then signs it also. "Jasmine."

Despite the warmth against my sides, I go cold. This was supposed to be friends time, and even from across the state, she manages to intrude. They've been on a couple dates now, and they're going to a haunted house on Halloween. Despite Liam's claustrophobia, which I'm not sure Jasmine even knows about.

I guess things are going well. And I'm happy for them. I really am.

Liam stands as he answers the phone; as he walks away, he reaches back and tucks in my tag.

Bowie rests their controller on their lap. "What's that face for?"

"What face? Nothing."

"Jacks."

"What?"

"What's going on?"

"Nothing."

But they keep studying me, their left hand going up to rub their right shoulder. I get this weird, quivery feeling in my chest and stomach. I glance back, but Liam's still out of sight, probably in the kitchen or something.

"Promise not to say anything?"

Bowie nods.

"I . . . kind of have a crush on him."

Bowie releases their shoulder. "I figured."

"What?"

"Come on. If anyone else tucked in your tag for you, you'd elbow them in the spleen, but you just let him do it all the time. And don't forget all those shmoodies you make him."

"He won them."

"You wanted to make them," Bowie says.

"Yeah, well, Jasmine took them over anyway." I sigh. "I shouldn't like him. He's dating my sister."

"So what are you going to do?"

"Nothing! He can't know. You promised."

"I know, and I won't say anything."

"Is it super obvious?"

"I don't think so." Bowie gives me a gentle smile. "But I know you."

My stomach is twisting itself into knots. All the Nerds and Smarties and Snickers I ate earlier threaten to make an encore appearance.

Bowie rubs their shoulder again.

"You hurting?"

"Little bit," Bowie says. "Two thousand yards of butterfly this morning."

"Want me to work on it?"

They accept my diversion with grace. "Sure."

Bowie runs up to their bathroom to grab the Tiger Balm. When they return, they pull off their shirt and sit between my knees. I squeeze out some Tiger Balm and start working it in, digging my thumbs into the crunchy spots, using the heel of my hand to work on the knots.

My hand turns cool and tingly as I work, the menthol and camphor tickling my nose as I press against Bowie's rich brown skin. Their shoulders are broad and round, with little striations from their strong muscles. They remind me of Liam's shoulders, the way he looked with his shirt off in the changing room, the way he looked in his underwear, and I'm glad I wore jeans today because they won't show my embarrassing reminiscence.

I've worked on Bowie's shoulders dozens of times and never gotten ~~an erection~~ excited. But I can't stop thinking of Liam, who's in the other room, talking to my sister.

I'm a terrible brother.

Bowie grunts when I hit a tender spot.

"Stop?" I ask aloud, but they make the sign for more. I dig in with my elbow, and Bowie tenses for a second before relaxing. I keep wiggling my elbow, feeling the crunch in their muscles or tendons or ligaments or whatever it is that's hurting. I bite my lip, controlling my pressure, so focused I don't notice Liam's back until he blocks the TV.

My elbow slips, and Bowie arches away to avoid me hitting their shoulder blade.

"Oh." Liam stares at us, at Bowie with their shirt off. "Uh . . ."

"Hey," I say. Liam's still got his phone in his hand. "Good call?"

"Oh. Yeah." He scratches the back of his neck as I drag my thumbs along the sides of Bowie's neck. Bowie melts a bit. Liam just stares at us, this weird expression on his face, like maybe he wants me to work on him too.

"I can do you next if you need. Bowie said today's practice was rough."

"Oh. Yeah." Liam shrugs. "I'm good. Thanks."

"Okay." I finish rubbing the Tiger Balm in, and Bowie pulls their shirt on. "Lemme wash my hands and I can finish kicking your ass."

Liam laughs. "Fine."

We play a couple more rounds—I win them all—until the doorbell flashes. Bowie throws down their controller without even pausing, leaving Pichu standing there all vulnerable, and leaps off the couch to grab the pizza.

I pause the game. I might be competitive when it comes to *Smash*, but I don't take cheap shots.

"You hungry?" I ask.

Liam nods. He bites his lip, then looks at me. "Hey."

"Yeah?"

"Thanks for letting me hang out tonight. I didn't mean to somethingsomething."

"I'm glad you could come. I wish we'd hung out more before."

Maybe if I'd gotten to be friends with Liam before this year, things between us could've been different.

Then again, maybe it would've been worse. Maybe I'd have asked him out and he'd have gently let me down, but then things would've been awkward, and we'd have drifted apart.

Maybe he and Jasmine would've started dating way before that. Then she could've skipped Man Bun Nick and Stanky Tristan and possibly even Monsieur Baguette. Maybe they'd be an official couple, boyfriend and girlfriend, happy and going to homecoming and Sweetheart and prom together.

Maybe they'd have dated and broken up and I'd have an old, wrinkled list in the back of my notebook.

Liam's talking to me again.

"Sorry. What?"

"Oh. Just, it means a lot to me. Things at home are . . ." His face falls.

"What?"

He chews his lip for a second.

"How old were you when your parents divorced?"

"Seven. Jasmine was eight. Why?"

"Mine are getting divorced."

He says it so simply, like it doesn't bother him. But his lip quivers. I wouldn't notice if he wasn't right in front of me.

"I'm sorry."

"Don't be. It's . . . I guess it had to happen. But I'm just so tired of it all. Of trying to somethingsomething all the time."

"Sorry. Say again?"

"I'm tired of playing peacemaker all the time. And now Dad's packing up to move out. It's . . ."

"Weird?"

He nods. "And he keeps talking about, like, setting up a room for me at his new place. Asking me what I want. And I just keep saying yes to everything because I don't know how to tell him I don't want to live with him."

Ouch. I don't even know what to say to that. Before I can even try, Bowie flicks the living room lights on and off. We turn to find them at the switch.

"Are you two coming? Pizza's getting cold."

"Coming!" Liam offers me a hand off the couch, and I let him pull me up, ~~and I don't even hold onto his perfect hand for too long~~.

But he yanks me a bit too hard, and I nearly bump against his chest. I back away.

"Sorry."

"It's okay." I swallow. "You know it's okay, right? If you don't want to?"

I didn't want to move to Colorado with Mom.

He shrugs, like maybe he doesn't know. Or isn't sure.

When he saw my lists, he joked about being a people pleaser, but maybe he thinks he really is. Maybe he needs to remember it's okay to make himself happy too.

Before I can figure out how to say that, he shakes himself off. "Sorry. I'm here to have fun, not mope. Let's eat."

"You sure?"

"I'm sure." He gives me a little smile. "You're a good friend, Jackson. What would I do without you?"

I blush. A good friend, but nothing more. "Win at *Smash* more often?"

He cracks up.

16

November blows in on the backs of two thunderstorms, one tornado warning, and workdays every Saturday—even the one after Thanksgiving.

"Little more," I shout. "Little more. There!"

I turn my hands like I'm twirling invisible knobs: It's not ASL, but it's the universal sign for "lock down that light." Denise is up in the catwalk focusing, while I stand onstage directing her.

We're down to crunch time: Only two weeks until the show. The set is nearly done. The lights are mostly focused. Costumes are fitted and labeled. Next week we've got run-throughs every night, and then ~~Hell~~ Tech Week starts on Saturday.

While Denise and I work on the lights, Paige supervises the final bits of set painting. We've got a crowd of Theatre I students volunteering, plus Liam—the only cast member to show up—and, to my ~~chagrin~~ surprise, Jasmine.

They've been dating for six weeks now, whenever Liam's got a free night from rehearsal and swimming. He and Bowie both placed at Regionals, which is awesome, but also stressful, because now they have to train for State.

While Denise scoots down the catwalk to the next light, Paige jogs over to me. She's in paint-spattered overalls and these hot-pink Converse that have clearly seen a lot of love.

"Hey. Um." She shifts from foot to foot. "About your sister . . ."

"Is she being a perfectionist?"

"Yeah. She's kind of holding us up."

"I'll talk to her. Can you help Denise focus area three?"

Paige finds the spike mark downstage right while I head to the scene shop. Sure enough, Jasmine's standing right in front of one of the Gethsemane flats, her nose only a few inches away as she paints in the individual thorns on the patches of radioactive plants.

Liam's next to her, expertly scumbling the gray skies. All that swimming has given him the proper wrist dexterity to do it swiftly and accurately.

"Hey, Jackson." He reaches for my tag with his free hand.

"Hey!" Jasmine steps back. "How's it looking?"

Jasmine's thorns are immaculate: sharp, evenly spaced, and she's even done a little highlighting.

"They're perfect," I say, and she beams. "Too perfect."

She cocks her head.

"Remember, the audience is going to be twenty, thirty feet away. Even more. So they won't appreciate this level of detail. And we've still got a lot to paint."

"But . . ." Jasmine clamps her mouth shut as she studies Liam, moving back and forth across the huge flat in broad sweeps. His paint-spattered white T-shirt keeps riding up, showing off a strip of creamy skin above the waistband of his underwear. I blink and look away before Jasmine notices.

"Point taken."

"And Liam? Keep doing what you're doing."

He turns, gives me a quick smile, but keeps working.

"Aww, babe." Jasmine tugs him down to kiss his cheek. "My boyfriend is so talented."

Boyfriend.

It hits me like a Leko to the chest.

Boyfriend.

Liam blushes hard, like his cheeks have been painted too.

My mouth starts running on its own.

"You two are . . . like . . . official?"

"Well . . . uh." Liam swallows.

"I mean . . . I'm not seeing anyone else," Jasmine says. "Are you?"

"No. Of course not."

"So we're exclusive then."

"Yeah. Just, I told you, I want to take things slow."

"I know, I know," Jasmine says. "Somethingsomething putting a label on it, right? But it's our six-week anniversary!"

Boyfriend.

"Cool," I say, louder than I mean to. At least I think it's loud. My ears feel full, like someone dunked my head underwater, or like a storm is rolling in, one of those big summer thunderstorms you can feel behind your eyeballs the day before.

~~I can't be here.~~

"Anyway, keep up the good work."

After lunch—pizza onstage, a workday tradition, even though it's against the rules—Denise pulls Jasmine and a couple other painters aside to have them start working on the backdrop. We're doing one big, apocalyptic-looking upstage drop, gray skies and gnarled branches and vague crumbling buildings. I bring in line-set 15, where we normally hang the cyclorama, as Denise gives out directions. Once everything's locked off, she comes over to the rail.

"Hey. Can you find Liam and get his fake blood sorted out?"

"Okay."

Fake blood is a complicated thing. It has to look good to the audience—in multiple lighting situations—not stain costumes or skin, and preferably be nontoxic.

If Cam was the one getting bloody, I wouldn't care so much, but I don't want to poison Liam.

I grab the plastic bag of ingredients—corn syrup for viscosity, red food coloring and cocoa powder for color, distilled water for volume, and a little bit of cornstarch for clumpy bits—and head into the scene shop. The big doors are cracked open now, after we moved the flats out, but I still have to push my way through.

Liam's inside, at the huge paint sink in the corner. His back is to me, and the water is running as I approach.

"Liam?"

He spins around, startled, flinging orange-tinged water across the floor. He's got his smoothie bottle in hand.

"Jackson! Hey."

"What are you doing?"

"Nothing." But he's still holding the smoothie bottle in hand. "Ah, just cleaning up."

Jasmine made him a mango-grapefruit-oat-milk smoothie this morning but I never saw him drink it.

"Everything okay?"

"Yeah." He bites his lip. It's red, and I can't tell if it's from pizza sauce or making out with my sister.

Boyfriend.

"Can I be honest?"

"Sure." I can't be honest, but he can.

"It's so sweet of Jasmine to make me smoothies, but, um . . . I like yours better."

Heat flares behind my chest, like someone lit an incandescent lamp. "I've got a bit more practice."

"Yeah, well . . ." Liam looks down, realizes his bottle is still dripping onto the floor, and drops it behind him in the sink. "Did you need something?"

I hold up my bag. "We've still got to test your fake blood."

"Oh. Right."

We clear off some space next to the compound miter saw and get to mixing.

"Okay. How about this?" I hold up a white plastic spoon, coated in fake blood.

Liam nods. "Looks good."

"Right. So . . ." Now it's my turn to blush. "We have to, ah, test it on your skin?"

"Sure." Liam holds out his arm. I use the back of the spoon and make a stripe of red across his smooth skin. It immediately breaks out into goose bumps, even though the scene shop is feeling way too warm. His arm is powerfully corded, strong enough to cut through the water like a dolphin. Gentle enough to tuck in my tags when they stick up.

Boyfriend.

I clear my throat. "Lift?"

He does; the fake blood starts running down, too quick.

"Too thin. Sorry."

"It's okay." He grabs paper towels from the stack I brought over, wipes it off.

I add more corn syrup and cornstarch, and we try again. This time it trickles down in beads. He grins. "Very dramatic."

"It feels okay?"

"It's fine."

"You're going to have it all over your face and chest. You sure?"

"I'm sure." He dabs his finger in it and tastes it. I make a face, but he just laughs.

"What? It tastes like candy."

"Gross."

"Oh yeah?" He dips again and tries to boop me on the nose. I knock my stool over trying to get away from him, but he cackles and starts chasing me with his bloody finger.

"Nooo!" I yell, but I'm laughing too, laughing so hard I can barely breathe as I dart around racks of flats and carts of broken lights and buckets of paint.

But Liam is tall, and long-limbed, and ~~I don't try that hard to avoid him~~ eventually he catches me, smearing red across my cheek.

I give him my best glower, but he just laughs.

He's standing right in front of me, breathing hard, his ~~nipples~~ chest showing through his T-shirt. Tall and handsome and strong and fast and *boyfriend*.

Jasmine's boyfriend.

I back away. Far away, until I bump against the rack where we store old flats.

"You're a jerk," I grumble.

His smile falters.

"I was only joking around. Sorry."

"It's fine." I go to the sink to wash myself off.

He's not a jerk. I'm a jerk. All he wanted was to tease me, like friends do. But every time he touches me I want to fall apart.

I never want him to stop touching me.

I'm a terrible brother.

When I turn back, drying my face with a paper towel, he's a few steps away. Giving me space.

"Sorry," he signs. "Sorry sorry."

I shake my head. "It's fine."

I summon up a smile that would make Dr. Lochley proud.

Maybe I'm a decent actor after all.

"Let's get back to work."

17

If I have to murder an actor during dress rehearsal, does that count as first or second degree?

The last week of techs were fine: Paige wrangled the stage crew for scene changes; Denise and I worked out all the lighting cues; Dr. L and Mr. Cartwright and Miss Benayoun, the conductor, argued about sound cues and how many bars of music to give each scene change.

The show came together. Became something more than the sum of its parts.

But now that everyone's in costume, it's like they've forgotten how to do a show. Actors run from one side of backstage to the other, like they haven't been making the exact same entrances for weeks. Asher accidentally sings the same verse three times in a row. Poor Liam nearly falls into the pit at one point, but in a surprising display of moral fortitude, Cam yanks him back.

I never thought I'd actually be grateful to Cameron for anything.

I'm seated at the tech table, hemmed in with Dr. Lochley to my right, Denise to my left, with a huge bag of ~~forbidden~~ mini candy canes in front of her.

I've got an iPad mirroring the screen of the lighting console back in the booth; its glow lights up my stage manager notebook.

"Light cue 158 go," I say over my headset. It's a special in-ear one Denise found online, that I can wear instead of my right hearing aid. It's not perfect (then again, neither are my hearing aids), but it's enough to get by—as long as Dr. L or Denise is on comm too, to catch what I miss.

"Spot Jesus, go."

Liam stands at center stage, in his costume of ripped black jeans and a clean white T-shirt, except it's not so clean anymore, as his makeup has stained the collar beige and there's a black streak of eyeliner on one shoulder. His hair has been gelled and styled into an angular, aggressive rock star look. Heavy eyeliner frames his blue eyes. They shine when the lights catch them, like someone stole a bit of the summer sky to make them.

"Light cue 159 go." The stage goes darker, leaving Liam bathed in blue backlight, with only the followspots lighting his face.

He's a glowing sun.

If I weren't such a heathen an atheist I would probably appreciate the symbolism.

The soldiers appear in the wings as he's singing the last notes of the song, and he looks right at the tech table, right at me, and I lose my breath. I know he's doing it because I'm a friendly face, a familiar presence in the audience, but I wish he'd look away. Look at Dr. L, who is obsessed with proud of him; look at Denise, who he's spent every work day learning tech from; even at Cam, who's waiting in the wings to kiss him.

He doesn't know the ache he kindles every time he looks at me. He doesn't know what it's like to watch him onstage, a blazing star, and want him to shine on me instead of on my sister.

And then he does that thing some people can do where he lets a single tear roll down his cheek. And it's gentle, not a squint-and-squeeze-it-out type tear but a true oh-I-didn't-realize-I-was-crying tear, and it feels like he's reached into my chest and ripped my still-beating heart out.

I forget to breathe. Denise elbows me.

Time for Judas to ~~kiss~~ betray him.

"Light cue 160 go."

"Have I polished my shoes?" Dr. Lochley asks slowly, rhythmically, raising her hands over her head. Onstage, the cast mirrors her.

"Yes, I've polished my shoes," they chant, bowing and rising in (nearly) perfect sync, smiling into the empty house.

I'm smiling too: no emergency stops, no scene change disasters, like the time someone dropped the jar of Eliza's marbles in *My Fair Lady* during the scene change and Miss Benayoun had to vamp the orchestra for three straight minutes while we chased them down.

Liam's standing center stage, shirtless, our perfectly formulated fake blood running down the valley of his chest and sticking to the ridges of his abs. His hair is held down by the plastic crown of thorns I found at a religious supply store.

I was worried I might burst into flames the moment I stepped through the door, but I made it out unscathed, except for the handful of pamphlets stuffed into my bag at the checkout counter.

Liam catches my eye and beams at me. He's breathing hard, like he just swam a race, and even though there aren't any followspots on him right now, he's still so luminous I have to look away.

Dr. Lochley claps her hands once, says something to the cast I can't catch, and they all scatter to get out of costume and ready for notes.

As I gather my stuff, Dr. Lochley pops back to the tech table.

"Nicely done, Jackson," she says.

I hide my smile as I stuff my binder into my backpack.

"You've really come into your own as a somethingsomething. I'm proud of you."

I think my face might set the theatre on fire. Maybe it's good the fire marshal came by this semester.

"Thanks," I manage.

She squeezes my shoulder and heads back toward the stage, where Cam is crouched on the apron, trying to get her attention.

Denise elbows my side. "She's right. You did good."

"Nah." But my smile might actually break my jaw. It's ~~nearly~~ enough to make me forget my exhaustion. After a full day of classes, then a dress rehearsal, my brain feels like a shmoodie left in the car on a sunny day.

I climb the woogedy stairs from the house to the stage—we'll pull them out before the show—and head backstage.

In the wings, actors elbow each other, making their way to the dressing room or the scene shop, which we're using as a makeshift dressing room as well. Most people try to get the real thing, though; no matter how much I sweep or vacuum, there's always the risk of sawdust and splinters in the scene shop.

I check the props table, make sure the dimmer rack didn't throw any errors. Paige pulls the cross offstage and sweeps. She's honestly amazing: If I mentor her well, maybe she can take over for me when I graduate.

When we finish, Paige goes to check the dressing room, while I take the scene shop. I open the door slowly—so anyone indecent has a chance to get decent—then let myself in. It's empty, except for ~~a very shirtless~~ Liam.

He's cleaned the fake blood off his chest, and wiped off his makeup, but his cheeks are still pink. And when he spots me, he signs, "Help."

He points to the crown of thorns, tangled in his feathery hair.

"Hold on." The scene shop has been transformed for tech week: its gray brick walls no longer lit by harsh fluorescents but by the warm glow of incandescent PARs stationed around the room. Two huge mirrors have been laid on their sides on the worktable, propped up by the miter saw and the band saw, to serve as makeup mirrors; on the opposite wall, where we store flats in huge steel racks, are more mirrors, regular IKEA ones standing up for people to check their costumes.

I gently shove Liam into a seat so I can reach him better. He's still too tall, and he's radiating more heat than usual, even though the scene shop is chilly. I untangle a strand from the back of his head, right where there are two whorls. I never noticed Liam has two whorls. He's quiet as I work, though he winces when I accidentally tug too hard.

"Sorry."

"It's fine. Keep going," he signs. His eyes in the mirror follow me as I work, slowly disentangling the crown. Once I get the back free, I move to his front. This close I can really see the effect of the eyeliner. His eyes are two pools of water, and I think I might drown in them. He's still looking right at me, and between that and his bare chest, throwing off heat like a furnace, I think I might pass out.

I can't look down: I'll just see more of his chest. Even though he's slouching, his abs still show, which I didn't think was actually possible. There's a sheen of sweat coating him, so the light catches on all the ripples and ridges that make up his front. I focus on the center of his forehead instead, willing him to not look anywhere in the vicinity of my jeans, which are feeling tight and uncomfortable.

I think about light cues and Dr. Lochley's notes and to-do lists until I finally free the last lock of hair and hoist the crown overhead. "Got it!"

Liam laughs and stands, and suddenly he's looming over me again, his chest still flushed from the show.

I try to back away, but I'm trapped against the workbench. All I can do is curve myself away from him so he hopefully won't ~~feel~~ notice the front of my jeans.

"You okay?" I ask. "I didn't hurt you?"

"I'm good."

"Good." It's hurting me, standing next to him.

~~I never want to stop.~~ He is Jasmine's *boyfriend*.

"You should get dressed for notes. I'll put this away."

"Yeah, I better . . ." He steps back, letting me out.

I don't look back as I run out of the scene shop.

18

As chaotic as dress rehearsal was, opening night is surprisingly smooth. Actors hit their marks, I hit my cues, spots hit their targets, orchestra . . . hits the right notes or something.

I'm in the booth at the back of the house, next to Dr. Lochley, who's listening in on comm in case I have trouble making anything out. Even from here, at the back of the house and with plexiglass separating us, I can tell Liam's crushing it. The audience goes wild every time he's on stage. Cameron too. It's like there's lightning bolts between the two of them.

"Light cue 305 go." The backdrop lights up in a blue-red-green fan. "Light cue 306 go." The fan turns into a full rainbow, chasing left to right, for *maximum gayification,* as Denise called it.

Cameron's singing his heart out for his big number, "Superstar." I try not to be annoyed at him for his talent. There are plenty of other reasons to hate him, after all; I update the list quite frequently.

CAMERON'S BREAKUP LIST (V. 38):
~~FUTURE PROBLEMATIC WHITE BOY~~
TREATS TECHIES BADLY

GLOWED UP EVEN MORE SINCE WE DATED
BASIC WHITE BOY LOOKS
ALLERGIC TO ONIONS
ALWAYS MAKES THE CAST
CONSTANT PDA WITH PHILIP
ABLEIST
GETS TO KISS LIAM
USED THE WORD *MOIST* IN A SENTENCE

I go through the cues one after the other, calling spot changes and lighting changes that perfectly match the emotions and the music, my feet tapping along to the beat.

"Light cue 325 go." As the song winds down, Jesus is supposed to enter stage right, bearing the cross for his crucifixion, so he and Judas can share one last look of longing. But Liam's not on his mark.

Cameron looks stage left, but he doesn't miss a beat. He keeps singing, turns back to the audience instead, singing out toward the house like it's his long-lost lover, though he does spare another glance toward the wings.

"Where's Jesus?" I ask over comm. "Light cue 326 go."

Paige answers over comm, voice faint and crackly. "No idea."

"No idea," Dr. L repeats. "Can anyone find him?"

"Light cue 327 go. Spots on Judas go."

The song is building to a climax, and I can't make Paige or Dr. L out: There's too much cross talk.

Suddenly Dr. L's hand is on my shoulder. "Go find him. Hurry." She gestures for me to pass over my binder so she can call the show.

I only hesitate for a second—my binder's got more than just stage manager notes in it—but this is a Theatre Emergency. I sneak out the booth and through the back doors as quietly as I can.

And then I'm sprinting down the halls, past the FACS classrooms and through the temporary black drapes we hang to keep the audience away from the cross-hall behind the theatre. It's rapidly emptying, though: Everyone's headed toward the stage doors for the crucifixion and finale.

I duck into the bathroom next, to check if he's having a code brown. "Liam? You in here?"

No one answers, but I check all the stalls just in case he's too embarrassed to say anything. I wouldn't blame him: A code brown during a show is the ultimate nightmare. My first year, Cody, this senior who played Eliza's dad in *My Fair Lady*, had a code brown during dress rehearsal, and everyone called him "Cody Brown" the rest of the year.

But the bathroom is deserted.

I run for the stage doors next. As I reach for the handle, the door opens and hits me in the face. I stagger back and cup my nose.

"Sorry!" Tori says.

I shake my head. "Have you seen Liam?"

"Somethingsomething putting his crown on."

Scene shop, then? "Thanks."

There's a trickle from my nose, but I ignore it as I slip backstage. The stage is dark, except for the blue glow of a scene change, and bare save the block that Paige will lock the cross into once Liam's dragged it onstage. It's the marbles all over again. But thankfully Miss Benayoun is vamping like a champion.

The scene shop is dim, the lights only at 25 percent, bright enough to find your way and check your makeup but not bright enough to risk spilling out.

"Liam?" I ask, quietly as I can. But if he answers back I don't hear it. I make my way farther in, around the costume racks arranged haphazardly in the open space. I trip on someone's makeup bag, another person's shoes. I wipe at my nose with the back of my hand; it comes away dark.

Dr. Lochley always talks about bleeding for our art, but I don't think this is what she had in mind.

In the back of the scene shop is a nook with the ladder to the catwalk. There's no actual door stopping students from climbing up, just a chain drawn across the rungs.

I poke my head in the nook. There's no lights in there, but a pair of naked shoulders catch the glow from outside.

"Liam," I say. "You're on."

He startles and turns around, drops the crown of thorns he was holding. His eyes are big, and his face is sweaty.

His lips move, but I don't catch it.

"What?"

He's got tear tracks on his face, which I'd never seen from him during this scene, but emotions are always at their highest on show night. He's going to bring the house down.

"What are you doing in here?" The nook is tiny, and his frame fills the space, his bare chest dewy from sweat and alarmingly *not covered in fake blood*. "Shit, we've got to get you ready. You're supposed to be getting crucified!"

I drag him out of the nook, grab the jar of stage blood, and scoop the crown off the floor, smacking it against my jeans to get the worst of the dust off. "Here. Put this on."

His fingers close around it mechanically, but he's staring at me. More tears pool in his eyes, but then he blinks them away. "You're bleeding."

"It's fine. What were you doing in there? Aren't you claustrophobic?"

"There's no door. It's not so bad."

I shove the crown at him again. While he puts it on, I uncap the stage blood and start trailing it across his neck, his brow. There's no time. I sniff to keep the real blood from dripping down my nose, but he steps away.

"Liam!" I whine, but then he's back, holding a paper towel, and while I smear fake blood along his chest, he holds it to my nose, gently wiping at it. It doesn't hurt much; hopefully it's not broken.

Liam's chest is firm and warm, his skin smooth. I can feel the way he's put together, the muscles that pull him through the water so well it looks effortless.

He is ~~Jasmine's boyfriend~~ supposed to be onstage right now.

I shake myself, try to pull away, but his free hand covers one of mine, warm and soft. I look up at him. He takes a deep breath, sets his jaw, and nods at me.

"Thanks. I'm good."

"Right. Come on. The show must go on."

I grab the paper towel from him, take him by the forearm, and lead him out of the scene shop. Give him a gentle nudge toward Paige, who's standing there waiting with his cross. "You got this."

19

It's a standing ovation. Of course it is.

I watch from backstage right, next to Paige, bits of paper towel stuffed up my nostrils.

The cast joins hands and bows, gestures to the pit, then bows again one final time. They wave goodbye as the grand drape closes. There's a tiny hitch about a third of the way along, but Paige recovers before I even blink.

The gold curtains close for the last time, wobble for a second, and still.

"Great job," I tell Paige.

She shrugs, says something I can't make out, but gestures to my nose.

"I think it's stopped." I pull out the paper towels, sniff experimentally, but things seem dry. Dry and crusty. The cast is breaking up, heading to their dressing rooms. Liam spots me as I hang back against the flyrail. He's breathing hard, chest heaving, fake blood smeared everywhere. There's a smile on his face, a genuine one, but it's still a little fragile.

"Hey," he signs.

"Hey."

"Thanks. I'm sorry."

I wave him off. "It's fine."

He shakes his head.

"Talk later?"

"Yeah. You better go change."

He reaches for me, ready to tuck in my tag, but his hand is covered in fake blood. I lean away. "Ew!"

He blushes and pulls back.

"Go get cleaned up. I've got to close the booth."

Dr. L is already gone when I get back, the door wide-open. I pack away my binder (making sure Dr. Lochley didn't ~~notice~~ disturb any of my lists), then triple-check for food. I didn't bring anything myself, but last year ~~a GSA member~~ someone left a half-eaten bag of Doritos in the booth, and no one found it for days.

There were mouse poops everywhere.

The lobby is full of cast members, still in costume and make-up, greeting friends or family. A few people hold handfuls of roses. River, a senior in the chorus (she's way more of an actor than a singer), holds a bouquet that's got to be at least two dozen.

A shriek distorts in my hearing aids, and I spin to find Tori, hugging her mother and surrounded by her siblings. She's beaming, bouncing on her toes, and I don't think I've ever seen her happier in all the years I've known her. Senior year and a lead in the musical.

I spot Bowie's brown hand waving over the crowd and make my way through. They're holding a small bouquet of yellow roses.

I'm not a plant gay, and I will no doubt kill these flowers the same way I did all the other ones Bowie's gotten me, but I smile as I take them. Bowie got me a bouquet for the first show I stage managed, after they saw all the actors get them and me with nothing, and the tradition kind of stuck.

"These are beautiful. Thanks."

"Sure thing, Jacks. You did great."

I shrug, my ears warming. "You couldn't even tell."

"Yeah. That's how I know you were awesome."

They give me a side hug, and we hang against the wall, watching everyone else milling around. It's so loud, Bowie switches to sign to ask, "Where's your dad and Amy?"

"Coming to the matinee."

"Oh. I saw Jasmine earlier."

"Probably waiting for Liam."

Bowie must see something in my face, because they give me the most sympathetic look. I can't stand it.

But then: "What'd you do to your nose?"

"Ugh."

They hold their compact mirror for me while I clean the last bits of blood off. My nose doesn't look crooked or anything, just a little too big for my face, like always.

"Thanks."

"Sure."

There's a commotion in the lobby as more actors emerge to greet their families and friends. I spot Cam and Philip, talking to Cam's parents. I only met them a couple times, and they seemed nice. Maybe even a little bland. Not like the kind of people who'd raise ~~an egotistical monster~~ an actor, but I guess you never know.

Liam finally emerges, Jasmine already hanging off his arm, smiling and laughing. He's got a dozen red roses in his free hand, and it's hard to tell which is redder, the flowers or his cheeks. But the color drains from his face when Dr. L swoops in.

At first I'm not sure if she's going to congratulate him or castigate him.

"What's she saying?" I ask Bowie. "Can you tell?"

" 'You were spectacular. Your best performance yet. Could you feel it?' "

I'm so proud of him.

"Now she's talking about how the whole house was moved to tears." Bowie laughs. "She's laying it on a little thick. Was it supposed to have that long dramatic pause, though?"

"No, he was . . ." I shake my head. I know he and Bowie are friends, but he was so upset, so vulnerable, and I can't just tell his business. I don't even know what happened. "I dunno. But I better go finish up. Perkins after?"

"You know it."

I bump into Cam as I head backstage.

"Oh. Sorry, Jackson."

I'm so stunned I nearly drop my roses. In all the time I've known Cameron I'm not sure he's ever apologized to me—not even after a fight while we were dating.

But he's not looking at me. He's focused on Dr. Lochley and Liam. He's changed out of Judas's red leather jacket, and his shirt is unbuttoned, and he's sweaty and kind of smelly.

"Good show," I tell him.

"Thanks." He actually looks at me, and he's doing the puppy-dog eye thing, all vulnerable, and for a second I feel kind of bad for him. He's the one who had to cover for Liam. "You too."

I nearly drop my roses again.

"Thanks."

"You kind of saved the show, didn't you?"

I shrug, but I'm blushing. "Yeah, well, you covered. It was a team effort."

Cam gets this smile—this real, genuine smile—and I remember why I used to like him. He wasn't always Cameron Haller, Senior ~~Asshole~~ Actor. He used to be just Cam, the first boy I ever kissed.

"Thanks." He scratches the side of his nose. "It was definitely alarming when he didn't show up."

"I bet."

He crosses his arms over his chest. That softness in his eyes sharpens. "Philip said he missed his cue because he and Tori were hooking up in the scene shop."

"What? Ew. No," I say automatically. Not that hooking up is gross (I definitely would like to try that someday), but in the scene shop? With all the sawdust and stuff?

Also, there's no way. "Tori was backstage. He was alone back there."

"You sure about that? He came out all flushed, like he'd just . . ." Cam makes a gesture that's definitely not sign language.

"Don't spread rumors just because you're jealous of him."

Cam's face turns red at that. His eyes darken, like curtains closed behind them.

"Don't you have a stage to go sweep, Jackthon?"

Ass.

But I do need to finish post-show.

I leave my flowers and backpack on the corner of the prop table and get to work.

JACKSON'S POST-SHOW CHECKLIST:
DOUBLE-CHECK PROPS, NOTE ANY BROKENS
CHECK DRESSING ROOMS AND SCENE SHOP
LOCK ALL LINESETS
SWEEP STAGE
SET GHOST LIGHT
WORK LIGHTS OFF, DOORS LOCKED

"Good show tonight," I tell Paige as I wheel out the ghost light. "See you tomorrow."

"You're not coming tonight?"

I shake my head. "You?"

She shrugs. "Thought I'd check it out."

"Have fun."

Paige heads out, letting Liam and Jasmine in. They're holding hands.

"There you are," Jasmine says.

"Hey," Liam says. "You coming to the cast party?"

I snort. "Of course not."

"Jackson never goes to those," Jasmine says. "He something-something."

"I'm not really feeling it either," Liam says.

"But we have to go! All the other couples will be there."

Including Philip and Cam, no doubt. Another reason to avoid it.

Jasmine twines her arm through Liam's and leans in to kiss his reddening cheek.

"All right," he finally says. "Can you give me and Jackson a second before we go?"

"Sure. Meet you outside?"

"Thanks."

Jasmine heads out, and then it's just Liam and me and the awkwardness swimming between us.

He tucks his roses under his armpit to free up his hands. "You're really not coming?" he signs. He's up to full sentences now, which is pretty impressive, though he still uses English syntax sometimes.

"To the cast party? No way." I say it aloud and sign it too.

"Why?"

"I wasn't invited."

It's not that big a deal. It's not like I wanted to go. It'll just be a bunch of sweaty out-of-control actors ~~goofing off~~ ~~hooking up~~ making asses of themselves.

"But you're the stage manager."

"Bowie and I always go to Perkins."

"Oh." He presses his lips together into this weird half smile. "Did they get you the roses?"

"Yeah."

"That's sweet."

"Don't let them hear you say that."

Liam laughs, but then the smile slides off his face again. He steps closer.

"Thank you. For earlier."

"It's okay."

"It's not. I . . ."

He stares at his hands, like he's searching for the right signs.

"You can say it aloud if that's easier," I tell him.

But he shakes his head and pulls out his phone.

My dad took me out to dinner tonight before
the show
But we got into a big fight. Like, really big.
He told me he'd been cheating on my mom.
That's why they got divorced.

I accidentally drop Liam's phone.

"Shit! Sorry."

He waves me off, reaches for the phone the same time as me.
Our fingers brush and I pull back like he's shocked me. But I can't
even imagine.

And I can't stop this dread settling in my stomach.

During the second act . . . I don't know.
It really hit me and I started crying and
I just couldn't stop.
I'm sorry.
I messed everything up.

My heart is cracking in two. I hate seeing Liam hurt like this.

"You didn't mess anything up. It was fine." I look up from the
phone; Liam's tearing up again. "Do you . . . do you want a hug?"

I shouldn't be hugging him. Shouldn't be touching him at all.
But he's my friend, and he's hurting, and I can't just let him be
hurting.

He bites his lip and nods. I step forward and pull him into a
hug, resting my hands in the small of his back, a safe distance
above his ~~flat ass~~ waistband. His body is warm, like usual. We

smush the roses between us, the sweet scent of the flowers mixing with his deodorant. I squeeze him, try to tell him without words that it'll be okay. That he's my friend and I'm here for him.

But eventually he breaks the hug, wiping at his eyes.

"I wish something~~something~~."

"What?"

"I wish I could just go to Perkins with you."

"Hah. I don't think Jasmine would like that."

"Yeah." He sighs, blows out a slow breath through his lips. They don't look quite so thin when he does that. And even if they are thin, they're really nice, with a little bow in them.

They make the shape of my name.

"Huh?"

He's looking at me funny. ~~Like he caught me staring.~~

"Sorry. It's been a long day and my brain is done."

He switches back to sign. "It's okay. You sure you won't come? Bowie too?"

I shake my head. Honestly, it'd be a nightmare. Loud music and cross talk and I would just sit in the corner alone, talking with Bowie, assuming I could even convince them to come, while Liam ~~hooked up with Jasmine in an empty bedroom~~ danced with Jasmine or made out in a corner or just hung around, being one of the actors, feeling at home with them in a way I never could.

And even if I had been invited—even if I wanted to go—how could I now? When he's going to be with Jasmine, and I'm going to be there, wishing he wasn't. Wishing he was with me instead.

I need to get away from him. As far as possible. For both our sakes.

20

Winter break in the Ghasnavi household is always a little weird.

We don't really celebrate Christmas, but we don't *not* celebrate it. We do a tree and presents, and it's Mom's year to come visit us, so we'll do dinner and see the Plaza Lights and stuff. But it's not like we go to church or put up inflatable nativity scenes.

Even Amy, who was raised Catholic, seems fine with us doing the Hallmark version of Christmas, though she does go to Mass on Christmas Eve. Which works out fine, since that's when we have the awkward Mom-and-Dad-whole-family dinner.

Dad's a decent cook, with one ~~glaring~~ minor weakness: vegetables.

"Tell me if these are cooked enough." He hands me a fork and points at the pot of carrot chunks simmering on the stove.

"How long have they been going?"

"Forty-five minutes."

I poke at one of the carrots with the fork. As soon as the tines touch the chunk they sink in, and as I pull the fork away, the whole thing splits into three pieces, turning to ragged mush that sinks to the bottom of the pot.

"They're dead."

He's only half listening to me, though. "Good. Your mom should be here soon. Can you check on your sister and Liam?"

The door is open, and they're both sitting on her bed, shoulder to shoulder, listening to music. Liam's in a purple polo and a pair of jeans; his UT Austin hoodie lays over the back of Jasmine's desk chair. The way he's sitting, his shirt has ridden up a bit, exposing the bottom of his stomach, where a small patch of dark hair has started growing ever since State—the end of the season—where he won three of his events (100 free, 200 free, and the medley relay).

Bowie won the 200 IM and the 100 fly, setting a new school record. I don't think I've ever seen them smile so wide.

"You need something?" Jasmine asks. She's in her usual winter break attire: fuzzy leggings, lilac today, and a sweatshirt. I blink when I see it's for UT Austin too. I wonder ~~if Liam got it for her~~ what Dad will think.

"Dad says dinner's almost ready."

"Is Mom here yet?"

"Not yet. But if she waits any longer, we'll be having hot carrot water."

"Ugh." Jasmine rolls her eyes. Her hand is resting on Liam's thigh, nearly in his crotch.

I glance up and realize Liam's caught me staring at ~~his crotch~~ Jasmine's hand. His lips are slightly parted, but he doesn't say anything.

We haven't been hanging out much in the two weeks since the show ended. He's been busy with swimming. And I've been busy with post-show cleanup and organization and stuff.

~~It's not that I'm avoiding him.~~

I clear my throat. "Anyway. Come down soon."

Jasmine nods absently and scoots closer to Liam, like she's trying to climb into his lap so they can make out.

I beat a hasty retreat.

I suppose our dad has a type.

Because Mom is white, like Amy, with brown hair, like Amy, and brown eyes, like Amy, and freckles, like Amy.

But while Amy's a librarian, Mom's a doctor like Dad, which is doubtless one of the ~~million~~ reasons they got divorced: Both of them have to have the last word.

"More brisket, Angela?" Dad asks.

Now that they're divorced and live hundreds of miles away from each other, they act super friendly in a way they never did while married. So friendly it's awkward: some unholy combination of Iranian taarof and Midwestern niceness, rolled in a heavy coating of passive-aggressive let's-get-along-for-the-kids.

"I'm full, thanks. It was so good. Interesting texture too."

Dad pretends not to hear the backhanded compliment.

"Amy's got me hooked on this Instant Pot thing."

Mom nods. "How's she doing?"

Across the table, Jasmine looks at me and rolls her eyes. Mom doesn't dislike Amy—they actually get along fine, as far as I can tell—but that doesn't stop her from avoiding Amy as much as she can.

Dad starts telling a secondhand story about the library, but I quickly lose track of it. He's facing Mom, talking fast, and when she starts telling a story of her own, about the hospital, I think, I give up and tune out.

It's weird: When it's just me and Dad, or me and Mom, they're both pretty good about looking at me when they talk, but when they're together they get so focused it's like I disappear.

It sounds awful to say, but them getting divorced might have been the best thing that ever happened to me. Though I do miss Mom. She announced she was moving to Colorado not long after the papers were signed. Right after she and I had gotten into a big fight, and I told her I would never forgive her for breaking up our family. I still feel bad about that, because I do forgive her. But at least it taught me to be a lot more careful with what I say.

I got sent to therapy after the fight. I spent the first few sessions angry and inconsolable. But eventually my therapist had me do this thing where I made a list of all the pros and cons of them getting divorced. It helped me see that they were hurting—not just each other, but me and Jasmine too. And that ultimately, their splitting up was for the best.

MOM AND DAD'S DIVORCE LIST:
THEY FIGHT ALL THE TIME
JASMINE KEEPS CRYING
~~WHAT IF IT'S BECAUSE OF ME?~~
DAD CAN'T COOK VEGETABLES
MOM CAN'T COOK MEAT
THEY SHOUT ALL THE TIME
~~THEY FEEL GUILTY ABOUT MY DEAFNESS?~~
DOUBLE PRESENTS????

I guess that was sort of the start of my lists.

* * *

It takes me a moment to realize Liam's signing at me.

"You okay?"

"Yeah. Hard to follow."

"They never learned?"

Jasmine elbows Liam, asks him something I can't make out.

"She wants to know what we're saying."

"Tell her 'never mind.'"

Liam's eyes screw up and he snorts out a laugh, so loud everyone at the table stops talking and looks his way.

"Liam, where did you learn that?" Mom asks.

"Bowie's been teaching me."

"Jackson's Bowie?" she asks.

"Yeah."

Mom smiles. "They're great. Jackson, when are you and Bowie going to stop this weird dance of yours and actually start dating?"

I close my eyes and breathe. "Mom. We're never going to date."

"You never know—"

"I do know, Mom. Bowie's my best friend. My very platonic best friend. They're aroace. Not all queer people are dating each other."

"Okay, sorry," Mom says. "I just want you to be happy."

"I am happy. Okay?"

Mom raises her hands in surrender, and I slump back into my chair. Liam's staring at me, mouth hanging open.

"What?" I sign.

"Nothing."

The table gets quiet again, which is fine by me, because everything got super weird. I turn back to my food, scooping up a carrot that's had the strong atomic force boiled out of it, while Dad decides tonight is a fine time to ~~pester~~ ask Jasmine about college choices once again. Which is my cue to pull out my phone and mute my hearing aids.

As I'm doing it, a text pops up from Liam.

I miss him too, miss him so much it hurts. But being around him hurts more.

We should do something soon

We absolutely should not. Not unless Bowie's around. Because without the play as a buffer—without to-do lists, and Dr. L needing things, and a theatre to maintain—there's just me and Liam and the fact that every second I'm with him I ache. I ache and I want to cry, and I hate myself, because I want him to be happy, and I want Jasmine to be happy, and I wish the two of them had never met.

I'm a terrible brother and a worse friend.

But I can't tell him any of that. So I just answer:

Sure

21

Jasmine waves at me from my doorway. "Jackson?"

"Yeah?" I mark my place in the lighting design book Bowie got me for Friendsmas, which is what we call it when we give each other gifts in December for completely secular reasons.

"Can you help me for a second?" Jasmine fidgets with the hem of her blue Royals hoodie. I'm not sure why she even owns it; neither of us likes baseball. But she got it from Blake, her four-times-removed ex, and even though Blake was a total bust, she really liked the hoodie.

His breakup list is more wrinkled than most since she took a really long time to get over him. He still holds the record for longest relationship—three months, though once January rolls around, Liam will tie it.

BLAKE THE BRICK'S BREAKUP LIST:
~~RACIST HAIR?~~
TRIED TO PULL OFF WHITE GUY LOCS
SMELLED LIKE BURNT HAIR (NOT HIS OWN?)
NO NECK, HEAD SHAPED LIKE LEGO MINIFIGURE
~~REVERSE HITLER MUSTACHE~~
WEIRD FACIAL HAIR

ONCE ASKED JASMINE IF SHE SHAVED HER ARMPITS
ENCOURAGED JASMINE TO SHAVE HER ARMPITS
~~MEN'S RIGHTS ACTIVIST~~
TOLD GROSS JOKES

I never told Jasmine half of the stuff he said to me when she wasn't around, including a lengthy soliloquy on the merits of tongue piercings ~~when it came to blow jobs~~.

As much as Jasmine mourned the breakup, I was grateful for it.

"Jackson?"

"Huh?"

"I said, can you help me pick what to wear tonight?"

I follow her to her room, where she's got three different outfits laid on her bed.

"You know being gay doesn't make me good at fashion, right?" I sweep my hands up and down my faded *Into the Woods* shirt from the last Broadway revival. I didn't actually see it, but Mom found the shirt online for my last birthday.

"I know. But I need your help. Liam's going to be there."

I figured.

"Do the sweater and jeans, then."

"You think?" Jasmine runs a hand over the red dress with the heart neckline that I ignored. "It's not . . . I don't know, plain?"

"It's cute."

Jasmine's nostrils flare. "Cute is for first dates. This is a party. I'm trying to, you know. Move things forward."

"Gross!"

"Aw, don't be weird."

"I'm not being weird. Your body is your business." But my face is catching fire. I don't want to think about ~~Liam and~~ my sister having sex.

"Don't be a jealous virgin," she teases, and that just makes the flames burn hotter.

Cam and I never got past kissing, though one time I did squeeze his butt while we were making out, and that felt pretty excellent. Cam had (still has, honestly) an excellent butt, probably from all the dancing.

"I'm not jealous!" I say, probably louder than I mean to, but my ears feel full, not from my hearing aids but from the churning in my gut. I don't want to have this conversation.

"Aw, don't worry. You'll find a boyfriend someday."

I don't want a boyfriend.

I want the one boy I can never have.

Dad and Amy are at a work party, and Mom's visiting her old college friends, but Bowie invited me over to hang out. Their parents are gone too—not that I mentioned it to Dad—so we make some boxed shells and cheese (the kind with the pouch of liquid cheese, not the weird powder) and play *Smash Bros.*

Halfway through dinner, Bowie drops their fork and runs a hand over their hair. They cut it after State, and it's in short waves now, with the sides faded. It looks crisp and cool, but I kind of miss their twists. I'm not used to Bowie with short hair.

"Are we going to talk about it?"

"About what?"

Bowie sighs—a heavy, dramatic one, and with their swimmer's lungs they can really put a lot of oomph into it. "Come on, Jacks. True biz."

I sigh back. "Liam and Jasmine are at a party tonight."

"He mentioned it."

"They're going to have sex."

Bowie makes a face.

"I know. But the thing is, she's happy. So happy. And I should be happy for her, right? But all I can think is I wish it was me." My stomach swoops. "Not the sex part. Just . . . being with him." ~~The sex part would be fine too, though.~~

I stop signing, rub my hands over my face. My eyes are burning and I don't want to cry into my shells and cheese.

I'm a horrible, selfish brother. And worse, I'm a terrible friend to Liam.

Because I don't want him to be happy. Not with her.

"I wish I'd said something. Before it was too late."

Bowie purses their lips. They're wearing the gold lipstick I got them for Friendsmas, and it looks stunning.

"That really sucks."

"It's whatever. He probably doesn't even like guys. You think he'd have mentioned before if he did, right?"

"Maybe," Bowie says. "Everyone comes out at their own pace."

"Yeah, but he's friends with you and me. We wouldn't judge."

"That doesn't necessarily make it any easier."

"I guess." I pick my fork back up and shovel more shells into my mouth.

At least there's always carbs and cheese.

"Enough about me," I say. "What about you?"

"What about me?"

"You hear any more from those recruiters?"

"Yeah, the one from Texas." They don't quite meet my eyes.

"We've been emailing back and forth some. I think I'm going to apply early decision. He thinks I can get pretty close to a full ride."

"Oh."

It feels like a cold stage weight dropped into my stomach.

I knew Bowie was thinking about Texas, but I always thought it was the same way I thought about UCLA: great program, but too far away from home.

Too far away from my best friend.

I thought they were picking Ohio. I thought they'd be closer to me.

But instead they're picking Texas. With Liam.

"That's cool," I manage, though my fingers feel like hot dogs as I form the signs.

It never really felt real before. That we'd be splitting up.

It still doesn't.

"Nothing's sure yet," they say.

It's definitely sure. There's nothing Bowie can't do once they set their mind to it.

"Even if I do go, I'll be home on breaks. And I'll come visit you. We'll still be best friends. College won't change us."

How could it not? They probably won't even think about me, except when they come home—assuming our breaks even line up—and then we'll have an awkward hangout where neither of us will want to admit we've grown apart and changed too much to really be best friends anymore.

My shells have congealed into a sticky mess, but I keep eating them anyway.

What else is there to say?

22

Amy and Dad pick me up from Bowie's around eleven. Well, Amy picks me up, and Dad is also there. Being short like me, he's kind of a lightweight.

When we were younger, Dad used to drag me and Jasmine to all his work parties. We'd stand around all dressed up, awkwardly interacting with a bunch of kids we didn't know, while Dad got tipsy off a single glass of champagne and spent the night telling medical jokes with the other doctors.

Eventually Dad stopped feeling like he had to show us off, and I'm not sure if it's because he realized he didn't need to impress anyone, or because he realized me and Jasmine weren't that impressive measured against a bunch of kids who were piano virtuosos or lacrosse champions or Johnson County residents.

Amy tries to talk to me while I buckle in. There's a light drizzle falling on the windshield; the forecast for tomorrow is freezing rain, which is always miserable.

"Huh?"

"You have fun?"

I shrug. Dad's head lolls in the passenger seat, and Amy shakes her head as she pulls away.

It's a short drive home, and Jasmine's car is in the driveway when we get there.

~~I wonder what she and Liam did tonight.~~

Dad rallies enough to make it up the stairs with Amy's help; Jasmine doesn't emerge from her room, but the lights are on, spilling from her doorframe.

I knock on her door, but when she doesn't answer, I knock again louder.

"Jasmine? You asleep?"

Still nothing.

I crack the door slowly, just in case she's changing or something.

But she's not. She's lying facedown on her bed, still in her jeans and sweater. Her rain-soaked boots drip onto the bedroom carpet—a disowning offense in the Ghasnavi household.

"Jasmine?" She doesn't answer me, but her shoulders are moving up and down like she's breathing hard.

Or crying.

A cold fist clenches in my stomach.

"You alive?"

She raises a hand before letting it flop down onto the bed again.

I approach her cautiously, like a wounded animal. Her duvet is rumpled from where she flung herself on top of it. "What's going on?"

She shifts around and turns her head enough to look at me. She's got tear tracks running down her cheeks, staining them black and purple from her makeup. Her puffy upper lip quivers.

"He broke up with me."

Liam broke up with her.

Liam. Broke up. With Jasmine.

It hits me like an out-of-control set piece, driving all the air from my lungs.

They broke up. They're not together anymore.

I clamp down on the strangled laugh trying to fight its way out. I'm a terrible brother. Quite possibly the worst in the world. Bottom ten for sure.

Because my first thought isn't even to comfort my sister. No. It's relief, flaring deep in my chest like a ghost light.

Maybe bottom five is more accurate.

Jasmine's still crying. I sit next to her and rub circles into her back. Just like I always do.

They broke up.

"You okay?" I ask.

I already know she's not. She never is.

She slowly sits up. I lean away to grab the Kleenex box, nearly toppling off the bed before I right myself.

There's a weird spot on her covers, and it takes me a moment to realize it's a smear of her makeup. It looks like a drama mask—the tragedy one—and another cruel laugh threatens to erupt.

Bottom three. For real.

Jasmine blows her nose, dabs at her eyes.

"What happened?"

~~I don't want to know.~~ I have to know.

"We were at the party. I thought we were having a good time. We wound up in an empty room. I thought . . ."

Thankfully she doesn't finish that sentence.

"But he said he wanted to talk about something. And then he said . . ." Jasmine blows her nose again, lets out this long sad sigh. "He said he'd been somethingsomethingsomething didn't think we should date anymore. That he somethingsomething, and it wasn't fair to lead me on."

She's talking too fast, her face all screwed up so I can barely read her lips.

"And then he said he hoped we could still be friends." She nearly wails that last part.

As far as breakups go, pretty much all of Jasmine's have been worse.

"I'm sorry." And I'm proud of myself for actually meaning it. I am sorry. I don't want Jasmine to be hurting.

If only they'd never dated in the first place. If only I'd warned Liam off. Told Jasmine not to go for it.

Admitted I like him.

"I should've seen this coming. He's been—" But then she's off again, and I lose the thread entirely.

"Can you talk more clearly?"

"Sorry." She sniffs hard. "He's been weird since the cast party. You know? And he kept talking about taking things slow. I thought he was being a gentleman. But I was the one who asked him out. I'm the one who called us official. I'm the one . . ." She reaches for another Kleenex and dabs at her eyes, though she misses a large streak of mascara. "I was going to tell him I loved him."

I feel like I've swallowed a crescent wrench.

Jasmine loved him?

"But it was always like . . . he didn't like me as much as I liked him. He was always holding back." She blows her nose. "Oh god. Was there someone else?"

"No," I say immediately. Liam could never do something like that.

"How are you so sure?"

"Did he ever tell you why his parents got divorced?"

"He never wanted to talk about it."

I swallow. "His dad was cheating on his mom. It tore him up. So no. I don't think he would cheat on you."

"He told you that?" Jasmine sniffs. "He never told me. He never talked to me!"

I rub Jasmine's back in circles as she cries, her hair tickling the back of my hand. It's still styled in the loose waves she spent hours putting in with a curling iron, even though her hair would already have a natural curl to it if she didn't straighten it twice a year.

She takes a shaky breath. "I just don't understand."

My sister's classic refrain:

I just don't understand.

I just don't understand why Mom and Dad are splitting up.

I just don't understand why Nick, Jason, French Class Guy, Blake, Tristan, Animation Guy, Dominic, and all the others broke up with me.

I just don't understand.

What's to understand? Sometimes things don't work out. Your boyfriend dumps you for being a techie. Your parents argue constantly. That guy in class doesn't notice you.

~~The boy you like goes out with your sister.~~

"I'm sorry. But at least he wants to be friends?"

159

She snorts, blowing a snot bubble out her nostril before she wipes it away. "You're joking, right? I'm never talking to him again. Liam is dead to me."

"Jasmine . . ."

"Here." She reaches for her nightstand, comes back with a purple glitter pen and a sheet of paper. "Do the thing."

"What thing?"

"You know. Make a breakup list."

"No."

Jasmine gapes at me. "I know he's your friend, but I'm your sister. You're supposed to be on my side. You're supposed to somethingsomething."

"What?"

"You're my brother. You're the only one I can count on."

"I don't want to do this, Jasmine."

"Come on, you love making those lists. You can find fault with anyone."

"That's not fair."

"Yes it is. You think love won't last, so you come up with reasons why it's not worth trying."

I feel like she's stabbed me.

"That's not true. Why are you being such a jerk? I'm not the one that dumped you."

As soon as I say it, I wish I could take it back, because Jasmine cries even harder.

"You're right. I'm sorry." She sniffs. "I just liked him so much. You don't know what it's like. You've never had your heart shattered into a million pieces."

I have. Every time I saw them together.

"Please?" She's crying again, harder than ever. "I need you, Jackson."

My heart cracks. She needs me.

"Ugh. Fine."

The good thing is, Liam already made his own list. It was all jokes, but Jasmine doesn't need to know that. I uncap the garish purple pen.

LIAM COQUYT'S BREAKUP LIST:
TOO HANDSY
PEOPLE PLEASER
RAZOR BUMPS IN WEIRD PLACES

"How would you even know that?" Jasmine shoves me. "I've got them in weird places too."

"I don't need to know that."

"What else?"

I wiggle the pen between my fingers and think. This would be a lot easier if Liam actually had any faults.

FEATHERY CHLORINATED HAIR
FLAT ASS
MISSED HIS CUE OPENING NIGHT

"Come on. None of these are even real faults."

"Fine. You do it."

But Jasmine shakes her head. "I can't. He was perfect. He had the most beautiful eyes. And I liked his flat ass, it made mine look better. And his shoulders were so strong. And his abs . . .

god, you ever see him with his shirt off? Of course you did, you saw the play."

I mean, it's all true, but it's all physical. I think about what he said. How he feels like people only see his body. And it makes me so mad. He deserved better from Jasmine.

"Do you hear yourself?" I snap. "Did you even know him or was he just a slab of meat to you?"

Jasmine blinks. "Oh my god. You're right. The only good thing about him was his body." She straightens up, sniffling, wiping away her tears with her mascara-stained Kleenex. "Put that down."

"What? No. That's too mean."

"So? How's he going to know?"

"I'll know."

"Jackson. Please." Her eyes have dried, but her lip is quivering again. "Can you just do this? For me?"

"Fine. But you can never tell him."

"I won't."

"Promise."

"All right. I promise."

So I add it.

BODY IS HIS ONLY REDEEMING FEATURE

"Good. More. I bet that's why he got cast too. Keep going."

I hate myself, but I keep writing.

ONLY GOT CAST FOR HIS LOOKS
GETS AWAY WITH THINGS BECAUSE HE'S
~~HOT~~ CONVENTIONALLY ATTACTIVE
DOESN'T CARE WHO HE HURTS

Guilt settles into my stomach like a stage weight. Liam worked hard for his role. He works hard for everything he does. He's a good friend.

And I'm a horrible one.

But Jasmine has stopped crying. She leans her head against my shoulder, reaches for the list. She scans it over, then looks at me and finally manages half a smile.

"It's perfect."

ACT III

23

"I can't say I'm surprised," Bowie says.

"Really? Why not?"

They arch an eyebrow. They're wearing silvery eye shadow today, and their nails are done with this pearlescent polish that changes color in the light streaming in from the kitchen window. It's beautiful, and I kind of want to ask them to paint mine, but my hands get trashed so quickly there's no point. Maybe my toes?

"Pass me the orange?"

I hand it over, and Bowie starts zesting it into the bowl. They're making some of their signature brioche French toast for my birthday brunch.

Having a birthday on New Year's Eve really sucks: It's impossible to have a party, since everyone's busy with other parties; and the weather is usually miserable (there's a "wintry mix" today); and worst of all, it gets swallowed by all the other December holidays.

I've had more than one birthday present wrapped in discount Christmas paper that Dad bought at Target on December 27. (He refuses to go on December 26, which he insists is nearly as bad as the day after Thanksgiving.)

Brunch with Bowie is one of the few things I look forward to each birthday. Their parents used to cook it, but Bowie took over once they got good enough in the kitchen. Mr. and Mrs. Anderson still stay close, though, to dispense a little of the secret ingredient (a tiny splash of booze) to the French toast batter. The alcohol all cooks out; it's not like they're letting me and Bowie drink.

Bowie finishes zesting the orange and turns to me.

"Just stuff Liam said."

"Like what?"

Bowie presses their lips together. "I think sometimes he got a little uncomfortable with how . . . intense she could be. You know? Like PDA, constantly texting. Constantly showing him off to her friends. I think he felt like a trophy."

"He never mentioned anything to me."

Bowie arches an eyebrow. "Can't imagine why he wouldn't complain about your sister to you."

"Fair enough." I sigh. "I wish he had, though. I wish . . ."

Bowie pauses as they crack eggs into a fresh bowl. Egg white drips down their fingers as they sign, "Wish what?"

"I wish I could tell him how I feel. But now it's even worse. He's not just dating Jasmine. He's her ex."

"Yeah. That sucks." They nod toward the stove. "Is that griddle hot enough yet?"

I hover my palm about an inch above the cast-iron surface. "Yeah."

"Good. Enough moping. Brunch doesn't cure everything, but it does make most things better."

* * *

After an obligatory family dinner at this new Mexican restaurant on the Plaza—the kind where they mash your guacamole table-side—we go back home to open presents.

Another drawback of having a birthday on New Year's Eve: If you don't get home early, you're stuck on the roads with all the drunk drivers. Which is only marginally better than being stuck at home with Mom and Dad. Mom's not drunk, but she's definitely more ready to argue with Dad after splitting a pitcher of fancy margaritas with Amy.

"I'm just saying, there are more options than following in your footsteps," she tells Dad.

"I don't care if she follows in my footsteps. Jackson's not going to. But to not even go to college—"

"She didn't say she isn't going, she just said she wants to wait a year."

At dinner, Jasmine announced she wants to take a gap year and stay with Mom in Denver. ~~Because nothing says *Happy birthday!* quite like announcing you're going to move away, just like Mom did.~~ At least Dad's disapproval has given her something besides Liam to mope about.

She sits stiffly next to me, cake barely eaten. It's a hazelnut one Amy picked up from this Swiss bakery in South Plaza.

"And what about financial aid? Scholarships? You know her college fund isn't where we wanted it to be."

"And rushing into things will magically fix all that?" Mom says.

"Can we not right now? Please?" Jasmine asks. "Forget I said anything. God."

She shoves away from the table and stomps up the stairs. Mom shoots Dad a look and goes to follow her.

Dad sighs, then he gets up too, leaving his half-eaten cake behind. It's just Amy and me. She gives me a sympathetic smile.

"Never a dull moment around the holidays, huh?"

"Guess not."

"You ever think about doing a half-birthday thing in June instead?"

June 30th is basically July 4th, so everyone will be distracted with hot dogs and fireworks. But still, I say, "Maybe."

Amy gives me a grin. The kettle is finally boiling, so she gets up to make tea, while my phone buzzes in my pocket. When I pull it out, I freeze.

It's from Liam.

> Happy bday!

My face heats up, and not from all the jalapeños I had with dinner.

He remembered.

> Thanks!

> You doing anything fun?

> Had dinner with the whole family

> I take it that's a no?

I snort.

"What are you laughing at?" Amy asks.

I look up, hugging my phone to my chest.

"Just texting."

"Tell Bowie hi!"

I bite my lip but don't mention it's not Bowie.

I hope it's okay to text you

Why wouldn't it be?

I'm sure Jasmine told you we broke up

I hope you don't hate me

I don't. I'm sorry things didn't work out

We're cool

We were friends before and we're st

*still friends

Yeah

Thanks

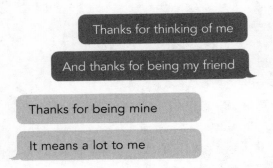

Thanks for thinking of me

And thanks for being my friend

Thanks for being mine

It means a lot to me

It means a lot to me.

I shake my head. It means a lot to me too. But now? After everything?

I don't know how it can ever mean anything more.

See you at school?

Yeah

See you

24

It's sleeting the first day back at school, icy drops that cling to Jasmine's windshield before melting away. The morning is dim and gray. I don't like the humidity of summer, but I miss the longer days. I hate going to school when it's still dark, and if we've got rehearsals, I'm usually leaving school when it's dark too.

We pull up into the golden cone of a parking lot light. Jasmine leaves the car running as she turns to me. Her lip is quivering, and tears have pooled in her eyes.

"Jackson . . ."

I was afraid she was going to ask.

"Can you do the list?"

"Do I have to?"

"Please? What if I run into him?"

"Fine." I pull it out and read it off as quick as I can.

Jasmine's spine stiffens and she blinks away her tears. "Thanks. What would I do without you?"

I shrug and stuff the list back into my notebook.

"One more semester to go," she says.

"Yeah." I clear my throat. "Are you really gonna move to Denver?"

"I think so. I don't know. Why does everyone expect me to already have things figured out?"

"Sorry," I mutter. "I'd miss you is all."

Jasmine gone in Denver. Liam gone in Texas. Bowie joining him a year later, while I'm up in New York or Chicago.

Everyone's leaving.

"I'd miss you too," she says.

I tighten my scarf, careful to keep it around my neck and away from my ears, and we head inside. The sleet is just heavy enough to be annoying when it hits me in the face, but not heavy enough to get us a snow day. Not that I didn't ask Amy like twelve times if she or Dad had gotten the robocall.

As we stomp our shoes on the mats, Jasmine gives me a nod and a "Bye!" and makes a beeline for Ellie. They link arms and head off toward first period, while I take my usual route up to my locker.

Now that swim season is over, there's no morning practice, so Bowie isn't there yet. But Liam is.

He smiles when he sees me. His cheeks are even redder than usual, and his nose is pink.

I can't help smiling back. I missed him.

Even though I just listed off a bunch of made-up faults to soothe my sister's broken heart. He doesn't need to know that.

He eyes the shmoodies in my hand with interest, and crap, I only made two. I had gotten used to Jasmine making him her terrible ones. But I can't leave him hanging, so I hand him mine.

"For me?" he asks, like I've just handed him a swimming trophy.

I nod.

He beams, uncapping the bottle to take a sip, and his lips immediately pucker. "Oh. It's good. Different."

"Pomegranates. They're pretty tart." Dad was supposed to make lavashak out of them, but he got called in for an emergency bypass and never got around to it.

So I broke them down myself—no sense letting them get all dry and hard—then blended (and strained) the arils into juice for shmoodies.

"I like it." Even one sip has stained Liam's lips garnet, and my stomach does a flip turn when he smiles, but then he looks past my shoulder. "Hey, Bowie."

Bowie tromps up, their black knee-high snow boots striking the floor so hard I can feel it.

I hand them their shmoodie, and with my hands free I can shrug out of my scarf and coat. Before I know it, Liam's tucking in my tag. I shiver, but not from his shmoodie-cold hand.

"Thanks," I say.

Bowie looks between us, pressing their lips together. But then they shrug and ask Liam, "How was your break?"

I excuse myself. I've got to check in with Dr. Lochley.

The crowd in the Theatre Hall is bigger than usual, everyone catching up with each other after break. There's a maze of bodies and backpacks and a dolly—laden with three giant potted plants, for some reason—between me and Dr. L's office.

Philip is sitting below the Theatre Board, his legs splayed out, and he acts like he's going to trip me as I pass. ~~Asshole.~~

The board is still full of flyers for Christmas shows: *The Nutcracker* at the Kauffman Center; *A Christmas Carol* at the Rep;

Nuncrackers at Just Off Broadway. Plus photos from *JCS* and printouts of reviews from the local news. But soon this will all come down, to be replaced with info on the spring show.

Except Dr. L still hasn't announced what it is.

She's at her desk with her phone cradled against her ear, working her way through a paper plate full of tater tots. The remains of several ketchup packets litter the desk; she rips another one open and squeezes it out as she listens.

I point toward myself and then the door, silently asking if I should leave, but she gestures for me to stay. The couch is fuller than usual: It looks like every script from the shelves in the props closet has been dumped on the floral print cushions.

Dr. L nods along with whoever's on the other end of the phone. She shakes the crumbs off her hand and grabs a pen from the *Wicked* mug she keeps on the corner of her desk, jots a few notes on the back of a napkin. She glances up at me and rolls her eyes.

"Yeah. Okay. Yeah. Got it."

She hangs up and leans back, then grabs on to her desk as the chair nearly topples over. Once she's righted herself, she picks up another tater tot and squeezes a zigzag of ketchup onto it.

"Jackson. How was your break?"

"Okay. You?"

"Good, good." She pops the tater tot into her mouth, steeples her fingers, and studies me. "What do you think about Shakespeare?"

"Shakespeare?"

She nods.

"Well, I know some people think he was fake, or didn't write his own plays, but I think he did."

Dr. Lochley laughs. "That's a start. How many of his plays have you read?"

"Just *Romeo and Juliet* and *Julius Caesar*," I admit. "For ELA."

"None of his comedies?"

I shake my head.

"Ah. Well, we were going to do *Cat on a Hot Tin Roof*—we've got the perfect seniors for it—but we can't anymore."

"Why?"

Her nose wrinkles, and her lips curl a little bit. "Mrs. Bashir heard from the licensing company for *JCS*. Apparently someone complained about us taking too many 'liberties' with our production. The school got fined."

The Toxic Andrew Lloyd Weber Fandom has gone too far this time. Though I suppose it could've been the Toxic Jesus Fandom.

Dr. Lochley finishes her last tater tot, then dramatically sweeps her empty ketchup packets into the trash.

"The fine ate up a good chunk of our spring budget. So we have to do something in the public domain. Something we can pull off with stock sets and costumes." She shakes her head. "And Mrs. Bashir has emphasized that something more 'traditional' might help somethingsomething."

"So what are we doing?"

"I'm narrowing it down. But don't worry. You'll know as soon as I do. I'll need your help to get everything ready for auditions."

"You can count on me."

"I know I can." She stands. "What would I do without you?"

As I round the corner of her office, I bump right into Cam. His phone clatters to the floor, facedown.

"Sorry! Is it okay?"

"It's fine. Try paying attention, Jackthon."

"Cam!" Dr. L calls, and I wonder if she heard what he said. If she's going to tell him off. But she just says, "You have a couple minutes to talk about college?"

Cam gives me a quick sneer and shoulders me out of the way. I shake my head. I can't worry about him right now.

25

Without rehearsal, I'm stuck at school until Jasmine or Bowie can give me a ride home. Which means I don't have a decent excuse when Bowie asks if I can help rearrange the choir room for the GSA meeting.

Granted, Bowie needs all the help they can get, since Cheyenne, the GSA president—a white senior demigirl—seems to have abdicated their responsibilities come down with the flu over break.

"Jackson! Good to see you, bro. How was your Christmas?" Braden swoops in, grabs a bunch of chairs, and starts lining up another row, treating it like some sort of race.

Getting *bro*'d my first day back isn't exactly an auspicious beginning to the year.

"You staying for the meeting?"

"Just helping Bowie. I heard Cheyenne was sick."

"Ah, well." Braden shrugs, then turns and salutes Bowie. "Our fearless VP will get us through it."

I've got no doubt about that. Bowie should just do a coup at this point.

Over Braden's shoulder, I spot Liam in the hall, backpack

slung over his shoulder. He gives me a little wave.

I wave back.

Braden notices and waves Liam in.

"Hey, bro. You here for the meeting?"

"Just looking for Jackson."

"Cool." Braden gives Liam a backhanded pat across the stomach; Liam's core is so strong he doesn't even flinch. "You should start coming. All are welcome, you know."

Liam shrugs, but Braden turns back to me with a dimpled smile and a wink. "You too. You're not still mad about *Rocky Horror*, are you?"

~~Yes.~~ No.

But Braden doesn't wait for an answer, just hefts another stack of chairs and gets to work.

Liam waves at Bowie, then signs to me.

"You want a ride home? I don't have anything today."

"Oh. Really?"

I've never ridden anywhere with Liam before.

Bowie gives me a gentle shove in Liam's direction. "Go on. Braden and I can finish."

"You sure?"

"Go, go. You might as well."

I've got about a million reasons that I might as well not.

But as Liam gives me a soft, questioning smile, I can't manage to think of a single one.

Liam's crappy brown Corolla pulls to a stop in front of my house, its idle engine vibrating my seat so hard I think my insides might liquify.

LIAM'S TOYOTA COROLLA'S BREAKUP LIST:
IT'S THE COLOR OF BROWN PANTS
UGLY BROWN CARGO PANTS WITH PLEATS
HEATER BLOWS SO HARD IT DRIES MY EYES OUT
GLOVE BOX WON'T STAY LATCHED SHUT
~~IT SMELLS LIKE HIM~~
~~HE'S RIGHT NEXT TO ME~~
~~HE DOES THAT THING WHERE HE PUTS HIS ARM ACROSS THE BACK~~
~~OF THE PASSENGER SEAT WHEN HE BACKS OUT~~

Liam's grip on the steering wheel loosens and he turns to me to sign.

"Hey."

"Hey?"

"You sure we're good?"

"Of course."

He nods. "Did you give me your own shmoodie this morning?"

I shake my head and press my lips together.

"Jackson . . ."

Caught.

"You looked like you needed it."

He lets out a slow breath and rests his hand on my knee.

I think I might literally melt on the spot.

"You're a good friend, Jacks," he says aloud.

"You are too. Your signing is getting really good."

His cheeks turn a beautiful crimson.

"Thank you."

His hand is still on my knee, and I think I'm having heart palpitations. Because he's touching me.

I know it's only friendly. Like him tucking in my tags. But he's touching me, and my knees aren't anywhere near my crotch but they're also not that far away, and it's just a hand, a warm friendly hand, but my jeans start feeling tight.

My breath hitches. "I better . . ." I reach for my backpack, and he releases me as I cover my lap with it.

"See you tomorrow?"

"Yeah. See you."

I wait for him to drive away, backpack held in front of me, teeth chattering—the sun's come out, and the roads are clear, but the wind is still biting—then let myself into the garage. The Crock-Pot is going: Amy must've started it this morning, but she and Dad are still at work. The house is empty.

My knee is burning from where Liam touched me. And so's another part of me, burning and fighting against my underwear, and thank god no one is home right now to see me.

I shouldn't feel this way, because even though he's not with Jasmine anymore, he's still off-limits. More off-limits than ever, because now he's broken Jasmine's heart and she holds grudges the way a theatre holds glitter: forever and ever, long past the heat death of the universe.

But I can't stop the way I feel about him. And I'm not sure I even want to.

My jeans are still too tight. I run to my room and lock the door just in case.

26

onday morning, another huge printed banner is waiting for me on the Theatre Board:

RHS Theatre Presents: William Shakespeare's Twelfth Night.

Dr. Lochley's put it up over all the other notices on the board; the pushpins beneath are dimpling the banner.

"So she finally picked a show?" Liam asks, sipping on his pineapple-mango-arugula shmoodie. (It sounds weird but it's super tasty.)

"Yeah." I heard on Friday, but Dr. L swore me to secrecy. "Have you read it?"

Liam shakes his head and stares at the sign.

"You going to audition?"

"I dunno."

"What? Why?" Liam's too good to not even try out.

He chews his lip and glances toward Cam and Philip, who are canoodling in the little vestibule by the stairs.

"You can't let them stop you."

"I'm not. But . . . you know they tried to start a rumor me and Tori were hooking up in the scene shop? That time I was late for my cue?"

I roll my eyes. "They're drama queens. And I'm allowed to say that."

Liam's eyes sparkle as he laughs. He sips his shmoodie, then licks off the little drop left at the corner of his mouth. I trace the movement with my eyes. His lips move but I'm still thinking about his tongue.

"What?"

He caps his shmoodie, tucks it under his arm, so he can sign.

"It's not just them. I don't exactly feel welcome."

"Some of the senior actors are jerks to everyone," I say aloud. "You can't let that stop you, okay? You're amazing."

"All right. I'll try. What about you? Are you going to audition?"

I laugh so hard I almost spit my own shmoodie out. "Me? No way. Someone has to stage manage."

Liam pouts. Actually pouts. It's so cute I think I'm going to pass out. My heart thunders extra hard and I back away a bit.

It was so much easier to deal with my crush when he was with Jasmine.

"That's not a good reason. Dr. L would find someone else."

"Well, maybe Paige can take over next year, but she's not ready yet. And besides. I *want* to stage manage."

Liam studies me really hard. And then he says, "It's not because the actors are awful to you too?"

"They're fine. It doesn't matter."

He gives me the kindest look then, all soft feathery hair and ocean eyes and I never want him to stop looking at me that way.

"It matters to me," he says. "I swear, if Cameron calls you 'Jackthon' one more time, I might drown him in the diving well."

It matters to me.

I can't pick that apart right now.

"I'm gonna be late to class," I tell him. "You going to sign up or not?"

"All right, all right. You got a Sharpie?"

Bowie asks me to meet them in the computer lab after school.

"What's up?"

"Look at this." Bowie waves at their screen. They've got a bunch of browser tabs open, for different caterers in town. "For the Winter Banquet."

I scrunch up my face. The GSA does a Winter Banquet every February, which is supposed to celebrate queer friendship and platonic relationships at a time of the year when most people are focused on romance.

Which is funny, given how many people have (allegedly) hooked up at the banquet.

"Shouldn't someone from the GSA be helping? Where's Braden, anyway? Isn't he banquet chair?"

"Tennis practice."

"Cheyenne?"

"College visit."

"You shouldn't have to do the work of three people."

Bowie rolls their eyes. "You're one to talk."

Uncalled for. Though they're not wrong, I suppose.

"So what do you need?"

"I've got to find somewhere with gluten-free, vegan, and onion-free options."

"Onion-free?" My stomach sinks like I've swallowed a sand-bag.

Bowie's lips curl, but they nod.

"Braden made an overture to Cam and Philip."

"Gross."

"They're the most popular queer couple in school. He figured if people knew they were coming, they'd want to come too."

"Super gross."

Bowie shrugs. "If it raises more money . . ."

"Yeah, yeah." I sigh. "Fine. What've you got?"

Bowie gives me a bemused grin. They've got orange eye shadow on today, a vibrant shade that matches their brand-new UT hoodie. Because after talking to the recruiter more, they've decided to apply early decision.

For real.

I look over the options on-screen, pushing away the knot of dread in my stomach. How many more afternoons will we have like this—just the two of us, hanging out, plotting how to not poison Cam with onions?

I don't want to think about it.

Jasmine's leaving. Liam's leaving. ~~Mom left long ago.~~

I don't know how much change I can handle.

27

"**S**omethingsomething monologue and a soliloquy?" Liam asks. We're in the Theatre Office, me working on my stage manager binder, him browsing Dr. Lochley's shelves.

"You can do either."

He shakes his head. "What's the difference?" He signs it too.

"Oh. A monologue is delivered to another character. A soliloquy is delivered to the audience or yourself. Like an internal monologue. So in *Hamlet*, 'To be or not to be,' that's a soliloquy, but in *Julius Caesar* the whole 'Friends, Romans, countrymen' thing is a monologue."

"Huh," Paige says from her spot on the floor. She's helping me sort the inventories I made of our sets and props and costumes. With the budget so tight, we need to reuse or repurpose anything we can. "I never knew that."

Liam nods and turns back to the shelves, pulls out a slim blue volume with *Best Monologues for Boys, 2001–2010* on the spine. I can't believe they gendered a monologue book.

Liam thumbs through it while Paige types away on her laptop, updating the scenery spreadsheet, and I mark up the script for *Twelfth Night*.

Dr. Lochley's thinking about doing the show in the Little Theatre, either in the round or in a thrust configuration, where we block off the south side of the house and use it as a backdrop.

Liam flaps his hand to get my attention.

"Hm?"

"What about sonnets?"

"Well, they're not really monologues or soliloquies, they're more like poems. Like the one you did for *JCS* auditions."

"You remember that?"

"Of course." I remember everything about it. Well, I don't remember the words, but I remember the way it felt like he was talking just to me. I remember the way my arms broke out into goose bumps.

Liam's cheeks color as he pulls out a slim yellow volume of sonnets.

"Hey, didn't this get damaged somethingsomething?" Paige points to one of the flats on our list: part of the garden of Gethsemane that got snagged on the dimmer rack because the actors carrying it were goofing off.

"Oh, good call."

Paige is really sharp, with a great mind for details, which lets me focus on the big-picture stuff. We're kind of a perfect partnership.

As we work, Dr. L rounds the corner, tote bag slung over her shoulder and Cam trailing in her wake, talking too low for me to make anything out.

But Cam's mouth shuts once he sees we're in the office.

"Sorry, we're in your way," Liam says, more to Dr. L I think, because Liam's eyes narrow at Cam.

"No worries." Dr. L drops her tote bag on her desk with a thud I can feel through the floor. "Looking at sonnets?"

Liam nods.

"Ambitious. What about you, Paige?"

"Somethingsomething monologues."

I whip around to face her, my mouth hanging open. Did she say she was looking at monologues?

Is she auditioning?

I thought she was going to be my ASM. In fact, I was kind of counting on it.

"I've got somethingsomething, give me one second." Dr. L sits, gestures to Cam to take the seat opposite her desk as a pile of scripts slides off her desk.

She sighs but ignores the mess. "Anyway, I know Tisch was your first choice, but—" I lose what she says as she ducks under her desk to find the book she needs.

Cam winces, and his shoulders hunch up.

Tisch . . . like NYU?

Did Cam not get in?

A really small, really mean part of me does a little dance, because for once Cameron didn't get what he wanted. But the rest of me actually does feel kind of bad.

I know how I'd feel if my dream schools fell through.

"Right," Cam finally says.

Dr. L emerges from below her desk, a bunch of books in her arms. "Well, I think it's premature to panic, don't you? Ah, here we are!" She extends two slim pink volumes toward Paige. "Take a look."

"Thanks." Paige stands to grab them.

I can't believe she's auditioning.

I can't believe she didn't tell me.

Dr. L turns back to Cam. "NYU is just one no. Let's wait and see what the others say."

My jaw drops. He really didn't get in.

Dr. L sees me gawking. "Jackson, did you need something?"

I shake my head. "Just getting ready for auditions. We can go."

I risk another glance at Cam, whose face has gone pale, like he's got mime makeup on. He's staring at the corner of Dr. L's desk.

We scurry out into the hall. I pause in front of the Theatre Board. Sure enough, there's Paige's name, right below Madison's.

"You're auditioning, then?" I manage to ask her.

"Yeah." She shrugs. "I figured it would be fun to try. I probably won't make the cast, though."

"That's cool," I say, proud of myself for sounding like I mean it.

Paige hoists her backpack. "I'll send you the spreadsheet when I finish?"

"Great. Thanks."

She heads off down the hall, and then it's just Liam and me. He crosses his arms and leans against the Theatre Board. His biceps strain the fabric of his T-shirt. I trace the cords of his forearms with my eyes.

"Well, that was awkward," Liam says, and I snap out of it.

I shake my head. "I'm not mad at her for auditioning."

Just . . . sad.

"No, I meant with Cam back there."

"Oh. Yeah. I feel kind of bad for him."

"Why? He's always awful to you."

"I know, but if I didn't get into NYU I'd be . . ."

Crushed. Heartbroken.

"Don't worry. You'll get in." He gives me a wicked smile. "Maybe Cam didn't *pay his dues* enough."

I honk out a laugh, then cover my mouth, because I don't want Dr. L to hear me.

Liam's smile softens. He reaches behind me and tucks in my tag, fingers brushing the back of my neck. "These tags are out of control. If I get a role, you should let me cut them all off."

"No way, then the little corners will itch."

"Oh. Well, we can't have that." He bites his lip.

"Who says you get another reward for getting a role, anyway?"

His smile turns into a smirk. He's still standing close to me, warming me with the body heat he always throws off like a furnace.

"You're saying I don't get one?"

Is he flirting with me?

He can't be.

I've been down this road before. Thought he was flirting, thought there was something between us, only to find out I'd read him wrong. That day in the catwalk, when I felt something—and thought maybe he did too—he'd already agreed to go out with Jasmine.

I keep wishing for something that's never going to happen. I must've smelled too many paint fumes in the scene shop while I was inventorying the flats. Or maybe the school has a carbon monoxide problem and I'm actually getting poisoned. The catwalk isn't nearly as well ventilated as it should be.

"What am I going to do with you, Jacks?" he asks, shaking his head.

I roll my eyes. "I don't know, but if you're not careful I'll start using some of Jasmine's shmoodie recipes."

He laughs, giving a theatrical little shudder. But then his smile fades.

I don't know why I decided to bring up my sister. But the memory of her will always be hanging between us.

"Sorry." I clear my throat. "I didn't—"

"It's fine." He waves me off, but his mouth has gone all tight. "It is what it is."

Still, I want to crawl back into the little hidey-hole in the catwalk, cover myself in ~~asbestos~~ dust and disappear. Live my life as the Phantom of the Little Theatre. Pine after Liam from the shadows. Make friends with the mice.

Actually, maybe that last one is more Disney than Andrew Lloyd Weber. Though it turns out both Toxic Fandoms are equally litigious.

"Hey. You need a ride home?"

I shouldn't.

"Sure."

I can't help myself.

28

After a tense week of auditions and callbacks—all the seniors stressing about their last show ever—Dr. Lochley works her usual Friday afternoon magic. When the last bell rings, the cast list is up and she's out of the building before anyone even realizes she's gone. She printed it on regular paper this time, not a huge banner, so the actors crowd around the Theatre Board to see it.

It seems that Dr. L decided some malicious compliance was in order. Mrs. Bashir said to do something more traditional—and it was tradition, in Shakespeare's time, for women's roles to be played by men.

Because right at the top of the cast list:

Viola—Liam Coquyt.

"You got it!" I grab Liam by the arm, shaking him as he stares at the cast list.

His lips make a *wow*. It's too loud for me to make out anything: Everyone's crowded around, all the seniors jostling to see who else made the cast.

Cameron got Olivia, which, gross. And Orsino went to Jamilah, a junior like me. I spot her black headscarf in the crowd, surrounded by people congratulating her.

But one more name catches me by surprise.

Sebastian—Paige Turner.

I should be happy for her. That's what a real friend should do. But I always figured, hey, she'd audition once (like me) and then not get a part (like me) and then be firmly on the tech path.

Now she's leaving me for the dark side.

I should've seen this coming.

PAIGE'S BREAKUP LIST:

~~ABANDONED TECH~~

COMMITMENT ISSUES

~~LOST LIAM BACKSTAGE~~

IRRESPONSIBLE

WASTED MY TIME MENTORING HER

GOING TO TURN INTO A MONSTER

~~TRAITOR~~

DISAPPOINTED DENISE

NEED TO FIND A NEW ASM

I don't have my notebook on me; I'll have to write it down later.

"So is the whole show gender-swapped?" I ask.

"Somethingsomething, I think."

"Huh?"

Liam's fingerspelling is still a little slow on people's names, but he's come a long way. "Philip and Asher are Sir Toby and Sir Andrew. Oh, and Madison got Feste!" Madison's nonbinary. They're a senior, and mixed like me, Mexican and white. Feste is perfect for them: They've got killer timing and the kind of body language that makes them look like they're in a stand-up comedy bit, all big shoulders and round stomach and cocked hips.

"Good for them." And I mean it. Madison's never done anything objectionable to me.

"Yeah." Liam's smile slips a little; some of the other actors are throwing nasty glances his way. But they have no right to treat him badly just because he discovered his talent late.

"We should go celebrate!" I say.

"What, really?"

"Yeah . . . unless you don't want to?"

I can't decide if I want him to want to or not.

But then he smiles, and I would do anything to see him smile. "All right. Let's go."

TJ's Coffee is this little shop about a block from the Natatorium, but in the opposite direction from Perkins. The smell of roasting beans warms me as soon as I step inside, and a wall of hot air gets me to finally stop shivering. The heat in Liam's car only came on for the last mile of our drive.

Liam's in his sweatshirt and beanie, no coat or anything. I don't know how he's not cold. Well, I do: It's because his body is constantly throwing off heat like a solar flare.

I'm wrapped in a warm black peacoat, with all the buttons done up, and an emerald-green scarf that Khanum, my grandmother on Dad's side, knitted for me.

"What do you want?"

"My treat," he says. "What do *you* want?

"But we're celebrating you."

"But I'm . . ." He struggles to think of another argument.

I save him the trouble.

"Don't try and out-taarof me. I'm Iranian *and* Midwestern. There's no winning." I poke him in the chest as I say it, but then I remember how firm and warm his chest was when I smeared fake blood all over it, and I blush and let my hand fall.

"Taarof?"

"Don't worry about it. Just tell me what you want."

I order his mocha and get myself a London Fog, then join him at a tiny table in the back corner.

When I pass him his mocha he pulls off the top to cool it. I leave mine on and sip; cold tea is an affront.

"How can you drink it so hot?" he asks, switching to sign. The music isn't too bad in our little corner; I can hear okay. He just does it.

"I'm Iranian."

I spell it out, because the sign for Iran is basically a thumbs-down, and that always felt a little racist to me.

"You have any family back there?"

"Maybe some second cousins? My grandparents moved here in the 1980s. Brought my dad and uncle."

"You have an uncle?"

"He's in St. Louis. So are my grandparents."

"Cool." Liam sips his mocha and winces. "Still hot."

I sip my tea and wrap my hands around the cup to warm them. TJ's has a back door, and people keep letting in gusts of cold air.

"You sure you're warm enough?"

"I'm fine."

"You're basically shivering. Here."

And just like that, Liam peels off his sweatshirt. Right in front of me.

He's got a white T-shirt on underneath, and it rides all the way up, exposing his abs and chest. He yanks it back down with one hand; with the other, he offers me his sweatshirt.

"You'll get cold!"

"I'll be fine." He keeps holding it out.

I shouldn't accept it—I've literally got my coat right behind me, hanging off my chair. But he's offering it to me. ~~And I'm a glutton for punishment.~~

His sweatshirt is warm and coated in his scent, chlorine and citrus, cedar and skin. I pop out my hearing aids and slip it on. It's too big: The sleeves cover my hands until I shove them up. Liam's grinning at me, biting his lower lip.

"What?"

"Your hair looks cute."

I reach up to fix it until I realize what he said.

Cute? He had to have used the wrong sign. He still gets things mixed up sometimes.

But I blush nonetheless, put my hearing aids back in, grab my tea to keep my hands busy.

Liam picks his mocha back up and blows on it, then finally takes a decent sip. My tea's already a quarter gone. Why order a hot drink if you're going to let it cool?

When he puts it back down, he says, "I wish we'd gotten to be friends sooner."

"Me too. I'm glad you tried out."

"Oh? Is that the only reason we're friends now? I finally joined Theatre?"

"Not the only reason," I say. "But we got to hang out more."

Which was the ~~best~~ ~~worst~~ best thing to ever happen to me.

"What made you audition, anyway? You already have college all sorted out."

Liam scrunches his lips. "I don't know. It looked fun."

"That's it? It looked fun?"

"I've spent the last four years—no, ten—swimming nonstop. My parents said that was the best way to get into college, so I kept at it."

"You didn't like it?"

"I love swimming, but . . . I don't know. It always felt like it was for my parents. For my future. But Theatre, that's just for me." He gives me a tiny smile.

"That makes sense."

"Good. And I'm really glad I did."

"Yeah?"

"It's amazing, getting up onstage and becoming someone different."

"I guess."

"What about you? You never wanted to act?"

"I used to. But I like doing tech better. I'm good at it."

"You really are. I don't know anyone as talented as you."

I sip my tea and try to cover my blush. Besides. He's the talented one.

I raise my cup. "To Viola."

Liam laughs and taps my tea with his mocha. "To our fearless stage manager."

Fearless?

If only he knew.

196

* * *

Jasmine is in the kitchen when I get home, and my heart leaps up into my throat, because what if she recognized Liam's jalopy and realizes I was with him?

Not that she told me I'm not allowed.

But instead, she's hunched over her iPad, looking at internships in Denver.

I always kind of figured Jasmine wouldn't stick around after graduation. After all, I'm not either.

But going to live with Mom . . . I don't know.

~~It's like she wants to get away from me.~~

"Hey," she says.

"Hey." I drop my shmoodie bottles in the sink to wash them, but Jasmine waves at me. I turn the water back off. "Huh?"

"You have Liam's list on you?"

"Right now? Really?"

I don't want to read it off. Not after spending the afternoon with him.

At least I remembered—barely—to return his sweatshirt to him before getting out of the car.

"Please? It's been a rough day." She sighs dramatically. "I need you."

"Fine." I finish washing, haul my notebook out of my backpack, and flip to Liam's list.

I wish I'd never made this thing.

"*Liam Coquyt's Breakup List . . .*"

29

Monday brings our first read-through. While Dr. Lochley continues her Shakespeare unit in Theatre IV, showing clips of the David Tennant and Patrick Stewart *Hamlet,* I sit on the stage, wrangling scripts.

Since *Twelfth Night* is in the public domain, Dr. L printed copies herself—but she forgot to collate them. So I spend the whole class sorting the still-warm pages like some frenzied card shark, dealing out acts and scenes for thirty-three players, until my hands are covered in paper cuts and smell like toner.

The bell rings, bringing its usual mad dash for snacks or the restroom before rehearsals start and the rest of the cast arrives. Paige is quick to show up; she gives me a wave before getting drawn into conversation with Jamilah.

Philip and Cam aren't far behind, but something weird is going on with them. They spent the last hour sitting upright, with a couple inches between their shoulders, instead of intertwined like usual. I wonder if it's because Philip got a bit part. Or because Cameron is still stewing over being rejected by NYU. I feel bad for him, but maybe it's healthy for him to experience being the rejectee, rather than the rejecter, every once in a while.

When Liam shows up, he doesn't even ask if I need help; he just tucks in my tag, grabs a stack of folding chairs, and gets to work. I stare at him, following the flexing cords in his forearms as he unfolds the chairs. My heart tries to switch places with my lungs.

He catches me looking, and for once I'm thankful for the abysmal work lights in the Little Theatre, because the ghoulish downlight will make it hard to see my blush.

He gives me a toothy grin and keeps working. I pick up the pile of scripts and follow behind, saving one of the nicer ones for him.

When read-through is finally done, I turn my hearing aids off as I clean up. Trying to keep up with all that ~~old-timey language~~ iambic pentameter while the cast mumbled their way through the first reading has my brain feeling like a bruised persimmon.

"What can I do?" Liam signs as I sweep the stage.

"Stack the chairs?"

"Got it."

When that's done, I set the ghost light and close the doors behind us. Dr. L is in front of her office, the door closed behind her and her scarf wound around her face, stuck talking with Cam. I give her a little wave, but she doesn't notice.

"Hey," Liam asks. "You want to help me study lines? This is way harder than the musical."

"I don't know how much help I'll be."

"Come on. I bet you already have the whole play memorized."

I don't. Not yet, at least.

"Please?"

But helping him means spending time with him. And I can't quite stop myself.

"Okay."

Every day after rehearsal, Liam drives his crappy car to TJ's, where he insists on paying for my tea with the spending money his dad keeps giving him out of ~~guilt~~ love.

Which means every day, when Jasmine asks me if I need a ride, I tell her I'm getting one from Bowie. Or from one of the cast members. Or taking the activities bus, which generally leaves well before rehearsals are over, but she doesn't seem to notice the discrepancy.

And then Liam and I sit together at the little corner table that's somehow become our usual spot over the last two weeks.

He cups his hands around his mocha to keep them warm—the polar vortex is so bad, even he's cold—while I recite Orsino's lines.

"Come, boy, with me; my thoughts—"

But I'm cut off when the back door opens again, letting in a burst of air so frigid my spine seizes and my jaw clenches shut.

"Come on," Liam signs. "Sit here. You're freezing."

"I'm fine." Unfortunately, my body chooses that moment to give an involuntary shudder.

"Really. The heater's closer." He points toward the vent in the ceiling.

"It's easier to see you from here."

"We're nearly done." He scoots his chair closer to the wall, makes room for me. "Come on."

I sigh but finally give in, scooting my seat around to sit next to him, but accidentally tip over my binder. When I pull it up my heart does a divebomb toward my stomach, because it's open to a breakup list. But thankfully it's just Jason's.

Liam laughs. "Neck beard?"

"It was bad." Neck Beard Jason was a year ahead of Jasmine (and Liam). In addition to the neck beard, he also had halitosis and was an overly aggressive Xbox apologist.

He sighs. "I guess you did end up making one of those for me, huh?"

"What?" My heart flutters. "Of course not."

The lie's out of my mouth before I can stop it.

"Really?"

I nod, keeping my lips sealed before I can say anything else.

Liam sighs. "I probably deserved one."

I don't know why he would think that; he didn't do anything wrong. But before I can argue with him, he shakes himself.

"Now come on. It really is warmer over here."

He's right, it really is, though how much is the heater and how much is his body I'm not sure.

"Better?" Liam scooches over until our shoulders are touching.

I nod, because I've lost the power of speech. Does he not notice how close we are?

"Great. Where did we leave off?"

I flip back, find my spot, clear my throat. "Come, boy, with me; my thoughts are ripe in mischief. I'll sacrifice the lamb that I do love, to spite a raven's heart within a dove."

"And I most . . . uh . . ."

"Jocund, apt . . ." I prompt.

"Jocund, apt, and willingly, to do you rest, a thousand deaths would die." Liam slouches a bit, and his knee accidentally presses against mine. But he doesn't move it. "This is impossible."

"Come on. You're nearly to the end." I do my best impression of Cam as Olivia, which basically means trying to sound as self-important as possible. "Where goes Cesario?"

Liam snorts at me. "Okay, Cam. You sure you don't want to act?"

"Positive."

"Okay, okay." He takes a sip of his mocha and then rests a hand on my knee. The knee he's pressing against. And even though the rest of me is still chilly, that knee might actually be on fire. It's hard to breathe with him so close, with him pressed against my shoulder and touching my knee. Two points of contact. His warmth and scent wrap around me like an electric blanket.

I shake myself. "Where goes Cesario?"

"After him I love, more than I love these eyes, more than my life, more, by all mores, than e'er I shall love wife."

Liam's looking right at me as he says it, and I can't look away, even though I don't remember what comes next, because he's too close to me, and he's talking about love, and I've spent the last two weeks pretending to be Orsino, who Viola loves.

My own lips are chapped, and I lick them, and do Liam's eyes track the movement? But that doesn't make sense. He's not talking anymore. Did he lose the spot?

He leans closer. I think he's angling for the script, but instead his shoulder brushes mine. The hand on my knee is still warm, and my heart's pounding hard. Can he feel my heartbeat? Do knees have a pulse point?

But he's so warm, and the coffee shop is so cold, so I lean a little closer too.

Liam swallows, and his hand grips my knee even tighter, and it's so nice and warm that I lay my own hand on top of his. And I'm not sure, but did he look at my lips again?

"Liam?" I manage to say.

Jackson. His lips make my name but I can't hear anything over my own pounding heart. And is he learning closer or am I?

What is happening?

No, I'm definitely leaning in, because he's warm and he smells nice and he's one of the best people I know, and maybe his head is angling just a bit? Because suddenly our noses are brushing, and I can feel his breath on my face, and he's staring right at me until I close my eyes and bring my lips to his.

ACT
IV

30

I. Am. Kissing. Liam. Coquyt.

It's soft, gentle, no tongue, not even any open mouth. But despite how thin and chapped his lips are, they're warm and perfect. And then it's over all too soon. He leans away and looks at me.

My lungs are about to burst from holding my breath. Did he not want to do that? Did I misread everything? Is he mad at me?

But his hand comes up to my face, and he traces the shell of my ear, the line of my cheek, the dip of my chin. Tingles buzz across my entire body, like that time I got very slightly electrocuted plugging in the fairy lights for the ballroom scene in *Cinderella*.

And then he's leaning in again, and I'm meeting him, and this time it's him who presses his lips to mine. His hand moves to cradle the back of my head, and it's warm and soft as his fingers slide through my hair, and I keep kissing him back harder, and then he uses his lips to press my mouth open.

His tongue meets mine, and it's like he's doing this choreographed dance, and I don't know the steps so I just let him lead. I taste the chocolate of his mocha, feel the heat of his breath. My own hand squeezes his—the one on my knee, not the one on my neck—because if he accidentally shifts he's going to find out just how much I enjoy kissing him.

My heart's hammering like I just did an entire scene change on my own when he finally breaks the kiss. I look up into his eyes: The pupils are dilated, black swallowing blue; his whole face is red, and he's smiling at me like he just saw a sunrise for the first time.

"Was that okay?" I think he asks, but I'm still too stunned to listen properly. He frees his hands, leans back a bit to sign, "Okay okay?"

"Yeah." I swallow. "What was that?"

"Did you not want me to?"

"I did." I shift a bit, angle myself so my crossed leg makes a barrier between us. "I . . . thought I started it."

His smile crooks to one side. "I'm pretty sure *I* did."

"Don't taarof with me," I say, but instead of teasing me more, he leans in and silences me with another kiss. This one slow, and lingering, and sweet.

When he breaks it, he smiles. "Sorry. You're cute when you're arguing."

"I wasn't . . ."

He blinks at me.

"We kissed each other."

"Yeah."

"So are you . . . um . . . I mean . . ."

"I like you."

He likes me.

Liam likes me.

My head spins. Can roasted coffee get you high?

"You like me."

"Yeah. I . . . do you?"

"Do I what?"

His face is already pink, but somehow it flushes toward crimson.

"Do you like me?"

Do I like him?

I like him so much I can't get the words out, of my mouth or my hands. So I just nod.

Now it's my turn to go crimson. My ears and the back of my neck burn. So does my chest, somewhere deep inside, because I like him. And he likes me.

We like each other.

And he dated my sister. The breakup list I made for him—lied about making—is still burning a hole in the back of my binder, inches away from us.

"We can't tell Jasmine," I say.

"Oh, god." He leans back and runs a hand through his hair. "Jasmine. I never should've . . ."

He clamps his mouth shut.

"What?"

He switches to sign.

"I never should have dated her."

"Why did you?"

"I don't know. I thought you wanted me to?"

I thought I wanted that too.

"And I thought you were unavailable. I don't know. Looking back it doesn't make any sense."

"You thought I was unavailable?" I haven't dated anyone since Cam. Everyone knows that.

207

"Don't be mad."

"At what?"

"I thought there was something going on with you and Bowie."

I snort. He's joking, right?

He's not joking.

"I know better now." He squeezes the back of his neck. "I don't know. I know it's no excuse for how I treated Jasmine. I just . . ."

"Just?"

"I just really liked you. So much. And I didn't know what else to do. I thought I could learn to like her. And I did, just not enough. She was always pushing and it was getting weird and then, over break, when you yelled at your mom about you and Bowie, I just . . . I knew I couldn't do it anymore."

"So you dumped her to be with me?"

Liam looks like I've punched him.

"I didn't mean it like that," I say. "Just . . ."

He blows a breath out of his mouth. "Somethingsomething awful, doesn't it? God." He rakes a hand through his hair. "I was so mad at my dad. Like father, like son, huh?"

"No. It's not the same. You didn't do anything wrong."

"Feels like it." He frowns.

I take his hand, twine our fingers together. "I could've said something too. Told you I liked you before all this happened. But I thought you were into her."

"She wasn't the one making me shmoodies. Well, not at first. And she wasn't the one who liked me for me. Not for . . ." He gestures up and down his torso.

I blush. "I like everything about you," I say, pulling him in for another kiss.

"I like everything about you too." He kisses my lips, my nose, then leans back. "So what do we do? What do we tell her?"

"Nothing. For now."

Liam opens his mouth to object.

"No. Listen. If we tell her, she'll go nuclear."

Not only that, she'll tell him about that list. The one I never should've helped make. The one I lied about.

"We have to give her time to cool off. Let her process the breakup. Move on. And then I'll figure out how to tell her we're . . ."

What are we? He likes me, and I like him, but what does that even mean?

"Seeing each other?" he offers. His lips curl into a gentle smile. "Together?"

"Together."

Me and Liam. Together.

Maybe I'm dreaming. Maybe a Leko fell from one of the electrics and hit me on the head, and I'm actually dying on the stage of the theatre and this is all a hallucination as my brain runs out of oxygen.

But then Liam leans in, and his nose brushes mine, and we're kissing again.

What a way to die.

31

"You're acting really weird lately," Bowie says.

"No I'm not." I hand over a pair of tickets to the sophomores who signed up for the banquet.

"Hm." They arch an eyebrow as they close the cash box. The GSA is still a cash-only operation. The Theatre Department mostly uses iPads and credit card readers for our ticket sales, but we also deal with about a hundred times more people than the GSA does.

"You sure you don't want to borrow one of the department's iPads?" I ask them as we have to turn away yet another student who wants to come to the banquet but only has a debit card.

"It's fine." They frown. "I said we should get one, but Cheyenne started going on about rainbow capitalism and credit card companies."

"Ugh. They're the worst. Where are they anyway?"

"Campus tours. You know they applied to, like, all the Ivies?"

I shake my head. Why would anyone want to go to a stuffy Ivy League school?

I mean, yeah, Yale's School of Drama is kind of famous, but NYU is still better.

"Well, it's still not fair you have to do all this on your own."

"I'm not on my own. Or I wouldn't be if you'd pay attention."

"I am paying attention!" I straighten out the pile of tickets and adjust the folding sign on our table.

They switch to sign. "Did something happen?"

Yes, something has happened. It's happened again and again. Every day at TJ's after we've run lines. And in Liam's crappy Toyota Corolla as it idles down the street from my house, because Jasmine absolutely cannot see us kissing when he drops me off.

"Nothing happened," I say, but clearly I doth protest too much, because Bowie narrows their eyes.

"What are you two talking about?" I stop signing to find Cam hovering in front of the table.

"Nothing," I say automatically.

Philip steps up next to Cam and passes over an ice cream sandwich. Cam thanks him with a little kiss on the cheek, then starts peeling it open.

"How'd you do?" Bowie asks.

Philip hands over a stack of bills. "Ten so far."

Ten? Bowie and I only sold four tickets today. ~~Braden might actually be right about them selling more tickets.~~

"Great." Bowie puts the cash in the box and adds it to their ledger. "Thanks for your help today."

Cam licks around the edge of his ice cream sandwich before it can drip. "Anytime."

I resist the urge to scoff, but only barely. Cam's helpfulness always evaporates any time there are sets to paint.

Cam gives Bowie a little wave, and me a curt nod, before taking Philip's hand and wandering off.

Once they're gone, Bowie switches back to sign. "So? If you

don't want to talk about it, that's fine, but don't pretend there's nothing going on."

"All right, all right." I look around the cafeteria and then lean in to shield our hands. I don't think there are any other signers at school (not counting Liam) but I'm not risking it. "You can't tell anyone."

"I won't."

I take a deep breath. "Liam and I kissed."

Bowie's eyebrows nearly fly off their face.

"I think we're dating now?"

Bowie's jaw drops too.

But before they can ask me anything else, Braden steps up to the table.

"Hey, bros," he says. "How're you doing?"

Bowie shakes themself, like they're snapping out of a dream. "Fourteen tickets," they say. "Not too bad."

Braden beams and nods, sending a lock of floppy hair over his forehead. He pushes it back. "So that's thirty-five in toto?"

"In total?" I ask.

"*In toto*. It's Latin, bro."

I glance at Bowie, willing them to meet my eyes, but their face is aggressively neutral as they keep their gaze fixed on Braden. "Right. We should have a good crowd Saturday."

"Sweet. I've got to somethingsomethingsomething meeting?"

"Sure," Bowie says.

Braden charges off. I don't know where he gets so much energy.

I straighten out the stack of flyers for the dance. They're in Papyrus—the worst font—but Bowie wouldn't let me help.

"We're not done talking about this," they sign to me, before spotting a pair of juniors heading our way. "Hey! Want to come to the Winter Banquet?"

Bowie catches me at my locker before seventh hour.

"Okay. Spill."

So I tell them everything. Well, not everything. I don't tell them about how Liam's lips feel, or the way he likes to play with my hair while we kiss, or how I like to wrap my arms around him and feel the way his back muscles are put together.

"That's . . ." Bowie shakes their head. "Wow."

"Yeah."

"Does Jasmine know?"

"Of course not! You know how she is."

"So you're just . . . not going to tell her?"

"I will once she cools off." And once she stops asking me to repeat Liam's list every week.

And once I figure out how to tell Liam I might have accidentally kind of lied about not making a list for him.

"Be careful. With Liam and Jasmine. And with your own heart. Okay?"

I nod.

"But you know I'm happy for you, right?"

"I know."

Dr. L claps her hands once. "Let's set up for Act IV, Scene 3."

The actors clear the stage, Philip taking a spot next to Cam on the benches, while I get out the bench for Olivia's garden.

As I grab it and start dragging, Paige steps up and takes the other end.

"Oh. Thanks."

"Sure." She helps me get it into position. I haven't spiked anything yet—I won't do that until Dr. Lochley's 100 percent satisfied with the blocking, which won't happen until we start doing our whole-act run-throughs. "Hey. When's the first workday?"

"Not for another couple weeks. Did you want to come?"

"Of course."

"Oh. I'll let you know, then. It'll depend on Denise's schedule."

I can't believe Paige still wants to help. I kinda figured she'd blow workdays off like all the other actors.

I finish setting the scene with a couple potted plants, then retreat to my usual spot next to Dr. L, who tightens her scarf. "Right. Let's start with Sebastian pacing center stage. Olivia and the priest, you'll be entering stage right."

I'm only about 70 percent certain I catch all of Dr. L's notes—since she's blocking for a thrust, she's constantly turning, making it hard to read her lips. But I can follow along pretty well, thanks to all my sessions with Liam.

Learning the script, not making out, though the latter is definitely my new favorite part.

It's our last scene of the day; Dr. L has Paige, Cam, and Shira—who plays the priest—run it through one last time, once she has the blocking the way she likes.

"Perfect! Perfect. Let's call it for today."

She retreats to the benches, where her tote bag rests.

"Hey, I missed a couple things," I say to her. "Can you . . ."

But Cam comes up to her other side. "Dr. L? You have a sec?"

214

"Sure, Cam. I'll be with you in a second, Jackson." And then she follows him out of the theatre.

I shake my head, stuff my binder into my backpack, and drag the set off-stage so I can sweep. ~~Whatever.~~

As I finish, a shadow falls across the waxed floor. Liam's standing in the doorway, silhouetted against the sunset from the big windows in the hallway.

I hate how, in the winter, the sun starts setting before rehearsal is even over. But I love how Liam looks in the golden light.

"Hey. What're you doing here?"

"Waiting around for you," he says. "How was rehearsal?"

"Fine." I gesture around the Little Theatre. "Tough to hear everything."

Liam nods and hoists my backpack so I can get my arms through it. When I turn around, he signs, "Sorry."

"It's whatever."

"You all set?"

"I was . . ." I glance toward the doors closest to the Theatre Office; Dr. L still hasn't come back.

"Waiting for Dr. L?"

"Yeah. Got a few questions."

"Ah." He looks around, then signs to me: "I wish I could kiss you right now."

If I could pop out my smile and stick it on a stand, it would outshine the ghost light. Which I suppose I still need to set.

"Me too."

As I wheel it out, Liam asks, "You excited for Saturday?"

"What's Saturday?"

Liam's eyes bug out. "The dance?"

215

"Oh. I dunno. Bowie's really stressed."

"I've noticed." Liam gives me a sly grin. "You going with any-one?"

I grin right back. "Why? Are you asking me to a dance?"

"I know we have to keep things quiet, until you can get Jasmine to come around. But . . ."

"But she won't be there," I say. "And if anyone asks we can say we came as friends."

"Exactly. So . . . you wanna go to the dance with me?"

Warmth fills my chest.

"I'd love to go."

The smile he gives me makes me wish I could kiss him.

I almost do.

But he straightens and looks past me, out into the hallway, where Dr. Lochley's headed for the stairs, tote bag in one arm and coat slung over the other, still talking to Cam.

Guess she won't be coming back to answer my questions.

Liam presses his lips together.

"It's fine," I tell him before he can say anything. "I'll catch her tomorrow."

"Okay."

"Come on," I say. "Let's go study lines."

And then make out.

32

"**H**ow many more tables do you need?" an older man in a blue Community Center polo shirt asks. The Winter Banquet is being hosted in one of their meeting rooms.

Bowie rubs their head, looking over their clipboard and tapping their foot. Cheyenne was supposed to be here to deal with decor, but they texted they were going to be late, so Bowie had to take over, in addition to managing the setup and caterers.

"Five more rounds, two more eight-footers. Oh, and two more carts of chairs. No, three."

The man nods and disappears into the back hallway. Bowie takes a deep breath.

"Hey," I tell them. "You got this."

"Thanks, Jacks. It's just, I really want tonight to go well."

"Why don't you leave the tables for me? You go talk to the event manager."

"All right."

I grab my tape measure out of my backpack and start checking placement, because you never know when the ~~Toxic Safety Fandom~~ fire marshal might show up to rain on everyone's parade.

Cheyenne finally arrives, blown in on the winter wind. They're my height, but wearing chunky boots that give them a couple inches over me, and they've got long, luxurious blond hair. If I had hair like that I would be sweeping it around dramatically every chance I got.

"Sorry I'm late," they say breathlessly. "Had to something-something."

They hold up a plastic bag with a Trans Pride flag sticking out of the top.

Even though the night's theme is Starry Night—like the Van Gogh painting, not like creepy looming cardboard cutouts of celebrities—one wall is supposed to be covered with as many Pride flags as can fit.

"Can you somethingsomethingsomething?" they ask, looking around the room wildly and talking faster than I can make out.

"I have no idea what you just said," I tell them. "Say again?"

"Sorry." They flip their hair over their shoulder and start talking super slowly, which honestly makes it worse. "Where's Bowie? Did somethingsomething?"

"Bowie's trying to find the event manager."

They keep looking at me expectantly.

"And Braden?" they finally ask.

"He's with the caterers."

Cheyenne rolls their eyes. "No. Did. Bowie. Talk. To. Him?"

I fight the blush coming on. Cheyenne's the worst.

"About what?" I ask.

"Never mind." They spin around, their hair slapping me in the face, leaving their bag of flags on the table next to me.

Yet another reason to avoid the GSA like ~~the plague~~ glitter.

Might as well hang the flags, though.

As I stand on my toes trying to get the ace flag into place, a hand takes the corner and gets it in exactly the right spot. I get a familiar whiff of chlorine and smile as I rip off a piece of gaff tape.

"Hey. You're early."

Liam tucks in my tag. "Figured you and Bowie could use a little help." He frowns for a moment. "Does Bowie know about . . ."

"About us?" I nod. "They kind of figured it out from me being happy."

Liam's smile is so big, I want to kiss it off his face, but not here, surrounded by GSA members. Still, he seems to know what I'm thinking, because he licks his lips.

"Liam, bro!" Braden says, swooping in and grabbing the bisexual flag. "You here to help out?"

"Yeah."

"Thanks, bro. You too, Jackson." He briefly wraps the flag around himself like a superhero cape. "You seen Cheyenne?"

"They went looking for you. Or Bowie. I couldn't tell."

He gives me a gap-toothed smile. "Honestly, sometimes neither can I."

He doffs the cape and hands it to me. "Anyway. Thanks again, bros."

"Sure."

And then he swoops away again.

Liam stares at me for a second before we both start laughing.

Somehow, in a twist of fate that would make great comedy and even better tragedy, Liam, Bowie, and I end up stuck at the same table as Cam and Philip. They're both dressed smartly, in matching shirts and vests, but they look more like waiters at a fancy restaurant than boyfriends.

Liam, on the other hand, is wearing handsome gray slacks and a black shirt that hugs his shoulders just right; and Bowie is a vision in their maroon three-piece suit-gown. They far outshine me, in brown slacks and a white shirt and a green bow tie I borrowed from Dad. I don't know why he owns bow ties; I've never seen him wear one, and he didn't actually know how to tie it, so I had to look up a video.

The room is packed and loud and there's music blaring, so I spend the meal with my hearing aids off, talking with Bowie and Liam in sign, while Cam and Philip alternate between staring at us, kissing, and picking at their (onion-free) meals.

After dinner, the DJ cranks up the speakers so loud I feel it in my chest.

Liam asks me to dance, and Cam, being physiologically incapable of letting anyone get more attention than him, grabs Philip and joins us on the floor. They take a spot next to us, dancing way too close for a school function.

Liam does a little shimmy, twirls me by the hand as Lil Nas X resonates in my rib cage. He's got decent moves.

But I've been to about a hundred Iranian weddings. So I swivel my feet, pivot my hips, roll my shoulders, show off my moves. Liam's face lights up like a followspot. He laughs, and tries to match me, doing his best to keep up, as more people crowd around us.

I catch a glimpse of Cam, whose mouth is hanging open. I guess he never knew I could dance. And I don't like the way he's eyeing me and Liam. If Cam suspects something, he might tell the whole department, and if the whole department knows, it won't be long before Jasmine hears.

So I give myself a bit more space—a *just friends* amount of space—and when Bowie finally joins us on the dance floor, we form a little triangle, jumping and laughing and dancing.

I'm still never joining the GSA. But this? This isn't so bad.

33

"**N**eed a hand?" Paige asks as I kneel onstage, spiking where the set pieces for Duke Orsino's palace are supposed to go.

"I got it."

She ignores me, though, leaning the fake column back so I can spike its corners.

"Thanks."

"Sure."

She offers me a hand up and we take our seats. Everyone's been antsy at today's rehearsal—too much Valentine's Day candy, probably—and I can tell the cast is ready to go.

"One more thing," Dr. L announces. "I know some of you are struggling with the heightened language, so Saturday we're hosting a movie night here in the Little Theatre to watch something-somethingsomething last minute, but I hope you can all make it."

You'd think Dr. L might have mentioned it when I was going over the week's schedule, since I'm the one who'd have to set it up. What if I had something else going on? Like a date?

Except me and Liam still haven't been able to go on a proper date. I haven't managed to tell Jasmine about us yet. I thought she was getting better, but this morning in the parking lot she made me recite his list twice before I could get out.

When Dr. L dismisses the cast, Liam hangs back to talk to her while I clean up. I'm sweeping the stage when Dr. L waves me over.

"Liam was just saying you've been helping him learn his lines."

"Oh. Yeah." I scratch the back of my head, keeping my face neutral. That's not all we've been doing.

"Well, it's working. Good job."

Liam's cheeks redden, and he fights a little smile.

"Thanks. I mean, I'm glad to do it."

"I might ask you to give Cam some help too."

I would rather swallow a Leko.

"What time is movie night?" I ask to distract her.

"Three o'clock. I guess it's more an afternoon than a night. You'll both be there?"

"If I can get a ride."

"You've got one," Liam says.

"Great!" Dr. L claps her hands together once, then starts packing her tote bag. "See you tomorrow."

We both watch her go; I only realize my hand's gone numb when the dust mop clatters to the stage.

Liam busts out laughing. "You should have seen your face."

"It wasn't that bad."

"I think you turned green for a moment."

I finish sweeping, set the ghost light, and grab my backpack. Liam's already got his on; a couple of the other cast members are hanging around, comparing notes.

"Hey." Liam glances around, then signs, "Happy Valentine's Day."

"You too."

I wish I could kiss him. I wish we could snuggle on the bench like ~~Cam and Philip~~ every other couple in the department.

But there are still witnesses. Actors taking forever to pack their bags. Others lounging on the benches still chatting.

If only we could go someplace private.

Then again . . .

"Come with me."

No one pays attention to us as Liam follows me out. No one ever notices the stage manager.

I lead Liam to the catwalk entrance, make sure the coast is clear, then slide my student ID into the gap between the door and the frame. It only takes a second before I feel it unlatch.

I flick the light on before closing the door. We're below the ladder, in the cramped entryway, and I suddenly remember Liam's claustrophobic.

"You okay?"

"As long as the light's on."

"Okay." I step closer. "Hey."

"Hey." He smiles as I pull him in for a kiss. He rests his hands on my waist, sways me back and forth like we're slow dancing.

Then he breaks the kiss, brushing his nose against mine before leaning back so I can see his hands. "I wish we didn't have to hide."

"Me too." I've got to tell Jasmine. I've got to. I just don't know how without everything exploding.

Liam pulls me closer, resting his chin in my hair. To think I used to mind how he loomed over me. Now it's like we fit perfectly together. He hums, the vibration passing from his chest to mine.

"I really like you," he says when he breaks the hug. "You're the only one who sees me."

Sometimes it feels like he's the only one who sees me too.

I kiss him again, and again, and again, until I'm dizzy with it.

I wish we could stay in here forever.

We're walking toward Liam's car when he stops abruptly and turns to face me. "Hey. What about the pool?"

"Huh?"

"You know how to swim?"

"I know how to not drown."

"We could do a swim date." He grins. "I could teach you to not drown better."

"I don't know . . ."

"It's perfect. No one we know will be there. And you still owe me a prize for getting in the cast."

"I do?"

"Yeah. And the prize is, I get to teach you to swim."

I bite my lip, mostly to stop myself from smiling at the mental image of him in his little Speedo that I've only ever seen from the stands . . .

"Come on. Please?"

"All right."

That night, Dad takes Amy out for a fancy steak dinner. Actually, I suspect Amy's taking Dad out, because Dad is many things, but he's not a planner of Big Romantic Gestures.

I make dinner for me and Jasmine: oven-baked popcorn chicken and shells and cheese. Jasmine's not allowed to help with pasta after the time she added the sauce *before* draining the water, and what was supposed to be fettuccine Alfredo turned into some sort of soup.

She sits at the table, looking glum. This is the first Valentine's Day I can remember where she's been single. Which means tonight is probably not the best night to broach the subject of Liam.

But I can't keep putting it off. We can't keep making out in parked cars and catwalk ladders.

We line our bowls with popcorn chicken before ladling in shells, so the chicken gets all cheesy and delicious, and sit at the table. It's quiet at first, as we eat and I work up my courage.

"I wanted to talk to you about something," I say.

"Sure. But first, can you do Liam's list?"

"Huh? During dinner?"

"It's Valentine's Day." She stabs her fork into her bowl. "Please?"

So much for talking to her.

I run up to my room and come back with my notebook. I set it carefully aside—don't want to get cheese on it—and recite Liam's list again.

Every word feels like a betrayal.

I can't keep doing this.

But when I finish, Jasmine seems bolstered by it.

"Thanks," she says. "I don't know what I'd do without you."

"You'll have to figure it out. You're the one moving to Denver," I say before I can stop myself.

Jasmine at least has the decency to look a little forlorn as she chews on a chunk of chicken.

I grab my water and take a big glug.

"I need to get away," she finally says. "From who I've been in high school. Do you get that?"

I shake my head. She's not going to magically change just because she graduates.

"I've spent the last four years getting my heart broken over and over. I mean, your binder's proof of that."

"You're more than your heartbreaks," I tell her.

"Maybe," she says. "But right now it doesn't feel like it. Especially Liam. I mean, we didn't even have a fight or anything. He just dumped me out of nowhere."

"It's been months, Jasmine."

"I didn't know my heartbreak was supposed to be on a schedule."

"It's not, but . . ." I swallow. "It's really hard on me too. He's my friend, Jasmine."

"I know." She sighs. "But I'm not ready to forgive him. All right?"

It's not all right.

What if she's never ready to forgive?

What if we're caught in this weird secretive limbo forever?

I don't know what to do.

34

Saturday morning, Liam texts me.

> What are you doing today?

> Before movie night?

Nothing much

Why

?

> There's public swim today.

> You said I could teach you!

I did say that.

> I'll drive us to the movie after?

Okay

After lunch, Amy drops me off at the Natatorium, two shmoodies clutched in my hands.

"Have fun. Don't drown. Tell Bowie I say hi."

"Okay." I might have ~~said~~ implied that it was Bowie giving me a lesson.

Liam's waiting for me, practically bouncing on his heels by the registration desk. He grins when he spots me.

"Hey. I already paid, so you're good to go."

"You sure?" I pull out my wallet, but he stops me.

"Don't try to taarof me. I know your secrets now."

I snort. That's not how taarof works, but whatever.

Liam leads me toward the locker room. I haven't been in one since first-year PE, which was definitely the stuff of nightmares. At least this one is cleaner than the one at Riverstone: It's got nice tile floors, pristine gray lockers, and it smells like baby powder instead of that weird mix of body odor and not-enough-deodorant that Riverstone's had.

"I always use this one," Liam says, dropping his mesh bag in front of locker 47. "I don't know why. You mind sharing?"

I shake my head.

"Great."

And just like that he pulls his shirt over his head. I've seen him shirtless often enough, but it's been a while. He's got a dusting of fine black hair on his chest now, and a little line that goes from his belly button straight down toward his underwear, which is black with a silver *Calvin Klein* stitched into the waistband. I guess he stopped shaving once the swim season ended.

Liam catches me staring, but he just grins. "Come on. Get changed."

He pulls out a swimsuit for me, baggy black trunks, because I told him I didn't have my own. I do, technically, but it fit me back in seventh grade, and ~~I like to think~~ I've grown a little bit since then.

Liam digs out his own suit: one of his purple team Speedos. Then, without even blinking, he pulls his pants and underwear down in one fell swoop.

And I don't know where to look. Do I look at *it*? Do I look away? Would it be weirder to look or not look? Do I keep my eyes on the lockers and pretend like I can't see anything at all? But it's not like I need to pretend to be straight. And it's not like I've never, you know, felt Liam when we were making out, if we were close enough.

"Jackson?"

"Huh?" Either my hearing aids are feeding back or I just literally squeaked. I've got a full-body blush coming on.

"You all right?"

"Uh-huh."

Except my eyes definitely dart down, and now I've officially seen all of Liam, and this might be the greatest day of my life, but also the last one, because I seem to have forgotten how to breathe.

Liam caught me looking too, and he blushes, bending over to pull his suit up quickly.

"Sorry. I wasn't thinking," he said. "On the team we kind of get used to it."

"It's fine."

"I didn't mean to somethingsomething."

"What?"

"I didn't mean to make you uncomfortable."

I shake my head. "I'm not."

"I can leave you while you get changed."

I swallow. I want to stuff myself into a locker and never emerge. But for some reason I say, "It's okay."

And then I pull my shirt over my head, and try to breathe and get my blushing under control, even though I can feel Liam's eyes on me as I pull off my pants and underwear, pull up the swim trunks and do the drawstring. Out of the corner of my eye, I catch Liam adjusting himself before tying his own drawstring, a sight that's burned into my brain.

Finally I breathe and look at him again. He's blushing hard too, red cutting sharp lines across his cheekbones. His eyes are wide, and he's smiling like he might honestly find me beautiful.

I feel like an octopus standing next to a shark: me in my baggy black trunks, short and soft; Liam in his team suit, lithe and dangerous and beautiful. But he keeps looking. And smiling. And blushing.

"Ready," I finally say when I can't take the tension anymore.

I stick my hearing aid case in my backpack, and Liam stuffs everything into the locker before leading me out the back door, past the little leisure pool—shallow, with slides and water cannons—and through the doors to the competition pool.

I've been in the stands countless times, but I've never set foot on the deck itself. The concrete is rough and scratchy and cold, but the air is warm and humid. No one is in the pool: Apparently swimming's not that popular on a Saturday afternoon in February. Liam sets a pair of towels on a low bleacher, steps up next to one of the starting blocks, and dives in smoothly.

When he surfaces, he pushes the hair off his face and gestures for me to join him.

I don't dive: Instead I sit on the edge, dangle my legs in.

"It's cold!"

Liam bobs in the middle of the lane, smiling at me. I never want him to stop smiling at me like that.

So I get in. Cold water rushes up the legs of my swimsuit, up my back, over my head. I bob up and shake the water off my face.

Liam comes up next to me as I grab the ledge. "Okay?" he signs.

"Yeah."

"Okay. Let's practice floating first." He fingerspells *floating,* so I show him the proper sign.

"Stop stalling. Come on."

I push away from the wall, floating until I bump up against the lane line and start to sink, but Liam's hand is under my back to steady me.

After that, he has me show him how well I can swim, which is not very. Apparently it's a bit closer to a doggy paddle than a front crawl. I'm out of breath after only a single length, but at least we made it to the shallow end, where we can stand.

"Here." He demonstrates his form, rotating his torso so he can bring his shoulder up and arm forward and scoop the water. I try to copy him.

"Don't kick so much. That's why you're out of breath."

"I thought I was supposed to kick."

"Use your kick to stabilize. Power comes from your arms and back."

He demonstrates again, and I copy him.

Not well enough, I guess, because he puts one hand on my lower back and the other below my abdomen to demonstrate what he means. Despite the cold of the pool, his skin is warm against mine, and I'm amazed the water doesn't boil around us.

Once Liam's satisfied I'm not going to kick myself to death, he swims lazily along with me as I make it up and down the length of the pool. It's probably like walking next to a toddler, with their tiny legs, but Liam doesn't seem to mind. He's patient and sweet and gives me the biggest smile when I get something right.

It's not like I didn't take swimming lessons before. I did, growing up, in our neighborhood pool actually. But none of those teachers ever took the time to make sure I understood.

I can't stop grinning as I come up at the end of another length. Even though I'm not kicking as much, I'm still tired after half an hour. But it's a good tired, one that I can feel in my chest and limbs. I feel strong, and confident, and proud.

"You did great."

"You're a good teacher."

Liam bites his lip and smiles. "I want to kiss you."

We're all alone—except for the lifeguard, some older guy with a white goatee—so I float closer to him.

"I want to kiss you too."

And so I do, drawing closer, but I barely get a peck on his lips before I bob lower, losing contact and getting a mouthful of pool water instead.

I sputter as I float back up.

"Smooth," he signs.

I roll my eyes, but can't help laughing.

After showering and drying off—in stalls, separately, because

I don't think I could survive actually showering with Liam, ~~not when I have shrinkage~~—and getting dressed, we go through the drive-thru at TJ's before movie night.

"I'm starving."

"Swimming does that," Liam says, checking both ways before pulling away. My tea and his mocha are in his cupholders, and I've got the bag with our cookies (peanut butter for me, snickerdoodle for him) flat on my lap.

"It was fun, though."

"Yeah?" Liam smiles so big as he heads toward Riverstone.

"Yeah. Maybe we can go again?"

"Really?" Liam looks like I just ~~stripped naked in front of him again~~ told him Christmas came early. "I'd love that."

I would too.

Dr. Lochley claps her hands once and the cast settles down. Everyone's crowded in the first couple rows of benches; a few are even sprawled on the stage floor, on blankets or flattened sleeping bags or random furniture pillows borrowed from ~~textbook storage~~ the prop closet.

I'm stationed by the doors, ready to turn off the house lights once she gives me the signal. We've got a projector set up, and a big folding screen, and a super-old DVD player that I had to use five different adapters to connect to the Little Theatre's sound system. But I got it working, despite not even being a sound person.

Denise was on a big call at the Kauffman Center today and couldn't make it, so it's just me. Well, me and Paige, who is standing by the DVD player and ready to hit play. She cocks her head to listen to Dr. Lochley's speech to the cast.

I can't make out a word of it, and I don't even try. It's for the actors anyway. I glance at Liam, who's sitting on the last row, saving a seat for me with his arm slung over the back of the bench. His hair is still a little damp from the pool, shining in the house lights. He catches me looking and gives a little smile.

I shake myself and wait for Dr. L's cue. She's got two movies for us to watch: one a recording of a staged production from London a couple years back, the other a movie called *She's the Man,* which is an adaptation set in the lurid world of high school soccer.

As I settle in next to Liam, I think he's going to move his arm, but he doesn't. Instead he shifts so he can run his fingers through my hair, playing with the ends and finding all the spots where it's about to curl if I let it get too long. He still smells like chlorine and lemon soap and a little bit of sweat.

I shouldn't be letting him do this, not in public. But Cam and Philip do stuff like this all the time. It's not fair. I shouldn't have to keep this a secret just because Jasmine can't get over him.

And it feels so perfectly peaceful. Like this is where I belong. Liam's laughter rumbles against my side. No one can see us in the back row, not without craning around, and it's too dark anyway. We're in our own little world.

So I relax against him. Liam brushes the shell of my ear, and I twitch a bit, but he avoids touching my hearing aids. Instead his fingers trail along my jaw, the back of my neck, and back up into my hair. It's hypnotic, sending tingles from my scalp all the way to my toes.

I never want him to stop.

35

It's long past dark as Liam and Paige help me fold up the screen. Cam has cornered Dr. L, like usual, so I just give her a wave, and she gives me a nod back. Paige takes the screen, while I gather up the pillows left behind by forgetful actors.

"Thanks," I say as I close the prop room.

Paige shrugs. "Don't mention it. See you?"

"Yeah. See you." I grab my coat and follow Liam out to the parking lot.

It's raining, one of those late-winter drizzles that somehow *smells* cold. Liam's only got a light jacket, but he shrugs at me and we run out to his car. Its remote unlock died before he even got it, but he unlocks my door with the key before running around to let himself in.

"Thanks." I rub my hands as he starts the car and waits for it to warm up a bit. We're beneath one of the streetlamps, but the rain streaking down the windshield turns the light into amber stars, shining across Liam's face.

"I had fun today," I say.

"Me too. It felt like . . . like we were on a real date."

My chest burns. "Weren't we?"

"I guess."

"We swam together. Kissed in the pool. Cuddled through two movies."

"Yeah. You're right." Liam sighs. "I just wish we didn't have to be so careful."

"Me too. But if the cast finds out, Jasmine will find out."

"Would it really be the end of the world?"

"It would." I chew my lip. "I tried talking to her the other day."

"Oh yeah?"

"But it didn't go so well. She's still just . . . I don't know. Hurt."

Liam purses his lips and blows out a slow raspberry. "Yeah. I really messed up, huh?"

"No. No. You didn't know I liked you. I didn't know you liked me. It was no one's fault."

"You don't have to say that," he says. "It *was* my fault. I could've turned her down. I could've told you how I felt. I should've been honest."

"But—"

"If I've learned anything from my parents, it's that honesty is the most important thing. So let me own my mistake, okay?"

"Okay." I swallow.

Honesty is the most important thing.

He still doesn't know about that list.

He thinks I'm honest.

"You sure it wouldn't help if I talked to her?" he asks. "Apologized to her face?"

"Definitely not." At least not without the fire marshal present.

"If you say so." He leans across the PRNDL to kiss me gently. "Thanks."

237

He backs out, his arm slung over my seat as he looks out the rear windshield, but as he puts the car back in drive it gives a sharp lurch and stalls, the engine's hum stilling beneath my seat.

Liam frowns. Turns the key to try and start it again, but nothing happens. And then the lights on his dashboard go out, and the wipers stop their rhythmic dance.

"Did it die?" I ask.

"No idea." He sighs. "I hate this car."

"Hey, it's okay." I crack my door open and look around, but we're the last ones out. The parking lot is deserted, and the rain's coming down harder, pelting my face with cold droplets. I slam the door shut again, trapping what heat there is inside with us. "What do we do?"

"Want to try your parents?"

"Dad's on call today, but lemme see about Amy . . ."

I text her, but she's in Overland Park. Worse, she's with Jasmine.

Liam pulls out his own phone. After a moment he says, "My dad can come get us." He bites his lip, brow furrowed. I lose his face as his screen goes dark.

"Oh. Okay." Except Liam doesn't look okay. "You sure?"

I can't hear his answer, though, between the dark and the rain hammering the roof.

"What?"

He opens up his Notes app.

I'm sure this is his old car anyway

"Ah."

Liam yanks the key out of the ignition, balls it in his fist. His screen goes dark again.

I reach for the hand clenched around his key; after a moment, he relaxes and lets me take it. I trace the tendons on the back of his hand with my thumb.

Eventually, Liam opens his hand up, flips it over so our fingers intertwine. Squeezes me gently, even though the car key is sandwiched between our palms. With his other hand, he types on his phone again.

> It'll be a while before he gets here
> At least half an hour
> Maybe more with rain

"Oh." I'm suddenly very aware that we're alone in Liam's car in a dark parking lot. Our warm breaths are already fogging up the windows.

I always thought that was just a thing on TV shows.

"What do you want to do?" I ask him.

Liam's hand clutches me tighter. The air in the car is still and close. He shifts and leans in. I brush my nose against his; his eyelashes flutter as he brings his lips to meet mine.

It's not like any of our other kisses. And we've had a lot of them at this point. But they've never been hungry like this. He pulls his hand out of mine; the car key falls somewhere to the floor as his hands go to my hair again, pulling me closer, and I wrap my hands around his back, because he is warm, and firm, and mine.

And then his lips pull away from mine, and I feel a weird whine lodge in my throat. The throat that he starts kissing. We haven't really done much non-face kissing, but it turns out hot lips on the hollow of my collarbone is maybe one of the greatest things in the universe.

"Don't," I practically squeak when he sucks on my neck. "You better not give me a hickey."

I feel his laugh against my skin.

But turnabout is fair play, so I push back against him, press my lips to the cord of muscle along his neck. I try to suck on it but accidentally graze it with my teeth. He seems to like it, though, trying to pull me to him, but the PRNDL jabs me in my rib cage.

"Ow!"

We break apart, breathing hard.

Liam scrabbles in the dark for a second; his hand comes back up, clutching his phone, lighting up his face so I can see.

"Back seat?"

My heart is pounding so fast I think I could yank it out and replace the engine and get Liam's crappy car running again. But I nod.

And then we're both out of the car, and I squeal as cold rain makes it down the back of my shirt, and then we're inside again, and it's even darker in the back seat, and Liam's hands are on my waist as he wraps himself around me, and his lips are pressed against my collar, and we fold ourselves to fit onto the seat.

And if I thought Liam playing with my hair was the best feeling in the world, it turns out I was wrong.

36

It's not like we go all the way. I don't even know what all the way means with two guys. In fact, we don't really go any of the way below the belt. But he pulls my shirt off, and I pull off his, and I let him give me more than one hickey that will be hidden beneath my collar.

And the whole time we kiss, I can feel him against me, and he can no doubt feel me, but neither of us says anything about that. We just kiss, and touch, and kiss.

Still, Liam's really too tall for the back seat of the car. And once we've kissed so much my lips have gone numb, I wrap my arms around him and he holds me and we just cuddle.

My whole body goes quiet as Liam plays with my hair, and I trace the contours of his spine with my fingers, and occasionally one of us pulls the other in for another kiss, but soft this time, generous and tender.

And I wonder what it would be like to get all the way naked with Liam. Not in a locker room but in my bedroom, or his, in warm lamplight instead of grayish fluorescents.

But my whole face burns as I imagine that, and I have to tuck the idea away for later. Much later. Because this is still so new, because Jasmine doesn't know, because there are secrets I still haven't told him, because I've never had sex and what if I'm not good at it? What if he doesn't like it with me?

I don't even know what kinds of things he likes. I don't know how much experience he's had.

The rain slows, but we don't move. I could stay in here forever. I've never felt like this before. Like for the first time in my life, I'm right where I'm supposed to be. It's scary. Terrifying. Because this has gone way beyond crushing. Way beyond liking. Or even like-liking.

I'm in love with Liam Coquyt.

The thrill of it runs through me, so strong I wonder if Liam can feel the electricity humming in my skin.

I love him.

I hold him tighter, and I feel his smile against my cheek. Everything is perfect.

At least, until the foggy windows light up with the glare of headlights.

Liam snaps up. There's no way we can get out without his dad knowing we were in the back seat together. I start to pull on a shirt but I realize it's Liam's, and Liam has the same realization, because my own shirt looks like a crop top on him.

So we switch as fast as we can, and try to pull on our jackets. Then Liam takes a deep breath, opens the door, and steps out into the cold.

I hang back as Liam stands, stiff-armed, while his dad hugs him and holds his shoulders. He's got Liam's height, and black hair, but his face is softer, cheeks less angular. He's got the same piercing eyes, though. And to my surprise, his smile is kind and open, just like his son's.

"You must be Jackson."

"Yes, sir." I don't know why I call him sir. I don't call anyone sir. This isn't the Navy. But I hold out my hand.

"Oof, Matt is just fine." He shakes my hand, then turns back to Liam. "Pop the hood?"

If he wonders what we were doing in the back seat, he doesn't mention it. Instead, he bends over the hood while Liam pops it. Matt shines his phone's flashlight inside, looks around before shaking his head. "It won't somethingsomething?"

"No."

"Let's try jumping it."

So they do, and despite having a lot of experience with running power for lights, I stand back and let Matt deal with the jumper cables, because car batteries don't have breakers and everything is still wet. Definitely not fire marshal approved.

Liam tries to start the car, but still nothing.

Matt sighs, scratches the back of his head the same way Liam does. I can't follow any of what he's saying to his son, but apparently part of it involved me, because he looks like I'm supposed to answer.

"Uh. Did you say something?"

He blinks, and I see the moment when he remembers I'm deaf. It never gets any less awkward.

"Sorry, Jackson. I can give you a ride home, if you'd like."

"Oh. Thanks."

* * *

My lips still feel a little numb from all the kissing, and my chest is tight from the awkwardness of the ride with Liam's dad, but still, I'm smiling when I put in the code to the garage, kick off my shoes, and step into the kitchen.

"Who was that?" Jasmine asks without preamble.

"Huh?"

"Who dropped you off?"

"Oh. Uh." I wasn't expecting a confrontation about this. "Liam's dad. His car broke down."

"So you were just going to get a ride with him?"

"Yeah? He's in the cast? He's my friend?"

I don't know why she's being weird about this. She knows we're friends.

Does she know we're something more now? Is it written across my face? Did someone say something?

Can she see one of my hickies? I thought we were being careful.

"How can you still be friends with him?" she asks. "After what he did to me?"

"He didn't do anything to you. People break up all the time." She should know.

How many boyfriends has she had?

"You knew he was my friend before you started dating him," I say. "Why are you being so weird about this?"

"I don't know!" Jasmine throws her hands up. "This is all somethingsomething."

"What?"

She takes a breath and seems to deflate a bit. "This was way easier when you hated all my boyfriends."

"I didn't hate them all."

"Yeah you did."

Well, they were all empirically terrible.

"It just feels like we're not on the same side anymore," she says.

"I'm on your side," I promise her. "Always."

Always, except when it comes to Liam.

When did I get to be such a good liar?

37

"Line?" Cameron calls.

Today's our first off-book rehearsal. The show's five weeks away, four if you don't count spring break.

Cam's usually pretty good about being off-book, but today he's struggling. ~~Maybe I should've helped him.~~

"Sure you have . . ." I wait to see if he picks it up.

Crickets.

". . . some hideous matter to deliver . . ."

Cam turns back to Liam. "Sure you have some hideous matter to deliver, when the courtesy of it is so fearful. Speak your office."

Liam doesn't miss a beat. "It alone concerns your ear. I bring no overture of war, no taxation of homage."

Liam's perfect. Just perfect.

"Line?" Cam calls again.

I don't even look at my script. I've basically got the whole play memorized at this point. Denise always says a stage manager should know a show backward and forward, and while I don't have the backward down, I think I could recite the whole thing from memory.

"Have you any commission . . ."

Cam picks up again, stumbling. He's never had this much trouble with his lines. I don't know if it's the Shakespeare or the pressure of senior year or if he's still torn up about that rejection from NYU.

I give Dr. Lochley a quick glance; she's tapping her pencil against her pursed lips, nodding along as Liam and Cam do the scene. She catches me looking and taps her pencil against my script, like I'll lose my spot if I'm not watching them. As if I haven't done this four shows and counting now.

I shake my head and mouth along with the scene.

"Good job, everyone," Dr. Lochley says. "We'll pick up with Act III tomorrow."

She slips her yellow legal pad back into her tote, grabs her director's notebook, and rewinds her scarf around her neck. Before any of the actors can swoop in, I sit next to her.

"Do you still have time to look over my portfolio with me?" I ask, holding up my iPad. There's a summer portfolio review Dr. L recommended, to help get ready for college applications, and she promised to help get mine into shape before the deadline.

"Of course! Come to the office when you're ready?"

While I put the furniture away, Paige grabs the dust mop and sweeps the stage behind me. I shoot her a smile as I finish up and find Liam.

"Hey. All set?"

"I've got to talk to Dr. L. I don't think it'll take too long."

"Okay. I'll be here."

I grab my portfolio and head to the Theatre Office.

Except when I round the corner, Cam's already in there, sitting on the couch with Dr. Lochley. His elbows rest on his knees as he hunches over. Dr. L's got a hand gingerly placed on his back.

"I know it's frustrating," she says, "but—"

Cam looks up and spots me. I can't figure out if he's surprised, or angry, or sad.

"Jackson?" Dr. L says. "You need something?"

"Uh. You said to come find you when I was done?" I hold up my iPad.

"Oh! Sorry. I've got to work something out with Cam first. We'll do it later, all right?"

Always later.

"Sure."

Liam's leaning against the Theatre Board, looking at his phone, but he straightens when he sees me. "That was fast."

I shake my head. "She's with Cam. Said we'd do it later."

Liam frowns. "She's always doing that."

"Doing what?"

"Putting you off every time Cam so much as sneezes."

"It's fine."

"It's not, though."

I shrug. "What am I supposed to do? It's not like I can complain about it."

"Why not?"

"She'll just think I'm jealous. She hates when people backbite."

Liam sighs. "Jacks. It's not backbiting. If you don't speak up, how will anything change?"

He's right, but also, he's wrong, because sometimes speaking up will just make things worse.

Case in point.

"Can we not talk about this anymore?" I've got this squeezing feeling in my chest. "Let's just go."

"Okay."

When we get in Liam's car, he glances around, then leans in and kisses me. "Hey."

"Hey. Careful." I look out the windows. Philip's car is still in the lot, but he must be upstairs waiting for Cam.

"Jackson. It's been a month. Would it really be so bad if people saw us?"

Maybe. I don't know anymore.

Jasmine hasn't asked me to recite Liam's list since his dad dropped me off two weeks ago. Maybe she's finally getting over him.

But I've been too nervous to risk our fragile peace.

"Jasmine's getting better," I tell him. "Give me a little more time."

He blows out a breath that makes his lips flap. "All right. Want to go rehearse lines?"

"I don't know. You seem pretty off-book already."

"All thanks to you."

"Thanks to your hard work."

He brings his hand up to trace my jaw with his thumb. I melt into his touch.

"Take the compliment, Jacks," he finally says.

"All right." I rest my hand on his knee. "So. Where to?"

Liam bites his lip. He meets my eyes, then glances down toward my lips, and then back up again. "My mom's not home."

"Oh?"

Is he suggesting what I think he's suggesting? My heart flies up into my throat like a poorly weighted lineset.

Liam's eyes widen. "Oh, god, that somethingsomething." He covers his face with his hands.

"What?"

"Sorry." He starts signing as he talks. "I just meant, um. We could hang out. And kiss and cuddle some? Not . . . uh, anything else."

I nod.

"I've never, um. Had sex. With anyone."

"Really?"

His eyebrows scrunch up. "What's that supposed to mean?"

I blink. "Just . . . you've seen yourself in a mirror, right?"

Liam blushes and shrugs.

"Take the compliment, Liam."

He grins. "What compliment?"

"You're hot, okay? Really, really hot. And thoughtful. And kind. And brave. And I . . ."

I can't say I love him. Not until I'm sure he'll say it back.

"I really, really like you," I say instead.

"I really, really like you too."

38

"So, what do you think?"

It's the Friday before spring break. Dr. Lochley finally agreed to go over my portfolio with me; that way I'll still have a week to work on it before the deadline.

She purses her lips as she taps around on my iPad, looking through my photos and documents, rearranging yeses into nos, maybes into yeses. Even one no into a maybe.

"If you have room," she says, about a picture of Madison from last year's production of *The Bad Seed*. "Now let's look over the layout."

My portfolio's not just a collection of photos, it's a whole website, with links to videos and stuff too. Dr. Lochley nearly stabs my iPad with the point of her pen before she realizes it, clicks it off and uses the soft nubby bit to swipe around.

"Hm."

Is that a good *hm* or a bad *hm*? I can't tell.

"I think you need to yes-no-maybe all this as well. There's too much going on, so nothing really stands out. But the bigger problem is, there's not a whole lot of you in here. Companies and universities and scholarship committees are going to be looking for candidates that bring something unique to their organization. You've got an Iranian last name, but you don't mention your disability anywhere."

"Oh." Heat creeps up my neck. I don't think she's trying to be ableist, but it's hard not to feel kind of weird about it. How am I supposed to talk about being hard-of-hearing in a portfolio, anyway? Take a picture of my hearing aids? ~~Make a log of all the times Cam called me Jackthon?~~

Maybe I could add that I'm fluent in ASL or something.

"Another thing that's missing is—"

Suddenly Cam bursts into the room. I jump, my elbow knocking my iPad against Dr. L's coffee mug. I save the iPad from getting splashed, but that doesn't stop the coffee (well, it's mostly cream) from sloshing onto her plate of tater tots.

"Sorry!"

But Dr. L's looking up at Cameron. "Good morning?"

"I got in!" Cam holds up his phone. The screen has gone dark, though, and he has to tap around and unlock it again before setting it on Dr. L's desk right on top of my iPad. "I got into AMDA!"

Their upside-down logo glows on the screen. Dr. L's face lights up as she stands and grabs Cam's shoulders.

"That's terrific!" She picks up his phone, skims it twice, then smiles back up at him. "I'm so excited for you."

"Me too." Cam runs a hand through his hair. He's been growing it out for the show, and he seems to think that the slight waves at the end count as texture. "I can't believe it."

"Believe it. You've earned this."

Dr. L pulls Cam to the couch and starts telling him about AMDA, and New York, and all the experiences he's going to have, and I lose the thread immediately. Cam spares me an absent nod hello as he listens.

And I just sit in my seat, forgotten. Dismissed.

Again.

This wave of anger crashes against me. At Cam, for always interrupting. And at Dr. Lochley, for always letting him. Always picking him over me.

I can't stand it. I stuff my iPad into my backpack, and despite my heavy stomps, neither of them seems to notice me leave.

I feel like I'm going to explode. I'm so tired of Dr. L giving up on me the minute Cam enters her orbit. Liam's right. It's not okay.

DR. LOCHLEY'S BREAKUP LIST:
ONLY PAYS ATTENTION TO ME WHEN SHE NEEDS SOMETHING
ALWAYS TELLING WEIRD STORIES
~~SCARVES NEVER MATCH HER SHIRTS~~
FAVORS ACTORS OVER TECHIES
~~ABLEIST??~~
~~LOSES THE DEPARTMENT MONEY WITH TERRIBLE CHOICES~~
TREATS ME LIKE A GLORIFIED ASSISTANT
LETS CAM ~~BULLY ME~~ GET AWAY WITH EVERYTHING
~~DOESN'T CARE ABOUT ME~~
NEVER LISTENS TO ME
NEVER HELPS ME WHEN I NEED IT

I take a deep breath, rip off the list, and stuff it in the very back of my binder where no one will ever see it. I don't really hate Dr. L. I just needed to vent.

But just once, I wish she'd pick me over Cam.

* * *

In seventh period, Dr. L doesn't bring up my portfolio, and how we never finished. And she doesn't at rehearsal, either.

She does make sure I note the changes in blocking. And has me sit in different seats to check sight lines. And asks if I've updated the prop list. And has the whole cast congratulate Cam on his acceptance to AMDA. No one claps harder than Philip, even though he looks a little sad too. He didn't audition for AMDA. I'm not even sure he's going to study Theatre after he graduates.

They're probably doomed to break up. Maybe they were from the start.

Still, that doesn't stop them from cuddling in the very last row of benches, ignoring their scene changes until I have to go up and shout at them.

"Can you just cool it, Jackthon?" Cam disentangles himself from Philip. "No need to get jealous."

I roll my eyes.

I'm not jealous of Cam for getting into AMDA, and I'm certainly not jealous of him and Philip. Not when I have Liam.

"Whatever. Can you join us onstage or do you need me to fill in for you?"

"Like you even could."

Given I know his lines better than him . . .

After rehearsal, Dr. L packs and is gone before I'm even done sweeping. Liam heads out too—he's got an awkward dinner with his dad.

"Sorry to leave you," he says, tucking in my tag and squeezing my shoulder for just a bit too long. With the other actors still packing up, there's no way we can kiss goodbye, but his quiet, knowing smile makes everything a little better.

Once I've swept and set the ghost light and closed up the theatre, I head down to the choir room. Jasmine's already gone, shopping with Amy at Target tonight, so I've got to wait for Bowie to get out of their GSA meeting.

I take a quick peek in through the choir room door. Cheyenne's gone again, so Bowie is running the meeting. They spot me, give a quick nod, and I retreat out of sight. The last thing I need is for Braden to notice me and try to *bro* me into submission.

I slide down the wall beneath a trophy case and pull my iPad back out, but after a few moments staring at it, I just get angry again. So I put it away and pull out my stage manager binder. It's getting way too full the closer we get to the show. The back folder is stuffed with three years of breakup lists. Maybe I need to find an archival system or something.

I scan Dr. Lochley's list again. I don't know what I have to do to make her see me.

As I sigh, a white sneaker taps against the sole of my foot.

I close my binder and look up. "Hey. All done?"

Bowie nods. They're in an orange UT hoodie, with matching burnt-orange eyeshadow. Their nails are a midnight blue, with electric-blue marbling and glitter (sealed in, so it's not dangerous).

I stuff my notebook into my backpack and stand. "Where was Cheyenne this time?"

"Out sick. Braden thinks it's a mental health day, but my money is on senioritis."

I snort and follow them to their car. The afternoon smells of spring rain and warmer days.

"We haven't done this in a while," I say once I'm buckled. Between rehearsals, and TJ's with Liam—or, lately, his mom's house when she's gone—plus swimming lessons on the weekends, not to mention the usual piles of homework we get, I've been super busy.

"Liam wasn't free?"

"Yeah. He's got dinner with his dad, so you know how that goes."

"I do know." But I've missed something. Bowie's face is carefully neutral, but their signs are more clipped than usual.

"What's going on?" I ask.

Bowie shakes their head.

"Are you mad at me for something?"

"You really have to ask that?" Bowie sighs. "When was the last time we actually hung out?"

"Sorry. I've been busy."

"Yeah, with Liam. I've noticed."

"What's that supposed to mean?"

"It's been two months of this and you only want to hang out with me when he's not available. You know how that makes me feel?"

I want to open the car door and throw up. Because I know exactly how it feels. Dr. L does it to me all the time. She did it to me just this afternoon. Again.

"You're right. I'm sorry." I swallow down my guilt. "And thank you. You want to hang out?"

Bowie rolls their eyes. "Can't tonight."

"But I thought—"

"I wasn't fishing to hang out with you. I'm actually busy. I do have a life outside of carting your carcass around."

"Sorry." I know they do. "I miss you is all."

"I miss you too," they finally say. "Even when you're being a butt."

"That's fair." I start to bite my lip but quickly stop. Now that I've got a boyfriend, I need to keep my lips in better shape. "I really like him, Bowie."

"I can tell."

"I think I'm in love with him."

I don't even think it. I know it. But it feels too huge to say with certainty.

"Wow." Bowie takes a deep breath. "Have you told Jasmine yet?"

I sigh. "No. I'm still working on it."

"You can't keep putting this off!"

"I know. But you've met Jasmine."

"I have. Doesn't change my opinion, though."

Can't they just be happy for me?

Bowie goes quiet as they start the car. Disappointment rolls off them in waves.

We barely talk the whole way home.

"See you," I say as I close the door.

Bowie just nods and drives off.

39

Amy goes all-out for Nowruz dinner: saffron-marinated salmon with sabzi polow, roasted chicken with zereshk polow, a whole platter of Persian sweets ordered direct from a bakery in California.

It's the one holiday of the year Dad always takes off; he's in charge of the haft-seen in the living room, and sorting out the sabzi from the little herb garden in the backyard, and picking out presents for me and Jasmine.

To my surprise—and Jasmine's utter shock—Dad got us both new phones.

"I figured it was time for an upgrade," he says. "Besides, there was a sale."

Even the deliciousness of dinner—and zereshk polow is my favorite—can't stop me from setting up my phone and texting Liam right away.

New phone!!

Happy new years!!

Thanks

How's break?

I miss you

Miss you more

It's okay

Mom wanted to know if I was okay with her "exploring the dating world again"

Awkward

Right?

"What're you smiling at?" Amy asks.

"Nothing."

But Amy shakes her head. "I know that smile."

"Huh?"

"Who is it?"

My face starts burning. Despite what I told Bowie, I still haven't found the right opening to tell Jasmine about me and Liam. I hoped that maybe, after Nowruz dinner, with her full of tea and sweets and presents, I might be able to tell her without causing an explosion.

But I wasn't planning on getting interrogated at the dinner table.

"No one," I say. "Show stuff."

Amy just shakes her head. "All right, keep your secrets. Tell us when you're ready."

"Tell us what?" Dad says, looking up from his own phone.

"Who's making him smile that way."

Dad looks at me. "You dating someone, Jackson?"

I must be turning redder than our tablecloth.

Before I can answer, though, Jasmine lets out a laugh. I stare at her.

"What's so funny?"

She shakes her head. "Nothing. Don't worry about it."

"Okay . . ."

But she shrugs. "It's just. You. Dating someone."

"What's wrong with me dating someone?"

"Nothing. But . . ." She waves her hand at me.

"What?"

"You're like, the most cynical person I know."

"What's that supposed to mean?" I ask.

"Oh, you know what I mean! You're not exactly the romantic type. You know?"

"I can be romantic."

"If you say so." She smiles. "Hey. When it goes south, I can always help you make a breakup list."

"It's not going to go south!"

Jasmine grins. I snap my mouth shut. I've all but confirmed it now.

"Come on. So . . . who is it?"

"I'm not talking about this right now!"

"Aww, don't be embarrassed."

"You can tell us when you're ready," Amy says.

I nod but keep my head down. My ears are on fire.

Jasmine waves.

"Hey."

"Huh?"

"I'm happy for you."

Let's hope she's still happy when I tell her who it is.

After way too much dinner and way too much dessert—and after FaceTiming our family in St. Louis—I go upstairs only to find Jasmine in my room.

"Uh. Hey?"

"Hey. Where's your notebook?"

"Huh?"

"Your notebook."

"Why?"

"I just . . ." She blows out a breath. "I need something."

"From my notebook?"

"I need Liam's list. Okay?"

"What?" I shake my head.

What could she need it for now? She hasn't asked about it in weeks. I thought she was over him.

I thought I could finally tell her about us.

"Sorry," she says. "But tonight just brought it all back. How much he hurt me."

"Can't you just be happy for me? Without making it all about you?"

Jasmine glares at me. "How exactly am I making this about me?"

"It means you always say we're in this together. That we can always count on each other. But at the end of the day, I'm supposed to be happy for you, but you're never happy for me."

Jasmine lets out an ugly laugh. "Have you met yourself? You're somethingsomething incapable of being happy. You've spent your life making lists of people's faults so you can push them away. You don't let anyone get close to you because you're so afraid they'll leave you."

"They always do!" I say before I can stop myself.

Jasmine rolls her eyes. "Just because you have abandonment issues, it doesn't mean the rest of us have to live in your cynical little world."

"Yeah, I'm so cynical," I say. "How cynical of me to think that just once, you could be glad that someone actually likes me."

"Yeah, well, just wait and see how long it lasts. Maybe then you'll know what it feels like to have your heart broken."

She stalks out of my room and slams the door shut.

I sink to my bed.

Guess I'm not telling her about me and Liam tonight.

40

"I'll pick you up at four?" Amy asks as I get out of the car.

"Sounds good. Thanks." I wave as she drives away.

Liam's waiting for me in the vestibule between sets of double doors. I let him wrap me in a hug, rest my cheek against his chest for a long moment, before we break apart and I get on my toes to kiss him hello.

"Hi."

"Hi." He reaches back and tucks in my tag. "How's break been?"

"Okay I guess. Yours?"

"Eh. Is it weird I'm kind of glad we go back to school tomorrow?"

"Not that weird." I am too. Jasmine and I are barely talking. "I missed you."

We've never gone so many days without seeing each other since we started dating.

"I missed you too." He kisses my forehead. "Ready?"

As we get changed—repeated exposure hasn't made the sight any less overwhelming and excellent—Liam says, "Sorry I something-something. Car's back in the shop."

"Again?"

"Some sort of coolant leak." He sighs and tightens his draw-string. "Mom thinks I should get a new one before college. Doesn't want me driving all the way to Texas."

"Oh." Even though we're still in the locker room, I feel like I've plunged into water. I don't want to think about Liam leaving for college.

I'm pretty sure that's a regular thing when your boyfriend's a year ahead of you. It doesn't mean I have *abandonment issues.*

The pool is way busier than usual, filled with parents praying their kids will swim off their spring break energy. A harried-looking mom is wrangling five kids in the far lane, trying to get them going in a line as they work on their doggy paddle.

Liam and I share one of the middle lanes. He has me swim a couple lazy laps, just to warm up, before he starts correcting my form again, demonstrating how he wants me to scoop the water at the catch, maintain even pressure on the pull, get my arm angle right on the recovery.

His signing has improved so much he barely has to fingerspell anymore, which is great, but he also doesn't have to demonstrate by moving my body around, which is disappointing.

I'm halfway through another lap when it happens. At first it feels like someone's grabbed my calf, and I kick harder to get loose, but that makes it worse. I've never felt pain like this before. It messes up my stroke, and my breath, and before I know it I'm bobbing and sputtering, drifting back toward Liam as he swims out to collect me.

"Cramp?" he asks, helping me back to the wall.

"Yeah."

I hold on to the wall as he helps stretch my leg until the cramp releases. I sigh with relief, but it's still sore.

"Come on, let's take a break." He leads me under the lane lines to a ladder—usually, we just pull ourselves out, but he can tell I can't do that right now. He spreads his towel out on a bleacher, has me sit, and wraps the other towel around my shoulders.

He sits beside me, has me spin a bit so he can get my leg on his lap, and presses at my calf. I hiss.

"Breathe."

"This ever happen to you?" I ask.

He nods.

"I'm never getting back in the pool."

He laughs. "When you've been swimming as long as I have, you get used to it."

I'm quiet as he works on me. We've touched each other plenty (all still above the belt), but this is different somehow. It's not exciting, exactly, but it feels tender and special in its own way.

Jasmine's wrong. This isn't all going to go south.

Liam cares about me. I care about him.

I love him.

"Am I a cynic?" I blurt out.

He pauses. "What?"

"Do you think I'm a cynic?"

Liam's brow scrunches up, and he releases my leg so he can sign. "What brought this on?"

"That's not a no."

He laughs. "No. I don't think you're a cynic."

"Really?"

"True biz. I think you're kind. And thoughtful. And way too smart for me. You're romantic and you're beautiful. Maybe sometimes you're a little too honest for your own good, but I like that about you."

I laugh and cover my face, because he's laying it on too thick, because he's wrong, because I'm not any of those things. But he makes me feel like I am. He makes me want to be.

"I like everything about you," I finally manage to tell him.

"Oh yeah?" He grabs my leg again, and immediately finds a really gnarly spot that makes me yelp.

"Not everything!"

He laughs, eases off, leans down to drop a quick kiss on my shin.

"Do you want to keep swimming or stay out here?"

I'm getting kind of cold, actually. And Amy won't be back for another hour.

"We can keep swimming."

It's warm when we step out of the Natatorium, or maybe it's just me, warmed on the inside because of the swim, because of Liam, because he's right next to me in his sweats and a hoodie, our shoulders brushing.

The sun shines on him, his flushed cheeks, his true-blue eyes, his raven hair shining where it's still wet. He looks at me, and smiles, and somehow the day grows even brighter.

My love for him boils over, so violently I can't hold it in anymore. I pull him against the side of the building, so we don't block anyone, and give him a kiss.

"Hey."

"Hey, you." He kisses me back, hooks his fingers in my belt loops. He looks down at me, and I look up at him, but it doesn't feel like he's looming. He's just with me. Always.

My heart's beating even harder than it did when we were swimming.

"I need to tell you something." I swallow. I can't keep this in anymore.

"Okay?"

"I really, really like you," I say.

Liam grins. "I really, really like you too."

I take a deep breath. "You make me feel good about myself. You listen to me. You see me. And I don't know if you know how much that means to me."

"Jacks . . ." he says, so soft I can only see the shape of my name on his lips.

"What I'm trying to say is I more than really really like you." I swallow down my nerves. "I love you."

I wait for him to say something back.

For him to love me too.

His eyes go wide and shimmery.

Did I mess this up? Why isn't he saying anything?

But then his lips curve up. And if I thought his eyes were bright before, now they're like follow spots on full brightness, and I'm transfixed in their beams.

"I love you," he says.

He loves me. He loves me!

I kiss him. It's like I've got a helium balloon in my chest, so full I might go flying off into the sky. I kiss him, and he kisses me back.

But all too soon, we have to come up for air. He smiles down at me, reaches back to play with my hair.

"I love you, Liam," I say. "So much."

"I love you too. I—"

But then he startles, steps on my foot and backs away to look toward the parking lot. His mouth has dropped open, eyes wide, not with joy but with something more like panic.

I turn and look.

It's Jasmine.

41

My sister and I have fought a lot over the years. From little spats when we were kids, arguing about what show to watch, to giant explosions once we were teenagers and Jasmine started dating a string of boys I hated. One time she didn't talk to me for two weeks after I told her I thought Dominic was homophobic because of something he said in class.

(Turns out he *was* homophobic, which Jasmine only found out after they went on a date that turned out to be a service at Dominic's church, where he and his parents tried to bully her into getting baptized. I guess I'm not the only one in the family who's had to deal with the Toxic Jesus Fandom from time to time.)

(Not that I'm not cool with Christians. I love going with Bowie to their church. But their church doesn't want to wipe me from existence.)

But I've never seen Jasmine looking the way she is now. Like she's about to burst into flames as she storms around her still-running car and up the sidewalk toward us.

Liam steps closer to me, as if he could diffuse her anger by sharing in it. But Jasmine's anger doesn't diffuse: It multiplies.

Besides, I'm the one she's mad at. I step in front of him.

She glares at me, tears in the corners of her eyes, but they're not falling. Her nose is too scrunched up in anger to let them.

"You!" She points at me, but nothing else comes out, like she can't find the words. "You!"

"Jasmine, listen. This isn't the way I wanted you to find out, but—"

"*This* is your secret boyfriend?" She cuts me off. Apparently she's discovered a few more words. "I can't believe you. The two of you. Behind my back. How could you?"

"It wasn't like that." I hold my hands up, to try and calm her, even though the waves of anger rolling off her make me feel like I'm back in the pool. "It only happened after."

But Jasmine ignores me. She's a steamroller when she gets this mad. She rounds on Liam. "How long were you something-something my own brother?"

"I wasn't."

She snorts, which makes her tears start to fall.

But Liam keeps going. "I made a mess of things, and I'm sorry. I was scared and I made some bad choices and I hurt you in the process. But I promise, me and Jackson only happened after."

"Like the promise of a cheater means anything."

Liam looks like she slapped him.

She knows she shouldn't throw that around.

"Don't say that!" I say. "Don't you ever say that. He's not a cheater and you know it."

But Jasmine's too busy being outraged. "All I know is my own brother betrayed me." She spins around, stalks back to her car. Shouts something over her shoulder that I don't catch.

"What?"

"She said you can walk home."

I stare at her car as it pulls away.

Suddenly I can breathe again.

I turn to Liam. "Are you okay?"

"Are you?"

I nod. "I'm sorry. I should've told her a long time ago. I should've—"

"No. You were right. There was never going to be a good time." He reaches for my hand and gives it a squeeze.

"Yeah."

"But at least it's all out there now. Yeah?"

"Yeah."

He looks past me. "Hey. That's my mom. We can give you a ride home. You don't have to walk. Okay?"

"You sure?"

"Of course." He leans in to rest his forehead against mine. "Love you."

I stretch up to kiss him. "Love you."

Amy's in the kitchen when I get home, dressed in a nice blue sweater and black dress pants.

"Oh, Jackson, good. Sorry I couldn't get you; your dad wants to take us to family dinner."

Family dinner is this thing Dad does when he unexpectedly gets a night off. He picks a restaurant, makes us all get dressed nicely, and takes us out.

It's the last thing I want to do tonight. Being stuck in a car, at a restaurant, with the glowing thermonuclear warhead that is my sister.

"Wasn't Jasmine picking you up? She got home a few minutes ago."

"I got a ride," I say.

"Ah. She didn't look so good."

I keep my mouth shut.

"Well, go get dressed, okay? I'll check on her."

"I'm not really feeling up to it."

Amy feels my forehead. "You're not sick?"

"No, just . . ."

"Jackson?" Dad asks as he comes down the stairs, wearing a deep maroon sweater. "Better get dressed."

"I'm not . . ."

"Jasmine's not feeling well," he says to Amy. "Cramps."

I'm pretty sure that's a lie; now that I think about it, I'm sure it is, because we share a bathroom, and I do notice when the supply of tampons under the sink fluctuates.

I can't believe she's playing the period card.

I'm kind of relieved, though.

"I'll go get dressed," I say.

I'm honestly relieved to disappear into the back seat of the car as Dad drives us to this Greek place he loves. With no Iranian restaurants in town, he's decided Greek is the next best thing. I pick at my pastitsio, tuning everything out, until Amy excuses herself for the bathroom and Dad knocks on the table to get my attention.

"Did you and Jasmine have a fight?"

"Yeah."

"What about?"

"I don't want to talk about it."

"If you change your mind . . ."

How could I explain any of this to him?

It's dark when we get back home, but the light in my room is on. My notebook's still open on my bed, all out of sorts—I was working on organizing it this morning—but I'm too exhausted. I stuff everything back in and shove it into my backpack.

After getting ready for bed—Jasmine's room is already dark, her side of the bathroom locked—I text Liam.

At least now we can be together for real.

Sorry about everything today.

I love you.

It doesn't take long for him to write back.

Love you

Monday morning, I find Dad in the kitchen, in a faded sweatshirt and plaid pajama pants. He's got the day off.

"Morning," he says into his coffee. "Jasmine left early. She asked if I could give you a ride."

"I can take the bus."

"I don't mind. Gives us some time together."

Which is not something Dad and I do very often. We don't exactly have much in common.

But on the road, he asks, "How's your portfolio thing coming along?"

"Okay I guess." I did my best with it over break, since Dr. L basically abandoned me.

"When do I get to see it?"

"Whenever you like."

We fall into silence again. Dad reaches for the radio and turns it on—he usually listens to NPR—but then he turns it off again. He asks me how rehearsals are going. And reminds me he wants tickets. And I ask him how the hospital is.

As we stop in the student drop-off, he turns to me.

"You know, your amou Sina and I got into the worst fights growing up. So bad I thought we'd never talk again. But sooner or later we forgave each other. Just give it time."

Time? Dad doesn't understand.

I don't think there's anything that can ever fix this.

"Thanks, Dad." I grab my shmoodies and head inside.

There's a crowd around the Theatre Board when I get upstairs, and it's covered in twice as much paper as it was Friday. I don't have time to deal with someone vandalizing it again.

But as I get closer, people start to notice me. The chatter gets quiet.

Paige spins around and stares at me, and there's something in her eyes. I don't know what it is. But I don't like it.

There's a familiar pair of shoulders near the front. Liam, standing right next to Dr. Lochley, her scarf half-unwound as they both stare at the board.

It's covered with my breakup lists.

ACT
V

42

There's the one for Cam. And the one for Philip. The other guys I've had crushes on. All the teachers who spoke slowly to me because they thought me being deaf meant I wasn't smart enough to follow along in class. Braden. Paige. Dr. Lochley.

Worst of all: Liam.

He keeps staring at it. Jasmine's added an item, in bright pink Sharpie:

CHEATER

And right in the center of the board is a fresh list entirely in her handwriting.

JACKSON GHASNAVI'S BREAKUP LIST:
SELFISH
CYNICAL
HATES EVERYONE
CONSTANTLY BACKBITING
JEALOUS
COWARD

And biggest of all:

LIAR

I think I'm going to be sick. I want to hide in the bathroom. I want to crawl into the hydraulics of the orchestra pit, descend into the bowels of the building, and never be seen again.

Anything to not have Liam looking at me the way he is. Like I broke his heart. Like he doesn't even know me.

"Liam," I say, because I don't care what anyone else thinks. But he has to understand.

"I thought you said you didn't do one for me."

"I . . ."

"Do you really think that about me? That all I am is my looks?"

"Of course not."

"Then why?"

I'm painfully aware of everyone staring at us. But I don't care. I have to make him understand.

"Jasmine was upset, and I didn't . . . I didn't think you would see. Or know."

"I thought you saw me," he says. "I thought you were honest."

"I do see you. I love you."

He shakes his head. Tears leak down his cheeks.

I made Liam cry.

I step toward him, but he backs away, taking a jagged shard of my heart with him.

Dr. L is trying to shoo away the crowd around us, but I don't pay attention to her. I need to fix this.

"I'm sorry."

What else can I say?

"Sorry? Jackson . . ." He looks over the wall of lists again, like he can't quite wrap his head around them. When he turns back, his eyes are still far away. "You're not who I thought you were."

The rest of my heart crumbles.

"Liam . . ."

"I can't be with you."

"You're breaking up with me?"

"I'm not sure we were ever really together."

It feels like he punched me right in the solar plexus.

I didn't think Liam had it in him to be cruel.

Maybe he didn't, either, because he looks down at his feet after saying it. Then he shakes his head and follows the rest of the crowd out, leaving me alone with Dr. Lochley, who gives me a look that tells me to stay.

She makes me wait while she takes down every single list. She's careful too, removing the pins rather than ripping them off. Staring extra long at the list bearing her own name.

When they're all collected, she turns to me. "Let's talk in my office."

I follow her in. My hand is wet, a combination of sweaty, nervous palms and a perspiring shmoodie bottle. Maybe I could drown myself in it. Or drink it so fast I get brain freeze bad enough to render me unconscious.

Dr. Lochley scoots her tray of breakfast tater tots out of the way and sits at her desk. I stay standing. I think my legs are going numb.

She stares down at the lists, then finally looks up at me.

A couple tears escape my traitorous eyes, but I don't sniffle.

"Jackson," she says. Her mouth hangs open, like she doesn't know what to say.

"I don't know how they got there," I blurt out. "Jasmine must've—"

Must've taken them from my binder. Gotten to school early and put them up.

Must've really been hurting.

"But this is your handwriting."

I nod.

"Well, clearly you're upset with me."

I wipe at my cheeks. "I was just—"

"But it's neither appropriate nor acceptable for you to be airing your dirty laundry like this."

"Jasmine—"

"If your sister posted them, well, I'll need to have a conversation with her as well." She eyes me. "Though perhaps that's a family matter. Still, they're yours. You wrote them."

I nod.

"Under the circumstances, I don't think it would be appropriate for you to stay on as stage manager. The cast needs to be focused on the show, not on whether you're filling your notebook with criticisms."

"What? But what will happen to the show?"

"We'll figure something out." Dr. L stands, gathers up my lists, and drops them in her recycle bin. "You're not who I thought you were, Jackson. I hope you'll take some time to reflect on who you want to be in the future."

I don't know if she heard what Liam said to me, or if she just happened to twist the knife by accident.

279

Hot anger leaps up my throat and out my mouth before I can stop it. "Yeah, well, you're not who I thought you were, either. I thought you cared about me. But all you care about is Cam and Liam and the other actors."

She stares at me.

"I do care about you, Jackson, but you're not my only student. I have a department to run."

"Well, good luck running it without me then."

I spin on my heel and leave.

I didn't know I had it in me to do that. Storm out of Dr. Lochley's office. Maybe I'm dramatic enough to be an actor after all.

But once I'm at my locker, the anger leaks away, and tears replace it. I wish Bowie was here, but they've already gone to class; the halls are empty. The bell's already rung. Maybe I should've gotten a pass from Dr. L, but no. I can't go to class like this.

One of the advantages to being me is, if I tell Mr. Denton, my APUSH teacher, that I was dealing with a Theatre Emergency, he won't question it. I'm trustworthy.

Except I'm not. Not when it really counts.

Not with Liam.

I hide in the bathroom, wiping my tears with the scratchy ~~sandpaper~~ single-ply toilet paper the school district stocks.

Eventually first period ends, if the sudden influx of people into the bathroom is any indication, and my tears have mostly dried, so I hike my backpack onto my shoulders and head to AP Chem.

What else can I do?

"You okay?" Bowie asks as soon as they see me.

I shake my head. If they press me I think I might start crying again.

So I just say, "I don't want to talk about it right now."

They squeeze my shoulder as we take our seats.

I didn't know it was possible to get stage fright without actually being onstage. But walking into Theatre IV seventh period feels like that moment when you're cresting the hill of a roller coaster and about to plummet.

I wait outside the door, pondering if I should skip again. But Dr. L knows there's not a Theatre Emergency, and worse, she knows I'm not the one to deal with them anymore.

Maybe I should go see my guidance counselor and drop the class entirely. It's a little late in the year, but then again, I'm just a TA. No one would miss me. I could replace it with a study hall; everyone would be happier.

I turn around and bump into Madison.

"Oh. Sorry."

"It's cool." They push their dark curls off their forehead. "You good?"

I shrug.

"I heard somethingsomething."

"Sorry."

"Why? You have one of those lists for me?"

I shake my head. They smirk.

"Not sure whether to be relieved or offended. You headed in, or . . . ?"

I shrug, open the door for them, but they gesture at me to go first, so now I'm trapped.

Everyone's eyes press on me as soon as I step in, a dozen stabs in my stomach. Rather than take my usual spot next to Dr. L's desk, I sit at the very end of the last row of benches and try to ignore the glances people keep casting my way. It's torture.

This has to violate the Geneva Convention.

After the longest forty-seven minutes of my life, the final bell rings. Normally I'd go grab a snack before getting the Little Theatre set for rehearsal, but that's not my job anymore.

Instead, I head to my locker to get my stuff. I've got to hurry if I'm going to catch the bus. I can't remember the last time I took it. I've always stayed late for rehearsal, or grabbed a ride with Bowie or Jasmine or Liam.

As I stuff my empty shmoodie bottle into my backpack, it catches on the corner of my binder. I pull it out and stare at it.

Jasmine's left all the breakup lists for her boyfriends in there. She only took the ones that would embarrass me. That would get me fired. That would turn Liam against me.

I should've burned them all. Or at least shredded them, which is probably better for the environment. And less likely to get the fire marshal involved.

I start ripping pages out of the binder. Scenes tear along their three-hole punches. Blocking charts crumple in my hands. Copies of Denise's elevations drift to the floor like autumn leaves.

I take everything and dump it into the nearest recycle bin. For the first time in forever, my binder is empty, except for the color-coded plastic dividers.

After a moment, I toss it into the trash can.

When I turn back, I find Bowie staring at me, a stack of flyers clutched in their hands.

"Jackson? What are you doing?"

I open my mouth to tell them, but nothing comes out. My hands are too shaky to sign it. Every feeling inside me has calcified, cracked and crumbled until my insides are nothing but dust.

"You gonna tell me what's wrong?"

I bite my lip because if I don't, I think I'm going to explode. But my eyes burn with the start of fresh tears.

Bowie stares down at their stack of flyers, but only for a moment. Then they dump them into the recycle bin—I catch a glimpse of an advertisement for StuCo's "Festive Egg Hunt"— and take my arm.

"Come on. Let's get out of here."

43

I follow them to their car like a lost puppy. The sun is out, which seems mildly homophobic since between the brightness and my tears, I can barely see. They pull out of the parking lot, headed vaguely toward home. My home or theirs, I'm not even sure.

Eventually I get my crying under control enough to say, "I got kicked off the play."

Bowie doesn't look away from the road, but their eyes bug out. "You what?"

"Jasmine posted my breakup lists all over the Theatre Board."

"What? Why?"

This is the hardest part to say.

"She found out about me and Liam."

"Oh." Bowie chews their lips, hits their blinker. "Yours or mine?"

"Huh?"

"Your house or mine?"

It takes me a moment to decide. Not only because I'm trying to calculate when Jasmine will get home, but also because I'm not sure if I deserve Bowie's friendship. Not when I've been such a butt.

"Yours."

"Okay."

The drive is quiet. I don't know what else to say, and Bowie's concentrating on getting around a traffic jam caused by a car pulled over on the side of the road. It's on fire, actual fire, with huge billows of black smoke coming from the front. At first I panic, thinking it might be Liam's—a fire is about the only thing that hasn't happened to his car yet—but it's not the color of cargo pants.

It *does* have a Riverstone student parking sticker on the rear windshield. Along with a bumper sticker for one of the more conservative churches in town. And then, next to the firefighters, I spot—

"Was that Dominic?" Bowie asks as we drive by. "Couldn't have happened to a nicer guy."

"Maybe Jasmine's gone on a vengeance tour."

"At least you've still got your sense of humor."

I'm not sure if I'm joking or not.

When we get to Bowie's, they let me in, and I immediately fall face-down on their couch. I wish it would swallow me whole. But before I can even get comfortable, Bowie prods me in the shoulder with their knee until I roll over.

"Uh-uh. Come help me with this basghetti."

"What's to help with? Boil water. Cook pasta. Drain. Add sauce."

"Nope. I need your help."

"Bowie . . ."

"Jackson."

They keep staring at me, one eyebrow quirked.

"Ugh. Fine."

So I fill a pot with water while they get out the spaghetti and a jar of sauce.

It's only basghetti if you make it with sauce from a jar.

"What happened?" they ask as we wait for the water to boil.

"You're going to be mad at me."

"Maybe. But I'm still your friend. What happened?"

So I tell them. About me and Liam getting caught at swimming. Jasmine freaking out. Stealing my lists. Liam breaking up with me. Dr. L kicking me off the show.

"You know the worst part? Right before it all happened, I told him I loved him."

Bowie's eyes soften. "You did?"

"And he said he loved me back." I'm crying again, tears pooling before streaking down my face to soak the collar of my shirt. "He said he loved me. But then he broke up with me anyway."

My lips quiver.

"I messed everything up. With Jasmine. With Liam. With you."

"Oh, we're doing me now?" Bowie asks.

I try to laugh and cry at the same time. It only comes out as a hiccup.

"I should've been a better friend to you."

"Yeah."

"I'm sorry. I know it was shitty. I made everything about my relationship."

Bowie adds salt to the boiling water and tosses in the pasta. They turn back to me, arms crossed.

"You did."

"I don't know why I did. But I'm sorry. I won't do it again. Please don't give up on me."

They look at me like I'm speaking French.

"Seriously, Jacks? Apologize in one breath, make it all about you in the next?"

I swallow. They're right.

"We've been friends since we were five. Do you really think I'd give up on you?"

"I don't know." I hug myself. "No."

"Good." Bowie purses their lips, blows out a breath. "I can be mad at you and still love you."

"I know. I'm sorry." Sometimes I can't help myself. "Jasmine says I have abandonment issues."

"Well, she's been pretty awful to you lately, but I'm not sure she's wrong."

"Maybe."

"I really think you should talk to someone about this, Jacks. Like . . . go back to therapy or something."

"You think?"

"I do."

"But my therapist was the one who told me to make lists in the first place."

"Are you sure they weren't supposed to be, like, pro-con lists?"

I shrug. "He always talked slow to me anyway."

"Sounds like you had a shit therapist."

"Maybe." I grab the tongs and stir the spaghetti. "I'm really sorry, Bowie. I messed up. And you're right. I'll ask Dad about therapy."

"I forgive you. And don't do it for me. Do it for yourself. Okay?"

"Okay."

"And I know you're scared about college. But it'll be okay. Did it ever occur to you that I'm going to miss you too?"

Honestly?

I'm not sure it did.

"But we can't let that stop us from chasing our dreams. I want you to reach yours, Jackson."

"I want you to reach yours too. You know that. Right?"

Bowie finally smiles. "I do."

When the pasta's cooked, I drain it, then Bowie cracks the jar and pours the sauce all over. I serve them a big pile and then myself.

"Carbs don't cure everything, but they come close," Bowie says. "It's going to be okay, Jacks."

I sigh. "But I don't know what to do."

"About what?"

"Everything. Jasmine. The show." I swallow. "Liam."

I feel another cry coming on and stare at the ceiling, but that doesn't help.

"I really hurt him."

"Yeah."

"You talked to him?"

"Not about you, but yeah, he seemed down."

"I didn't think I *could* love someone the way I love him." I wipe at my tears before any more fall into my basghetti.

Bowie sighs. "You've got a big heart, Jackson. A big heart, and an itty-bitty brain sometimes."

"Ouch."

"But that's why I love you."

"I love you too."

"It's going to be okay. Now dig in. The basghetti's getting cold."

44

The next morning, I wake up extra early to catch the bus. So early, I catch Dad in the kitchen, eating a stale croissant with fig jam smeared on top, sipping his coffee and doing a crossword on his phone.

"Oh. You're up early."

"Yeah. Taking the bus today." I eye the plastic clamshell of Saturday's croissants. They even look dry. I shake my head and start gathering ingredients for shmoodies.

I make three, out of ~~habit~~ hope.

"Amy said you're not doing the play anymore?"

"Yeah." I told her last night, when she saw Bowie drop me off. Thankfully she didn't make me get into it.

"What happened?"

I shrug. I don't want to talk about it. And thankfully, Dad doesn't press me.

"Hmm. Well, what are you going to do instead? I'm sure there's other clubs."

"You're not doing the play?" Jasmine stands in the door of the kitchen, still in her pink-striped pajamas, her hair coming undone from the braid she sleeps in.

I want to ask her what she thought would happen, but I'm definitely not going to do that in front of Dad. So I shake my head and run the blender.

While I pour out the shmoodies into bottles, Dad says, "What if you signed up for a sport?"

"I don't think I can join any teams this late." Also, seriously. What would I play?

"Just saying. Or maybe an internship somewhere. You're good with computers."

I'm good by Iraj Ghasnavi standards, which basically just means I was born this century. Dad's always on me about double-majoring, just in case theatre doesn't work out.

"Actually, I was thinking maybe I should start up therapy again?"

Dad blinks at me. "What for?"

"I'm just going through some stuff."

"You know you can talk to me about anything, right?"

"I know, Dad, but I think I need to talk to a stranger. A professional."

Dad only pouts a tiny bit. He's always acted like, since he's a doctor, he's a doctor of everything. But then, every Iranian man has an ocean of knowledge one inch deep. At least that's what Khanum says.

"I'll look some up. Or do you want to do that yourself?"

I nod.

"Okay." He stands and kisses my forehead. "Love you, Jackson."

He puts his coffee cup in the dishwasher and wanders upstairs to finish getting ready, passing right by Jasmine, who's still standing at the edge of the kitchen. She looks away when I catch her and goes to the pantry for her cereal.

I grab my stuff and walk to the bus stop. It's warm today, T-shirt weather, and I'm in a light blue one Bowie got me for the Friendsmas before last. I haven't worn it very often, since I'm almost always in black; the tag is still stiff and scratchy where it sticks up. I tuck it away and swallow back the wave of sadness that threatens to drown me.

Bowie's waiting for me at my locker, like usual. And even though I knew he wouldn't be there, I still kind of hoped I'd see Liam. Ready to tuck in my tag.

I hand Bowie two shmoodies.

"Uh. Thanks." They scrunch up their face and smack their lips after tasting one. "What is that?"

"Lemon, ginger, and kale. And a bit of honey."

Bowie shakes their whole body. "It's got a kick."

"Yeah. We're running a little low on fruit."

"You need a ride home today?"

"I'll take the bus."

"You sure? The GSA meeting won't run that long."

"I don't want to be a hassle."

Bowie rolls their eyes. "Just meet me after school."

"All right."

I keep my head down the rest of the day. It's not like I talk to anyone but Bowie, anyway.

Theatre IV is a nightmare. Again. But I stay in my corner, out of everyone's way, and they all ignore me as they pair up to do scenes from Tennessee Williams. A few times I look up from my chemistry homework and think Dr. L is watching me; but maybe I'm just imagining it.

It's honestly a relief when class ends, and I make a hasty escape. I join the tide moving down the stairs, jostling each other, until the crowd parts, some heading toward the student parking lot, others toward the Arts wing or the gyms.

The crowd thins, and for a second I think I'm hallucinating, but no: feathery black hair, broad shoulders. Liam's ahead of me, when he should be heading for rehearsal. I almost say something, but what is there to say?

Would he even answer?

I'm not sure I could handle it if he ignored me. So I stay quiet, following him with my eyes, until he waves at someone down the hall.

It's Jasmine.

He steps close, says something to her, and she says something back, and then they duck into the pottery studio.

What is going on? Why are they talking?

They can't possibly be getting back together. There's no way. But I can't stop thinking about them, alone in the studio. Wild scenarios spin in my mind, like a revolve gone out of control, flinging actors and set pieces off it into the wings. I'm so distracted, I don't realize what I'm doing until Bowie waves to get my attention.

"Jackson?" Their brow furrows up. "Everything okay? Did you need something?"

"Huh?" I shake myself off. I've wandered into the choir room. Not only that, I sat down.

Amidst the GSA.

45

I meant to linger in the hall. Wait for Bowie to finish. Do my homework. Instead, I've stepped right into the unicorn's den.

A strange hand claps me on the back. For a second I think it's Liam, getting ready to tuck in my tag, or maybe just rescue me, but no. This hand is callused, and it doesn't linger on my tag; instead, it gives my shoulder a squeeze and a shake.

"Glad you finally decided to join us, bro!" Braden drops into the seat next to me, leaving his arm across my back like we're old friends.

I glance from Braden's gap-toothed smile to Bowie, whose cheeks are puffed up like they're trying to contain a laugh.

"Uh . . ."

Braden finally takes his arm off me. "You know your tag is sticking out?"

"Oh. Thanks." I reach back and tuck it in.

"No worries, bro. It's nice to have you."

He looks like he really means it, as he pushes his swoopy hair off his forehead and turns to Bowie. "Cheyenne gone again?"

"Another college visit."

Braden shakes his head and turns back to me. "Well, you came on a good day. We could use your help, bro."

Mr. Cartwright emerges from his office and spots me. His eyebrows shoot up. Did Dr. L tell him about the lists? About me getting kicked off the play? I think about bolting, but it's too late for that.

I've already been *bro'd* into a corner.

I keep mostly quiet as Bowie runs the meeting. My hands itch with the urge to take notes—force of habit—but Nadine, the GSA's secretary, is already doing that, seated stage left of Bowie at a folding table. Bowie stays standing as they work through the meeting's agenda: an upcoming movie night, volunteer shifts at one of the local shelters, a *Mario Kart* tournament fundraiser.

I raise my hand.

"Why not *Smash Bros*?"

"We did that last year. It got a little messy."

I blink. I never heard about that.

Braden leans over. "Two drag queens got into something-something."

"Huh? Got into what?"

"A fistfight. I guess some people are really picky about which Bayonetta costume they wear."

"Wow." I never knew about the Toxic Bayonetta Fandom.

"Anyway," Bowie says. "*Mario Kart* is the name of the game, and Braden has gotten a few football players to work as security to prevent any more incidents."

Braden pounds his fist over his heart. I want to laugh, but it's strangely sincere of him. "I got you, Bowie."

I raise my hand.

"Yes? Jackson?"

"I can help. If you need anything. Like, tech-wise."

Bowie nods. "Great. I'll put you down. We actually need some-one to chair the event, if you're up for it."

Mr. Cartwright gives me a cheesy thumbs-up.

"Really?"

"Yeah. I think you'd be perfect for this."

"I don't want to take over if someone else wants to do it."

"You should do it, bro," Braden says, patting me on the shoulder. "You're like, a genius wizard with tech stuff."

I'm definitely neither of those things. But maybe I can help. I like being helpful.

Besides. A *Mario Kart* tournament sounds fun.

After, I help Nadine rearrange the chairs in the choir room, while Bowie and Mr. Cartwright are caught up talking.

Nadine's a sophomore, and she's a Lebanese American lesbian. The first time I met her I thought she was joking for alliteration, but nope. She's got copper skin and a large nose and the bright-est laugh of anyone I've ever met, and she laughs often. I'm not sure why we haven't hung out more—except she's never had any interest in Theatre. But she's cool, and she's Lebanese, so I've always felt a sort of Middle Eastern kinship with her.

"Thanks," she says as I move another stack of chairs back into place. "Glad you could make it."

"Me too."

When we're done, she wipes her hands against each other, even though the chairs weren't that dirty, and pulls her phone out. "Can I have your email? I can send you what we have about the *Mario Kart* tournament."

"Sure."

I wave bye and wait for Bowie to escape what seems to be a rather long-winded story from Mr. Cartwright about the internal politics of the Heartland Men's Chorus. Eventually Bowie puts up their hands.

"Sorry, Mr. Cartwright, I'm supposed to give Jackson a ride."

"Oh, sorry! I didn't realize." He turns to smile at me. "Great having you here, Jackson."

"Thanks."

We head up toward Bowie's locker.

"So. Your first GSA meeting."

"I guess."

"Who knew all it would take was a bad breakup?"

I snort. "Wow."

"Seriously. I'm glad. I worry about you sometimes."

"Huh? Why?"

"I don't know. You don't have much queer community. Or deaf community, for that matter." Bowie frowns. "Or even other Iranians."

"I'm fine. I have . . . had Theatre."

"I know." They purse their lips. "Sometimes it's like you get so caught up in what you do, you forget it's okay to celebrate who you are."

"Huh."

I don't think that's right. But maybe.

After grabbing Bowie's stuff, we head out, our path taking us by the Little Theatre. The doors are open and I catch a glimpse of rehearsal going on without me. Liam's in there; I still wonder what he was doing with Jasmine.

But it's none of my business.

"You doing okay?"

I shake my head. "He's never going to forgive me."

"You know I don't want to be in the middle of all this. But for what it's worth . . . I don't think he hates you. I think he's hurting, and trying to figure out how to move past this himself. But he's got his own baggage and most of it has nothing to do with you."

"You don't think he hates me?"

"I don't think he has it in him to hate anyone, to be honest. Even if he should."

I wince, but Bowie quickly says, "Not you. But sometimes I think he's too nice for his own good."

"I like that he's nice. I've got enough mean in me for both of us."

"You're not mean, Jackson."

"But all those lists—"

"Not knowing where to put your anger isn't the same thing as being mean. Still, I'm glad you're giving them up. We've got to find you a new outlet."

"Maybe my new therapist can help."

Bowie raises their eyebrows.

"Got an appointment next week."

"Good for you." They bump my shoulder. "Want to come over? Play some *Smash*?"

"Sure."

46

Amy takes me to my first therapy appointment Wednesday after school. Dr. Jacinto's fluent in ASL, which is a big step up from my last therapist. Then again, she's also a lot more direct than my last therapist. By the time our hour's up, I'm wrecked, not from listening but simply from thinking so hard. It's like someone pulled my brain out of my nostrils.

"How was it?" Amy asks as we head to the car.

"Good." I think. Dr. Jacinto asked me a lot of questions. Stuff about school, and my parents, and Jasmine, and Liam, but also stuff I wasn't expecting—like how it felt that my family still hadn't learned to sign.

I didn't even know how to answer that one. But it left me feeling weird and unsettled.

"You need anything on the way home?" Amy asks. "Want some Dairy Queen?"

"I'm good."

Amy's quiet again for a while. But then she says, "I know you probably just talked a lot to your therapist, but I'm here for you if you need anything."

"I know you are. Thanks."

As I sit on my bed, organizing brackets for the *Mario Kart* tournament, my phone buzzes. I grab it so fast I accidentally fling it off my bed. I scramble to find it. Is it Liam?

But no. It's Denise. She never texts me unless it's an emergency.

Tech starts soon. But I guess she doesn't need my help.

I nod, even though there's no one to see me, my chest going all warm. I miss Denise too.

I get off the floor, scoop up my overturned notebook—a tiny spiral-bound one—and find Jasmine hovering in my doorway.

We haven't talked much, aside from the bare minimum that goes with sharing a house and, crucially, a bathroom. I've been taking the bus in the mornings, riding home with Bowie in the afternoons, so we've been able to mostly avoid each other.

It's so awkward even Dad has taken to asking what's going on between us, but I haven't told him. I don't think Jasmine has, either.

She looks at me, a slight frown creasing the corners of her mouth.

"What?" I ask. "Dinner?"

"Can I come in?"

I blink at her. What could she possibly want?

But I guess my not saying no quick enough counts as a yes to her. She steps in, closes the door, and sits on the edge of my bed. I stay standing.

"Did you need something?"

"How was therapy?"

"Private."

"Okay." She tucks her legs up underneath her. "You probably heard I got a week of detention."

I hadn't heard that. "For what?"

"For putting up your lists."

"Oh."

I guess that's good? Though a week's detention hardly seems fair for imploding my life.

Though maybe I did that to myself.

"I heard you got kicked off the play."

"What did you think would happen?"

"I don't know." She puffs up her cheeks, then exhales. "I'm sorry about that."

I stare at her.

It's a little late for sorry.

"I was so mad at you. Like, madder than I've ever been in my life. You hurt me, Jackson. What you and Liam did really hurt."

"He didn't do anything except break up with you," I say, feeling suddenly defensive of him. "It's my fault."

"He and I talked a bit."

That's more than I've managed. I gave up on texting him, and the one time we made direct eye contact at school, he got a panicked look and turned the other way.

Dr. Jacinto thinks I need to give him space, and she's right. But I miss him so much it's turning me inside out.

"Jackson?"

"Huh?"

"I said, I talked to Liam."

"Okay."

"He apologized to me for . . . well. Everything."

"Everything?"

"For dating me when he liked you. For thinking things would just magically work out. For dropping me once he realized you and Bowie weren't together."

I wince.

"Somethingsomething, that was a really shitty thing to do."

"I'm sorry."

"I am too." She takes a deep breath. "I could tell you liked him. And I started to wonder if he liked you too."

"Really?"

"Yeah. Learning sign seemed like a lot for someone who was just a friend."

"Or a sister," I mutter before I can stop myself.

Jasmine stares at me for a long time. So long I start feeling awkward.

"So what now?" I ask.

"Don't get me wrong, I'm still mad at you. For a lot of stuff. You could've been honest from the start."

"Yeah. I could have. I didn't . . . I'd never felt like that before. About anyone. It took me a while to figure out. I'm sorry. I should've told you."

"I understand." She traces patterns across my comforter. "I'm not saying I forgive you. But I didn't mean to mess up your life."

"You didn't. I'll be okay."

"Good." She stands, fiddles with the hem of her shirt. "You don't have to keep taking the bus. I can give you a ride."

"I'll think about it."

She shrugs.

"I do love you, Jackson. Even when I want to kill you."

I snort.

"I love you too."

And for the first time in a long while, my sister smiles at me. It's small and uncertain but it's a start.

Maybe we'll be all right after all.

47

riday afternoon, after another Theatre IV spent hiding in the corner while the class works—they've moved on from Tennessee Williams to Neil LaBute, from dialogues to small scenes—Dr. L flags me down before I can leave.

Is she finally going to kick me out of the class? It's not like I'm contributing anything. I'm just making it awkward for everyone.

"You have a moment, Jackson?"

She's the one with places to be. Today's the last run-through before techs this weekend.

"Okay."

"Let's talk in my office."

I grab my things and march after her. The last time I was in her office is when she fired me. I never noticed before how it always smells faintly of tater tots.

She goes to sit behind her desk, but shakes her head and heads to the couch. She scoops off a pile of script books, takes a seat, and pats the other cushion for me.

I shrug off my backpack and sit.

"So . . ." I say.

"I'd like to apologize to you, Jackson."

"I . . . huh?"

She unwinds her scarf and rolls her neck. "I like to think I'm a big enough person to admit when I've made a mistake. Though sometimes I do need Denise to give me a kick in the pants."

She chuckles to herself.

"Anyway. I'm sorry I made you feel like I didn't care about you. Or that I prioritized everyone ahead of you."

My cheeks heat up.

"It's fine," I say, but she holds up her hand.

"I'm saying this not as an excuse, but as an explanation: There are fifty-odd students in this department, and twice as many I see in class every day. And if I don't listen as well as I should, or appreciate how much you do, or check in when you're not okay, it's not because I don't care. It's because I'm constantly in triage mode, and out of all my students, you're the one that always seems like you're going to be fine. But that's not fair to you. I'm sorry."

I don't know what to say. Except "Thanks."

"And one more thing."

"Huh?"

"I've spoken to Cameron. Let him know his behavior wasn't acceptable."

"Which behavior?" I mutter, but she hears me and laughs.

"Some things are beyond my power to change," she says. "But I made it clear if he said anything else unkind to you, or made fun of you, there would be consequences."

I don't know what that means.

"I understand if you're still mad at me, but I hope you haven't given up on Theatre. You're talented and hardworking and an asset to the department."

"Thanks." I manage a little smile. "And you can't get rid of me that easily."

Dr. L laughs. "I didn't think so. Now, I've got to get to rehearsal. I hope you'll still come see the show."

"I might."

"Good." She stands, gestures for me to leave first. Right as I round the corner, I bump into Paige.

"Oh," I say. "Hey."

"Hey."

I swallow. If Dr. L is big enough to do this, so am I. "You have a second?"

Paige crosses her arms. "I guess."

We used to be friendly. Maybe bordering on friends. Now there's a wall between us.

I put it there. But maybe I can make a crack in it, at least.

"I'm really sorry. About that list I made. I was being petty and you didn't deserve that. I think you're pretty awesome."

She nods. "Thanks."

"Seriously. I'm glad you're in the show. You're amazing. I was just . . ."

Jealous. Angry. Hurt.

Lots of things.

"Anyway. You didn't deserve that. So, sorry. And I hope, maybe, we can figure out how to be friends again. If you want."

"Apology accepted."

"Really?" I blink. "Just like that?"

"Just like that." She relaxes her arms. "I'm still a techie. Techies have to stick together. And so do friends."

My face is on fire, and my cheeks might cramp from smiling. "Yeah. We do. I'm sorry I forgot that."

She looks past me. "Well. You had a lot on your mind."

I glance over my shoulder, where Liam's disappearing into the Little Theatre.

God, was it that obvious? My smile melts away again.

Paige gives me a sympathetic shrug. "I better go. See you?"

She joins the crowd headed into the theatre. I tighten the straps on my backpack.

Paige and I are going to be okay.

Dr. Lochley and I are too.

Even Jasmine says we'll be okay eventually.

But Liam still won't talk to me. Won't even look at me.

That's his choice, though. I have to honor it.

Even so, I feel a little lighter as I head down the stairs to find Bowie.

Everything isn't fixed. But a few things are on the mend. Maybe that's enough for now.

48

"**A**re you done yet?" Bowie asks.

"Almost."

We're in the computer lab. Bowie's finished fighting with their Excel spreadsheet, but I'm still working on a list of equipment we need for the *Mario Kart* tournament. I'm pretty sure we can borrow it from the Theatre Department, now that Dr. L and I are talking again.

"I need food before the show."

"Okay, okay." I save my work and pack up so we can make a DQ run. Bowie gets some chicken fingers while I get a little Oreo Blizzard; we're still doing our usual post-show Perkins, even though I'm not in the show, so this is more a snack than anything else.

It's the sort of spring day that feels like summer came early: sunny, in the seventies, though still cool in the shade. We drive with the windows down—and my hearing aids off—and the wind feels like freedom on my face. Like the sky is vast and boundless, and our futures even more so.

Bowie's smirking as we hit a stoplight.

"What?"

"You're smiling."

"Am not."

"It's good to see."

I roll my eyes. "I guess I'm doing a little better."

"Good."

It turns out, even if they're a little on the weird side, the GSA crowd is pretty cool. Braden and I might actually become friends, despite his constant *broing*. And it turns out Nadine's parents own the little Middle Eastern Market in Gladstone that Dad's always getting Persian groceries from.

I still miss Liam. Maybe I always will. But I'm doing okay.

We eat in the parking lot, and I'm careful to keep the soft serve off my button-up. It feels weird to be wearing normal clothes instead of show blacks on opening night. Weirder still to have tickets to the show, even if Dr. L gave them to me for free.

Still, maybe dairy wasn't the best choice for a snack, because my stomach starts doing little flips when a familiar black Honda pulls up next to Bowie's car.

Cam emerges from the driver's side; Philip gets out the other, clutching a brown paper bag with the Big Burger logo on it. Cam sidles around the car and wraps his arm around Philip's waist, as they both head in.

Bowie's nostrils flare. "Those two are toxic."

I shrug and open the door. "Come on. We'd better go before the good seats are all taken."

Good seats being ones where I can see Liam the clearest. I hand over our tickets, take a couple programs, pick spots at the northeast corner.

"That's pretty cool." Bowie points at the set. It was only half-finished when I got fired, but now it's done, and it's phenomenal: the skyline of Illyria, with windows made of frosted gels twinkling like candlelight, courtesy of the flickering LEDs behind them. All built out of recycled flats.

"Yeah. It is." Denise has outdone herself. I wonder who else helped. Did Liam keep showing up to work days without me?

I thumb through the program; to my surprise, Dr. L didn't take me off the stage manager spot, though she did add Laken underneath.

Laken's a first-year girl who started showing up to our work days. She's heavyset, with clear-framed glasses and the kind of face that's super friendly when she's smiling and super judgey if she raises an eyebrow. She said she wanted to learn about sound and lights, but it looks like she got a huge promotion. I scan the catwalk, but I can't spot her; she's even shorter than me, and no one can see me in the catwalk unless I stand at the rail and lean out.

The house slowly fills with students and teachers and parents. Braden snags a seat house left, but not before giving me and Bowie a big wave that nearly knocks over his neighbor.

I wave back, trying not to laugh.

"I'm gonna run to the water fountain," I say with a little over five minutes to curtain. My DQ has left me all thirsty. "Be right back."

I leave my jacket on my seat and weave through the incoming audience. There's a small crowd still milling about, flipping through programs, chatting with each other or playing with their phones, even as the house crew tries to corral them inside.

I drink my fill, wipe off my mouth, turn—and am immediately knocked off my feet by someone slamming into my shoulder. Cam rushes past, without even pausing to apologize. His costume, a big plum-colored dress, is only half-done, and his wig is a mess.

He runs right into the bathroom while I pick myself up and readjust my hearing aids.

Philip's not far behind. He's in the hunter-green waistcoat and puffy shorts of Sir Toby; he's got wrinkles drawn onto his fore-head and a big bushy mustache spirit-gummed to his upper lip.

Philip looks like he wants to run into the bathroom after Cam, but before he can, Denise strides up in show blacks, a walkie talkie at her waist and a headset around her neck.

"What's going on?" she asks, then notices me. "Oh. Hey, Jackson."

"Hey."

"What happened to Cameron?" She pulls Philip aside so he's not blocking the bathroom. Some of the audience is staring at him; actors are supposed to stay backstage once they're in costume, backstage being the hall outside Dr. L's office, with black drapes to block it from view. Otherwise it breaks the illusion.

"Somethingsomething fine after dinner, then he got dressed and all of a sudden . . ."

"You had Big Burger," I say. I hadn't thought twice about it when I saw them, I was too distracted, but—

"Yeah, he'd never been."

"Big Burger has onions in their patties."

Philip's eyes go so wide the white powder on his eyebrows starts flaking off.

"Cam's allergic to onions," I tell Denise.

"Do we need to call an ambulance?" she asks. "Maybe something-something EpiPen."

"It doesn't kill him," I say.

"It makes him sick," Philip adds.

I meet Denise's eyes and mouth *Code Brown*.

Denise groans and grasps her forehead, massaging her temple with her thumb. "Great. Just great. Curtain's in five. Will he be all right by then?"

Philip shakes his head, sending the ends of his mustache flopping. "It could be hours."

"Poor guy." Denise stares at the bathroom for a moment, then turns to me. "Well, better go take your seat, Jackson. Not sure what we'll . . ."

She stops mid-sentence.

I know people talk about light bulbs going off, but I don't think I've ever seen one in person, until now.

"Jackson."

"Yeah?"

"You still remember all the blocking?"

"Yeah . . ."

"You have the show memorized?"

I nod. After all those hours helping Liam rehearse, how could I forget?

"Great. Come on."

"Huh?"

"You're going on."

"I can't!"

"Why not?" She takes my arm and starts leading me backstage, Philip trailing behind us.

"Dr. L kicked me off the show." Just because she apologized to me, it doesn't mean I'm allowed back in.

"This is an emergency." She waves her hand. "I'll deal with Tracy. You get into costume."

"But Cam's still in his."

"We've got plenty of dresses. We'll figure something out. Come on."

49

Denise finds this salmon-colored dress, with big sleeves that aren't period-appropriate, but this is an emergency. The neckline is a little low and shows the few scraggly dark hairs growing in the valley of my chest. Liam used to like tickling them.

I'm about to shake off the memory but that will ruin Jamilah's work on my makeup. Which is a rush job that mainly focuses on my eyes and lips. There's no time for a wig, plus if I wear a wig I won't be able to hear for all the hair scratching against my hearing aids—not to mention the risk of feedback—so I'm a short-haired Olivia, but whatever.

Laken pops her head in. Her show blacks and headset suit her. "How much longer?"

"Somethingsomething places," Dr. L says, yanking on the laces at the back of my dress, forcing the breath out of my lungs. I might actually be Dorito-shaped, like Liam, when she's done.

"Thank you, places." Laken follows Jamilah out, letting the prop room door swing shut behind her.

Dr. Lochley gives one last, fierce yank and ties me off. She swings around to my front.

"You sure you want to do this? You know you don't have to."

"The show must go on, right?"

"The show must go on," she agrees, thumbing away a bit of lipstick. "All set. You need a mirror?"

"Would it matter?"

She laughs. "At least let me take a picture. Your stage debut."

"Okay."

Dr. L pulls out her phone. "Thank you for stepping up. You didn't have to."

I think of everyone who worked so hard on the show. Afternoons of rehearsal and laughter. Movie night. Saturday work days. Liam.

"Yeah. I did."

Dr. L smiles. "Well then, break a leg." She opens the door for me. I step out into the hallway and bump right into Liam.

"Oh. Sorry."

He's in a dress too, a silver-blue number that perfectly matches his eyes. He's in full makeup and a black wig that's all curls and rings that perfectly frame his face.

He is breathtaking.

"Oh," he says again. We're chest to chest. "Jackson?"

"Hey."

I forgot how tall he is. I swallow and stare up at him.

"I better—" He nods toward the stage doors, where the actors are already lined up.

"Yeah."

But he doesn't move. Instead, he reaches back and tucks in the laces Dr. L knotted off. I can barely breathe.

"Break a leg," I manage to say.

"You too."

Madison, in their checkered fool costume, and Peyton, who plays Maria (Olivia's lady-in-waiting) stand in front of me, waiting for the scene change. My stomach ties itself into a clove hitch. There's bile in the back of my throat. I never should've had so much dairy.

The stage doors have their windows blocked with BlackWrap, so we can't see inside. I can't hear what's happening onstage, but Madison stands close, waiting for Peyton's cue.

The line of light along the bottom of the door goes dark for scene change. I reach for the door—force of habit—but Madison grabs it, lets Peyton go first, and follows. The door swings shut again.

My stomach unravels and ties itself into a bowline instead. Darcy, who plays Malvolio, steps up next to me. She's got a sharp, blue-black beard spirit-gummed to her chin and bushy eyebrows painted on over her real ones. She gives me a quick nod. I nod back.

I think I have to pee. I should've done that before getting into this dress. And I should've let Bowie know what happened, but my phone is still in my jacket. Are they worried? Annoyed?

Did I even remember to silence my phone before going out for water?

"Breathe," Darcy says.

It doesn't help at all.

But she grabs the door and prods me in the back to get me moving.

I step onto the stage, squinting at the lights. The audience is laughing, and for a second I'm convinced it's at me, that one look was enough for them to realize how utterly ridiculous I am, to confirm that I don't belong onstage, I belong in the back where no one can see or hear me. But then I notice Madison, making a fool of themself, and I relax a tiny bit.

They turn to me. "God bless thee, Lady."

I try to summon the way Cam always did this bit, so haughty and full of himself.

"Take the fool away," I command my retainers, two first years, Connor and Kieran.

But Madison gets a gleam in their eye, and they tell the retainers to take me away instead. They've got so much energy, and I don't know how I'll keep up with them because they have amazing comedic timing and I'm just, well, me. There's a ringing in my ears, not from my hearing aids but from every nerve in my body being electrified.

I make the mistake of looking out into the audience at one point and catch Bowie, their mouth hanging open, watching me perform. But then they sign a quick *You got this* at me, and they're right. I do got this. I match Madison beat for beat, I act from the inside out, I become the best Olivia I can become.

At least until Liam steps onstage.

He's in his Cesario costume now, a blue waistcoat the same hue as his dress from earlier, puffy shorts, and black leggings, which make his legs look about a mile long. The stage lights catch the shine of his raven hair. And just like Olivia, I'm smitten.

It's the easiest thing in the world, acting like I'm in love with him at first sight. Because first sight, twelfth sight, millionth sight, I will never stop loving him.

Liam meets my eyes, and my lungs fight against my corset. He's right in front of me. I stare at him, and he stares back at me, until I realize he's said his first line.

"Huh?"

That gets a chuckle from the audience. He blushes, even beneath his makeup, and repeats, "The honorable lady of the house, which is she?"

And I answer, "Speak to me, I shall answer for her. Your will?"

This is the most Liam's spoken to me since we broke up. And the way he's looking at me, I don't know if it's acting or if he really sees someone beautiful when he looks at me. I'm not sure I want to know.

My heart is pounding, but I think I'm actually having fun. I haven't done this since middle school, and I'd forgotten how amazing it is: the audience's emotions feeding me, the lights twinkling like stars high above, the feel of the stage beneath my feet. It's terrifying and glorious and there's nothing else like it. My body is flooded with adrenaline and there are times I forget who I am.

At intermission, Madison tucks a bottle of water into my hand. I'm sweating in the dress, and along my hairline, and the back of my neck. Even my underwear is chafing. I press the bottle against the back of my neck and against my pulse points.

"Drink," they say. "Hydrate or die-drate."

"Huh?" Maybe I heard them wrong. "Thanks."

"You did good out there."

I shake my head, but I can't fight the smile.

"Thanks."

Liam's last scene had him exiting stage right, but I'm back-stage left. Act III starts with our next scene together: the one where Olivia confesses her love.

And it's like I poured the water bottle all over myself.

How am I supposed to do this?

Before I know it, Laken is calling places for the second half, and the lights are dimming, and Peyton is leading me back on-stage. Everyone else *exeunts*, and then it's just Cesario and Olivia.

Liam and me.

50

hen he takes my hand to kiss it, I do a whole body shiver, because I remember those hands. His perfect hands. Holding mine. Playing with my hair. Demonstrating how to improve my front crawl. Curling around the steering wheel of his shitty brown car. Resting on my knee as we sat together in TJ's, memorizing his scenes.

I flub my next line and try to recover, but the adrenaline is gone. Instead there's weight pressing down on me. Guilt gnawing at my stomach.

Liam gave me his heart, and I wasn't careful with it. I was selfish and I was cowardly and I hurt him.

And yet here we are again. And I'm the one giving him my heart. But Cesario doesn't love Olivia, and he never will. That's not how the play goes.

The tears that spring to my eyes are very real as I plead, "I would you were as I would have you be."

And Liam answers, his voice raised, "Would it be better, madam, than I am? I wish it might, for now I am your fool."

He hasn't moved, but I feel like he slapped me.

I made a fool of him. I lied to him and I hurt him and I'd do anything to take it back.

I blink and the tears pooling in my eyes start to slide down my cheeks. Liam's mouth opens in surprise.

I've got another line, I'm sure of it, but it's gone. My whole mind is blank. No lines, no blocking, no lists. Just the boy I still love.

This is not how the show goes. But I step forward and take his hands. This definitely isn't in the script. I don't remember what's in the script.

Liam clears his throat and says, "My lady?"

That's not in the script either.

I swallow and look him in the eyes. "You're not the fool. I am. And I'm sorry."

He blinks at me. This isn't iambic pentameter. This isn't Shakespeare.

But it's the truth.

"I was afraid. Afraid of hurting my sister. Afraid of hurting you. Afraid of being hurt myself. But I love you so much. I love your smile and your laugh. I love your patience and caring. I love the way you tuck in my tags when they stick up. I'm sorry I hurt you. I'm sorry I messed everything up. But I will never, ever be sorry for loving you. That's the best thing I've ever done."

The audience is silent. Or maybe it's just me: Maybe I can't hear anything except for the beating of my own heart as I look into Liam's eyes and wait.

Whatever happens, I said what I needed to say. I might've just ruined the show, but there will be other shows. There's only one Liam.

Liam looks down at me. The stage lights glow like stars in his eyes. And gently, ever so gently, he gives my hands a squeeze.

His smile is a sunrise, slow, and subtle, until finally it crests the horizon and blinds me with its brightness. He brings my hands to his chest, which pulls me closer to him. I stumble a bit in my shoes; I'm not used to a chunky heel.

"I love you too. That's why it hurt so much." He lets go of one hand so he can use a thumb to wipe away my tears. "I never stopped loving you."

"Really?"

"Really."

For some reason that makes me cry harder.

He never stopped loving me.

Liam brings his other hand to my face and leans in.

And then he kisses me. In front of everyone. And I kiss him back. I want to stay in this moment forever.

Someone whoops in the audience. I'm almost certain it was Bowie. We break apart, smiling.

Liam drops his hands, signs close so only I can see: "Let's do the scene?"

I nod. Step back to my mark. Brush my hands across the front of my dress, as if I'm swiping away wrinkles, even though the whole thing is pleats. I clear my throat and pick up the scene.

"Cesario, by the roses of the spring, by maidhood, honor, truth, and everything, I love thee so . . ."

Have I polished my shoes? Yes, I've polished my shoes, I say in my head. My hand is in Paige's for our tandem bow as Olivia and Sebastian.

Paige and I break apart, her going stage right, me stage left, leaving room for Jamilah to come through for a solo bow as Orsino. The crowd whistles and claps, and then comes Liam, back in his Viola dress. He bows, reaches for Jamilah for their couple's bow, then gestures to all of us for the full cast bow.

Have I polished my shoes? Yes, I've polished my shoes.

We break apart, making for the stage doors, high on adrenaline and applause and the sheer joy that comes from a play well-played. The buzzing in my belly is so strong I feel like I've been zapped again.

Backstage, people pat each other on the back, laugh, and hug. I hang back, because even though I'm here I'm not really one of them. Not just because I got kicked out, and not just because of the lists, but because even when I was stage managing I was always apart.

Until Darcy grabs my hand, yanking me into the pack. I can't make out a thing anyone says, but I feel the sheer euphoria of a (mostly) successful show. No one seems mad at me and Liam for our little bit of improv.

Not even Dr. Lochley, who is hovering by Denise near the catwalk door. She mutters something, then hands a twenty-dollar bill to her wife, who laughs and kisses her on the nose.

I eventually excuse myself to the prop room to get out of this dress, because I'm pretty sure it's been smooshed by the press of bodies all around me, and it's getting uncomfortable. After I pull my shirt back on, a hand brushes my back to fix my tag.

I spin around and he's there. Right in front of me, smiling. He's still in his costume and makeup, and the fluorescent light of the prop room makes him look slightly ghoulish, but he's still perfect.

"Hey," he says.

"Hey," I say back.

I reach for his waist; the fake silk of his costume is slick against my palms.

"I'm sorry," I say again, so he knows it's me and not Olivia. "I'm so, so sorry."

"You don't have to—"

"I do." I clear my throat. "I liked you from the start and I didn't know what to do with it. I was jealous of Jasmine and then I felt bad for feeling jealous so I went along with her wanting a list. But I shouldn't have done it. I should've put you first. And I shouldn't have lied about it."

"Jackson—"

"And I shouldn't have been such a coward about telling her about us. You are important to me. Our relationship is important to me. I never should've kept it a secret. I'm sorry."

"Will you be quiet?" he asks.

"Huh?"

"I'm trying to apologize here too."

"What for?"

"For not telling you how I felt from the start. For dating your sister in the first place. For not giving you the chance to explain."

"That list . . . Everything on it was a lie. I was trying to talk Jasmine out of being in love with you. Trying to talk myself out of it. Because I didn't think you'd like me back."

"But I do."

"You do," I say, and I can't believe it. I've never quite understood the logic of musicals: how someone could have feelings so huge, so overpowering, they have to burst into song.

But now I think I could carry a whole showstopping number by myself.

"So what now?" I ask.

"What do you mean?"

"I mean . . . you and me?"

"Yeah. You and me." He pulls me in close.

And then he kisses me. It's soft and kind and sweet and over all too quickly. But he breaks it and smiles at me, so bright I feel like I'm back onstage, and it's too much. I hide my face against his chest, and he hugs me tight, resting his chin on my head.

"Are you getting makeup in my hair?"

"Yes. Deal with it."

"Okay."

We stand like that, holding each other, and I think time might've stopped. But then the door swings open.

"Oh!" Dr. Lochley says. "Sorry. I hope I'm not interrupting."

We break apart, but Liam keeps my hand clasped tightly.

Dr. L looks at our hands and smiles. "I should be upset with both of you for going so far off script, but that's probably the most interesting Shakespeare has ever been. You were both terrific."

"Thanks." Liam jiggles my hand.

"And I'm glad you worked things out. Best twenty dollars I've ever lost."

"You bet against us?" he asks.

"You two were being pretty dramatic about the whole thing," she says, a twinkle in her eye. "Now come on. Your adoring public awaits."

* * *

"You. Are. Ridiculous!" Bowie says when they spot me. But they're smiling, and it only widens when Liam comes up beside me, now free of makeup and back in shorts and a T-shirt. He missed a few spots, but it's cute.

"Sorry. I hope you weren't worried."

"I mean, I figured it was some sort of Theatre Emergency, but I didn't expect this. Did you poison Cam or something?"

"No. His boyfriend did."

Bowie's brow furrows, but then they say, "Big Burger?"

"Onions in the patties."

"Couldn't have happened to a nicer person," Liam says. Bowie lets out a cackle.

I spot Cam hovering by the bathroom door; he looks a little pale but otherwise fine as Philip hands him a Gatorade bottle.

Cam sees me looking and gives me a little nod. I'm not sure what for. But I don't have time to worry about him now.

"So," Bowie says, tapping their lip with their forefinger. "You two, huh?"

I grab Liam's hand. "Yeah. Us two."

"It's about time you sorted things out."

"Thanks."

"So. You need a ride to Perkins, or . . ."

"He's got one," Liam says. "We'll meet you there?"

"As long as you two aren't gross or anything," Bowie says, but they're still smiling.

"Deal."

"Come on." I pull Liam toward the stairs. "Let's go."

We make it all the way to the parking lot, Liam's hand in mine, but when we reach his car, he spins us around so he's leaning against the trunk and I'm leaning against him. His hands rest at my sides; mine link behind his neck.

"I missed you," he says.

"I missed you too."

I'm not sure which of us starts it, but we kiss again. We kiss and kiss and kiss, right where everyone can see us, parents and teachers and friends, and I don't care. I want everyone to know.

Liam kisses me harder, does this thing with his tongue that makes my knees go all woogedy, and I break the kiss and laugh.

"Hm, you know what I want?" he asks.

"What?"

"Mm. Onion rings."

I snort so hard I think I pop a blood vessel.

51

"**H**ave fun," Jasmine signs as I get out of the car. She's started taking online classes. And she says she's going to find in-person ones when she gets to Denver. She might even get Mom to join in too.

"Thanks."

I grab my backpack and three shmoodies and head into school.

Summer has come early—though if I wait ten minutes, we might get a late April freeze—and the warm air feels nice.

Mr. Cartwright is waiting by the backstage doors, with the Main Theatre already unlocked. "Hey, Jackson."

"Hey, Mr. C. Ready?"

"As I'll ever be."

We're the first ones here: The theatre is still dark, the ghost light still set. But I get to work readying it for the *Mario Kart* tournament.

I looked long and hard for other places to host it, but in the end, I asked Dr. L if the GSA could use the theatre if I was there to supervise. And she said yes, without even blinking.

So maybe next year, we (I can't believe the GSA is *we* now) can use it for more things.

The rest of the crew trickles in: Bowie, looking immaculate in a bright green jumpsuit; Braden, in his football jersey and shorts; Nadine, in the most amazing black pompadour I've ever seen.

But Paige shows up too, to help me run things. And Madison isn't far behind her. They signed up to compete.

So did a bunch of deaf gamers Bowie's dad introduced me to. I didn't even know there was such a big deaf gaming community in town. But I've already had a couple games of *Smash* with them.

I look down at the to-do list on my clipboard. We're nearly ready.

A familiar hand graces my back, tucking in my tag.

"Hey." I turn and kiss Liam hello.

"Hey, you." He kisses me again. "Where do you need me?"

"Help me bring in the screen?"

I don't really need help. I just like it when he's near me.

I bring in the lineset with the projection screen on it. Lock it in place. Paige is already in the booth, ready to focus.

I turn to go, check off my next item, but Liam grabs me.

"I missed you."

"You saw me this morning." We had another swimming lesson; Bowie came along too. It was really fun.

Not like I'll join the swim team next year, but still.

"That didn't count." Liam pulls me in, leans down, and kisses me. I kiss him back, then rest my forehead against his chest. Let him hold me.

I'll never get tired of being held.

Something crashes into us. I nearly fall against the rail, but Liam catches me.

"Huh?"

I shake myself off and find Braden and Madison wrestling. No, not wrestling; they're still standing, arms entwined, making out so hard they didn't even notice us. But Madison's using their long legs to guide Braden backward toward the scene shop.

"Sorry, bros," he manages to say before he's kissing Madison again.

I turn and stare at Liam for a long beat, until we start cracking up at the same time.

"What just happened?" I ask.

"No idea." His eyes twinkle. "Bro."

"Ugh. I hate you."

"No you don't."

Bowie waves at me. "Hey. Can you help me set up the sign-in table?"

"Yeah! Be right there."

Liam lets me go, but I grab him.

"Hey."

"Hey."

"I love you. I love you so much."

"Yeah? How come?"

"There are too many reasons." I grin at him. "I'll have to make a list."

ACKNOWLEDGMENTS

It'll come as no surprise that, like Jackson, I too was a Theatre Kid growing up. And though we're given to self-indulgence, I'll try to be brief.

Lu Brooks and Julian Winters, thank you for reading this back when it was called *Project Beautiful Rule-Breaking Moth* and had no plot. It took three years, but I think I found one.

Natalie C. Parker, Tessa Gratton, and Tara Hudson, thanks for helping me find that plot. I'll never look at a cold-cut sandwich the same way again.

Lana Wood Johnson, Ronni Davis, Mark Thurber, Julie Murphy, and Alex London, thanks for all the ears you lent when I was struggling.

Molly O'Neill, thanks for being honest with me—and patient enough to know I'd eventually figure it out. And thanks to the entire Root Lit team, for championing me and my career.

Ellen Cormier, thank you for making me kill most (but not all!) of my darlings. But seriously: Thank you for helping this book become its best self. Squish Pruitt, thanks for your keen eye and excellent suggestions. And to the entire Dial Team: I'm eternally grateful.

Afsoneh Khorram, thank you for letting me make fun of your exes, and for being the best sister I could ask for.

Thank you to all my theatre teachers—Jim, Val, Roger, Bea, Laura, Otis, Chuck, Peter—and especially Sheri Coffman, who got me through high school alive.

Thank you to the many deaf folks who generously shared their experiences and insights with me.

Thank you to my friends and my family. I love you all.

Most of all, thank you to the real star of this show: you, the reader.

CURTAIN CALLS

PUBLISHER: Jen Klonsky

EDITORIAL DIRECTOR: Nancy Mercado

EDITOR: Ellen Cormier

EDITORIAL ASSISTANT: Squish Pruitt

COPYEDITOR: Regina Castillo

MANAGING EDITORS: Tabitha Dulla & Nicole Kiser

INTERIOR DESIGNER: Jason Henry

COVER DESIGNER: Kaitlin Yang

PUBLICITY: Kaitlin Kneafsey, Shanta Newlin, Elyse Marshall

MARKETING: Christina Colangelo, Bri Lockhart, Amber Reichert, Felicity Vallence, James Akinaka, Shannon Spann, Alex Garber, Emily Romero

SCHOOL & LIBRARY: Judith Huerta, Summer Ogata, Venessa Carson, Trevor Ingerson, Carmela Iaria

SALES TEAM: Todd Jones, Becky Green, Enid Chaban, Trevor Bundy, Debra Polansky and their teams

SUBRIGHTS TEAM: Kim Ryan, Helen Boomer

PRODUCTION TEAM: Vanessa Robles